IT WAS LOVE AT FIRST SIGHT.

The moment Peter walked out onto the stage in his faded jean shirt and skintight beige Levi's, I fell head over heels in love with him. I mean, the guy was a vision. A tall, lean and bearded vision with a soft, mellow voice that sharply contrasted with his rugged features. He seemed to be a unique combination of sensitive human being and wild animal.

"Please God," I prayed like I never prayed before, "please let him come over here to say hello so I can meet him, PLEASE!"

The next thing I knew, I looked up and Peter was standing there in the flesh and shaking hands with Stanley.

Peter looked at me and grinned. "Is this your old lady or what?"

"No, you turkey," Stanley snapped. "This is my fian— I mean, my girlfriend, Shayna."

"SHAY!" I blurted. "My name is Shay." I never felt so strange in my entire life. . . . My heart was ticking away a mile a minute. His eyes were riveted to mine. No man ever gazed into my eyes like that before. Except for maybe the Man of My Dreams . . .

I LOST IT ALL IN MONTREAL

DONNA STEINBERG

AVON
PUBLISHERS OF BARD, CAMELOT, DISCUS AND FLARE BOOKS

I LOST IT ALL IN MONTREAL is an original publication of
Avon Books. This work has never before appeared in book
form.

AVON BOOKS
A division of
The Hearst Corporation
959 Eighth Avenue
New York, New York 10019

First Avon Printing, January, 1983

AVON TRADEMARK REG. U. S. PAT. OFF. AND IN
OTHER COUNTRIES, MARCA REGISTRADA, HECHO EN
U. S. A.

Printed in the U. S. A.

WFH 10 9 8 7 6 5 4 3 2 1

For my parents
and for Professor Abraham Ram

Mama may have, and Papa may have . . . but
God bless the child that's got his own . . .

> —Billie Holiday
> and Arthur Herzog, Jr.

I LOST IT ALL
IN MONTREAL

PART I

Oyster Bed

Chapter 1

I JUST LOVE getting into hot water.

Few things in life give me greater pleasure than getting into hot water up to my neck and just lying there until I'm drained; until I've steamed away every impulse to move or think. In this house a hot bath is the only chance I have to get away for a while, this evening my only chance to be alone. Or at least it *was* until Ma picked the lock with a knitting needle and came barging into the bathroom.

"Shayna Pearl . . . Shayna *Pearl!* Wake up, *Shayna Pearl!*"

"What? *What!*" I cried, springing to my feet and splashing water everywhere. "What happened?"

"Honestly," she clucked her tongue at me in disgust, "if I'd let you, you'd lie in that God*forsaken* tub and daydream your entire life away!"

"For crying out loud, Ma! Is that why you came storming in here like your girdle was on fire? To lecture me on the evils of daydreaming?"

"Never mind your shenanigans, Shayna Pearl! Stanley's on the phone. He says it's important. Something about tonight being the first night of the rest of your life if he had anything to say about it?"

"Well, what do you know?" I had to laugh. "I've been dating the guy for months now, and all along I thought he was a lawyer. I had no idea he was a closet fortune-teller!"

"Are you going to stand there all night like Lady Godiva or are you going to find out what this is all about?"

"Awwww, Maaaa . . ." I stared longingly at the steaming tubful of Jean Naté bubble bath, "I'm not in the mood for Stanley tonight." Lately, it seems, I haven't been in the mood for Stanley any night. Or day for that matter. He gets on my nerves, to be perfectly blunt. All he has to do is open his mouth to say hello and every hair on my body bristles. But go and tell *that* to Ma. She thinks Stanley Charles Drabkin, B. Comm. (Bachelor of Commerce), B.C.L. (Bachelor of Common Law), C.M. (Certified *Mensch*), is the greatest thing since Grease Relief.

"What do you mean, you're not in the mood for him?" She almost choked. "You think a boy like that grows on trees?"

"I've got my reasons, Ma. Can't you just tell him I'm not here or something?"

"I'll do nothing of the kind!" She grabbed the "It's Better In The Bahamas" bath towel from the rack and wrapped it around me. "Oh, my baby!" All of a sudden she threw her arms around me and hugged me to pieces. "I think this is *it!* The Night of Nights! I think Stanley is going to pop *the* ques—"

"Ma! You're squishing my boobs!" I cried, wriggling out of her grasp. "And I'm not your little baby anymore, for crying out loud. I'm twenty-three years old!"

"Boobs, shmoobs,"—she grabbed me by the shoulders and shook me so hard my teeth rattled—"didn't you hear me? I said Stanley's going to pop THE question!"

"No!" Suddenly it all began to sink in. "He's not going to propose tonight?" I don't know why the whole thing

4

came as such a shock. I mean, Stanley'd been dropping enough hints lately. Deep inside, I'd known it was only a matter of time before it came to this. "Not tonight?"

"Can you think of any *other* reason why tonight would be the first night of the rest of your life?"

"Propose as in m-m-marriage?"

"I'm willing to bet my life on it."

"M-m-marriage as in 'Till Death Us Do Part'?"

"Knock wood," she banged on the cupboard door.

"In that case, *don't* tell him I'm not here."

"I knew you'd come around once I mentioned the magic word."

"*Just tell him I'm dead!*"

"Shayna Pearl, God*forbid!* Bite your tongue!"

We both bit our tongues.

"If you don't mind," I told her, "I want to be alone now."

"I want to be alone . . . I want to be alone," she mimicked me. "What is it with you and this Greta Garbo routine lately? If you're not shut up in your room with those ridiculous stereo headphones blasting that awful rock music into your ears, you're lying there in that God*forsaken* tub . . . *shvitzing* yourself silly!" She gave me a worried glance. "Even your father who never notices anything, God*bless* him, has noticed that you've been acting peculiar these days. What's wrong with you, anyway?"

"What's wrong?" I didn't know whether to laugh or cry or what. There were so many things I'd been dying to tell her for so long. Things I'd kept bottled up inside me because I knew she didn't want to hear them. "You wanna know what's wrong?"

She threw her hands up to God. "Can't you just spit it out? You're the one with the college degree in Communications—so communicate!" She gave me another worried glance. "It's not something terribly wrong, is it?"

"Yes," I said. At least I thought so.

"Oh, pooh," she sneered, "what could possibly be so wrong with a Shayna Pearl who was *born* with the world as her oyster? Everybody should have your problems!"

So much for keeping things bottled up inside. I popped my cork. "You wanna know what's wrong?" I cried. "I'll tell you what's wrong. My *life* is wrong. All wrong!"

"What do you mean your *life* is all wrong? Couldn't you be a little more specific? Is it *that* time of the month again, or what?"

I stared at her in disbelief. I could become completely schizoid before her very eyes and she'd think it was *that* time of the month again. She and my father-the-gynecologist both.

"Well, is it? Do you want me to bring you some Midol? Pamprin? Darvon Compound? 222s?"

"Maaaa . . . Can I help it if I want more out of life than worrying about whether or not Stanley Charles Drabkin has Ring Around The Collar, Socks That Don't Cling, or Underwear That's Slowly Going Gray? Or if he prefers Stove Top Stuffing to potatoes? Or if I'm buying the right toilet paper for him to wipe his ass with?"

"Shayna Pearl!" Her mouth dropped open. "Either you're in shock or you've been watching too many television commercials lately. You don't know what you're saying!"

That did it. I had had just about all I could take. I sat down on the edge of the tub and burst into tears. "Oh, Ma, I don't wanna get married!" I wailed. "Not to Stanley . . . not to anybody! There's so many th—ings I want to do fi-ir-irst . . ."

"I don't understand." She sat down beside me and cradled me in her arms. "You've been seeing Stanley for months now. And he's so crazy about you. He'd give you the moon if you'd ask for it." She let out a heavy sigh. "I thought for sure he was The One."

"So did I," I sobbed. "All my friends were getting married and I felt so left out . . . like a freak or something . . . and he was just there . . . and you were so crazy about him . . . *every*body was so crazy about

6

him . . . and I thought I could, you know, grow to love him with time . . . and I tried . . . GodKNOWS I tried . . . but I didn't . . . I couldn't . . . I still can't . . . and I don't think I'll *ever!*"

All of a sudden she started to laugh.

"What's so bloody funny?" I cried. I was incensed. "My whole life is falling apart and you're laughing?"

"Oh, Shayna Pearl, sweetheart," she hugged me, "I know exactly what's bothering you!"

"You do?" My eyes almost popped right out of my head. "But . . ."

"It's all right, you don't have to explain. I understand."

"Oh, Ma!" I threw my arms around her. "Thank you!"

"Yes, it's the Bridal Jitters is what it is. We all get them. Even I got them before I married your father."

I jerked away from her just as surely as if she had slapped me. "The Bridal Jitters?" I knew all that understanding was too good to be true.

"Yes, that's exactly it," she smiled reassuringly. "It's only natural to be nervous about taking a big step like marriage. Nothing a little Valium won't cure though. I'll go get the bottle . . ."

"Valium?" I couldn't believe my ears. "I don't need Valium!"

"In fact, I think I'll take a couple myself," she said, massaging her temples. "I'm a wreck!"

"You're a wreck? What about me?"

"In that case, maybe I should bring you something stronger?"

Having resisted the urge to strangle her right then and there, I realized I probably never would. "You could bring me heroin, Mother," I told her as I got back into the tub and submerged myself up to my chin, "but I won't change my mind. So you can just go back to the phone and tell Stanley to find himself another wife!"

"Oh, my God, *Stanley!*" She smacked herself on the head. "I left him dangling on the phone all this time?"

"And you tell me *I've* been treating him like dirt lately?"

7

"Oh, dear, you got me so *farchadet* I don't know if I'm coming or going anymore!"

"Tell me about it."

"Hang on, Stanley dear!" she yelled as she tore out the bathroom door. *"I'm cominggggggg!"*

She drives me insane. The only way she's ever going to take me seriously is if I go out and commit some sort of heinous atrocity. Something twenty-three-year-old Jewish Princesses from pish-posh suburban Hampstead just don't do. Like getting arrested for prostitution or landing a job as a nude dancer at the Sextuple Club or something. Yeah, maybe that's what I have to do to get the message across. Become a nude dancer at the Sextuple. And then, when she drives down St. Catherine Street, in the very heart of downtown Montreal, and she sees my name up in lights—

APPEARING NIGHTLY . . .
SHAYNA PEARL FINE,
EXOTIC NUDE DANCER . . .
FEATURING THE BIGGEST PEARLS
THIS SIDE OF THE ATLANTIC

—she's bound to realize that marriage to Stanley is the furthest thing from my mind these days. That is, if she doesn't die of the shock first.

Oh, Christ, what am I saying? I don't want her to die! She's my mother and I love her. I care what she thinks of me.

That's my problem, you know. I don't hate her enough. Life would be so much easier if I just despised her. Then I wouldn't have to worry about disappointing her when I tell her that my future plans include, among other things, being a career woman and moving into my own place in downtown Montreal—or maybe even Los Angeles. And she *will* be disappointed. I guess you can even say she's laid down the law as far as I'm concerned; no daughter of Sylvia and Arnie Fine M.D., Ob. Gyn., leaves home without making a pit stop at the local synagogue to exchange vows. (Of course Dad agrees with her—he always agrees with her for the sake of keeping the peace around here.) My wedding day is supposed to be the Greatest Show on Earth and then some. Divorce statistics and Women's Liberation aside, Ma and Dad live for the day they can marry off their precious Shayna Pearl (so-named, I am told often enough, because I was born with the world as my oyster) to a Nice-Jewish-Professional-Boy-Type. They long to see their one and only daughter, the one and only certifiable twenty-three-year-old virgin in Hampstead . . . maybe even Montreal . . . possibly even the world . . . dress up all in white and walk down The Aisle. They just can't wait to hear the crunch of glass under my groom-to-be's foot.

I guess that's why they've been so anxious for me to marry Stanley ever since that night, some six or seven months ago, when he came to the house to pick me up for a blind date. The very moment Ma laid eyes on his feet (he was wearing, among other things, a very impressive pair of Gucci loafers) she decided (and Dad agreed, as usual) that Stanley was The One.

Naturally, Stanley's size twelve Guccis are not the only reasons why Ma and Dad think he's such a great catch. They do have at least four other very good, solid reasons. Firstly, Stanley's mother's maiden name just happens to be Gertie Blutstein—of *the* grocery chain Blutsteins, so Stanley is rich. Secondly, Stanley's father owns one of the biggest *shmata* businesses in Montreal, so Stanley is wealthy. Thirdly, Stanley's grandfather just died and left him a bundle, so Stanley is loaded. And fourthly, but certainly not lastly, Stanley's law firm, which specializes in representing various show business types like movie stars and rock singers, is raking it in, so Stanley has money. I mean, why else would they want me to marry an overweight, balding guy who has all the personality and sex appeal of a piece of gefilte fish?

Oh, yeah, I know, I know, he's madly in love with me. And he's precisely the kind of guy I'm supposed to marry. The kind who can afford to keep a spoiled-rotten (not to mention sheltered and pampered) Jewish Princess like myself in the royal manner to which I have grown accustomed. But it's not enough. I've had it with this whole ridiculous charade. I can't keep going through the motions my entire life just to please my family. I mean, what about me? What about how I feel? Don't *my* feelings ... *my* desires ... *my* needs count for anything? Doesn't anybody out there even care that I don't love Stanley? Or his money? Or his body?

The faucet looked like an erect prick. That's how I imagined it.

It always looks that way when I'm soaking in a hot tub and the bathroom gets all steamed up. Always. I reached up and caressed it with my foot, wondering what it would be like if it were the Real Thing instead of just a piece of metal jutting out of the wall. I tried to imagine what it would be like to hold it in my hands. To have it in my mouth. To slide it up in between my legs.

And then, suddenly, he appeared. The Man of My Dreams. The incredibly rugged, fantastically sexy Man of My Dreams. The star of my every fantasy. He was standing over the tub wearing nothing except the beard on his face and a towel around his waist. He's always bearded and he always wears just a towel around his waist. Except when he surprises me and wears nothing at all.

"Mm-mm, you look good lying there," he said, his baby blue eyes sparkling as they traveled up and down my naked body. Up and down. Up and down. "In fact, you look good enough to eat ..."

"Oh, you!" I laughed. It was a deep, throaty kind of laugh. My sexiest. "You're always saying that!"

"Well, it's the truth." He smiled down at me. "Hell, I get a hard-on just looking at you."

"Is that a fact?" I glanced over at his crotch to see if the familiar (but always tantalizing) bulge was there. It was. I reached out and ran my hand over it, tracing the outline with my fingers. I could just feel it grow, harden, expand until I thought it might burst right through the towel. "You wouldn't just be saying that, would you?"

"Of course not,"—he moaned from the pleasure of it all—"a prick never lies." He looked down at his ever-hardening hard-on straining against my hand, and then he looked up at me and grinned. "Never . . ."

"No, a prick never lies," I smiled seductively as my hand continued to caress him, to tease him, "I've never had a prick that's lied to me yet."

"We gonna do it in the bath again tonight?" His breath was coming in short gasps.

"Yeah,"—a shudder ran right through me as I anticipated the good things to come—"I just love doing it in the bath."

We were going at it something fierce when Ma's cold, frantic hand grabbed my shoulder.

"Shayna Pearl, for crying out loud!" she screamed into my ear. *"Will you stop daydreaming and take your Valium?!"*

"Jesus Christ!" I sat bolt upright.

"No, it's just me, your mother. Sorry to disappoint you."

"Holy cow!" My eyes scanned the length of the tub. There was no one in it except me, thank God for small mercies. "Holy Moses!"

"I'm not surprised you're having trouble recognizing me. There's so much steam in here, I don't think I'd recognize my own mother if I fell right over her, may she rest in peace." She waved her hand around in a vain attempt to clear the air. "These hot baths of yours are killing my wallpaper!"

"Ma!" I wailed. "What are you doing in here?"

"What do you mean, what am I doing in here?" She shoved a glass of water and two small green pills under my nose. "I said I was coming back with Valium, didn't I? It's not my fault you were a million miles away . . . for a change."

"Well, couldn't you have at least *knocked* first?!" I was furious. Furious with her for invading my privacy. Furious with myself for getting so carried away when I knew damned well that it's asking too much to have a sexual fantasy in peace around this house. But even more than furious, I was mortified. Mortified because I suddenly realized that underneath the murky bathwater, my right hand was wedged between my legs. God, I wanted to die. No, I wanted a fate worse than death. I wanted the drain to open up and suck me into the St. Lawrence River where I'd languish for all eternity while all the toilets and tubs of Montreal flushed an endless stream of filth upon my head. "How long have you been standing there, anyway?" I couldn't bear to look her in the face. "I never even heard you come in!"

"I just walked in this second," she said. "Here now, take the Valium and get out of that God*forsaken* tub already!" She looked down at the water and made a disgusted face. "Feh! That bubble bath of yours made such a thick layer of soap scum, nobody would ever know you had a body under there."

Thank God for soap scum. I carefully withdrew my hand. Being a card-carrying member of the Worldwide Order of Prudes, my mother holds Masturbation high on her "Strictly Taboo" list. I mean, it's right up there with Oral Sex, Premarital Sex and Sex in General.

"Shayna Pearl, please!" she pleaded. "Take the pills. The steam is ruining my hair. I just had it done today."

"I don't need Valium!" I pushed her hand away.

She looked at me and shrugged. Then she took the pills herself.

"Did you take care of Stanley, by the way?"

"Yes I did, by the way, how nice of you to ask!" She clucked her tongue in disgust. "A young woman of twenty-three shouldn't have to send her mother to make excuses for her, you know. Especially a young woman who's always *burtching* about wanting to take responsibility for her own life!"

"Oh, brother!" Funny how she never takes anything I

say seriously until it's time to throw it back in my face. "Gimme a break."

"The trouble is you only want to be grown up when it suits you . . ."

"Save the lecture, Mother! What'd you tell him?"

"He wanted to pick you up at eight-thirty but I told him that would be impossible."

"Oh, Ma, thanks," I cried, "I knew I could count on you!"

"So he's going to be picking you up at nine."

"*Oh, Mother!* I can't count on you for *anything!*"

"You have half an hour to get ready. Don't you think you ought to shake a leg?"

"No,"—I folded my arms across my chest and refused to budge—"I'm not going anywhere."

"*Arnie . . . Arnie!*" she called out for Dad. "*Come talk some sense into your daughter. She gets her* mishegaas *from your side of the family!*"

There was no response. There seldom is.

"Ooooo, that man!" she said between clenched teeth. "When he lies there in that God*forsaken* vibrating, twenty-four position E-Z chair with that damned newspaper over his face, the whole house could fall on him and he wouldn't notice!"

"The joys of marriage," I rolled my eyes around in my head. "I mean, there's just so much to look forward to."

"No man is perfect, Shayna Pearl."

"I'm not looking for someone perfect," I told her, "just someone different. Someone sexy, exciting, good-looking and strong. Someone who treats me like a person. Gives me space. Encourages my career. Values my opinions. Someone who makes me feel alive. Who turns me on!"

"Like who? Like that character with the long hair and the beard who you think is so wonderful? The one who starred with Barbra Streisand in that *A Star Is Born* movie you saw twelve times? The one whose posters you Scotch-taped to the walls in your room and wrecked the paint! What's his name . . . Kristofferson Kristofferson or something?"

"Kris Kristofferson."

"Right, him. You think *he's* going to come galloping by on a white horse and whisk you off into the sunset?"

"Or a reasonable facsimile thereof."

"Take it from me, a woman who knows more about life than you do, and save yourself a lot of grief . . . Mr. Perfect does not exist. So Stanley's not perfect? Surprise. Who is? So he's not exactly Kristofferson Kristofferson. I know why you're doing this. You're doing this just to aggravate me. You're always doing things just to aggravate me! Why couldn't you be more like your wonderful brothers? They've never given me a day's aggravation."

"You can't win 'em all, Mother!" I glared at her. I felt like spitting up. I always feel that way when she reminds me (as she does umpteen times a day) of how wonderful my wonderful brothers are. At thirty-one, identical twins Terry and David Fine, The Doctor and The Financial Consultant, respectively, are the closest things to perfection this side of God. At least to her and Dad they are. And so are their wives, Arlene and Eva, respectively. And so are their children, Melissa and Andrea, Victoria and Erin (plus one on the way any time now) respectively. And so are their semidetached homes right down the street at 8675 and 8677 Blossom Road, respectively. And so on and so on and so on. They're all so wonderful they make The Waltons look like delinquents. "What do you want from me, Ma, what? I mean, am I that repulsive, am I that sexless, dull and unattractive that I have to marry the first guy that shows an interest in me—just so I can fit into the family picture?"

"If we'd let you, you'd spend the rest of your life in a dream world . . . pining away for Kristofferson Kristofferson . . . waiting for some big-time movie producer to take you away from your job at the *Cote Saint Luc Weekly Register* and whisk you off to Hollywood to write screenplays!"

"Well, I didn't get a degree in Communication Arts to

Mirtazapine od

45 mg

30 owd

2 pills

mane thes

POINTS	VALEUR D'ÉCHANGE
10 000	10 $
20 000	20 $
30 000	30 $
Et vous pouvez échanger jusqu'à...	
500 000	500 $

Accumulez des points encore plus rapidement avec la carte de crédit Mastercard[MD] **Services financiers le Choix du Président**[MD]**. Pour en savoir plus, visitez le site pcfinance.ca.**

pcoptimum.ca

OBTENEZ DES RÉCOMPENSES À VOTRE IMAGE.

Inscrivez-vous au programme *PC Optimum* et obtenez des récompenses conçues pour vous, des invitations à des événements exclusifs ainsi que des offres spéciales sur les produits que vous achetez le plus souvent. Inscrivez-vous à **pcoptimum.ca**.

pharmaprix.ca

spend the rest of my life as Chief Schlock Processor and Drivel Writer for some two-bit suburban weekly! Or to be nothing more than some nobody's wife! As soon as I get enough firsthand writing experience I'm going to move on to bigger and better things."

"See what I mean?" she cried. "You have absolutely no conception of reality. You've been working—what?—*ten* whole months, and already you're going on to bigger and better things. A headful of ridiculous schemes and impossible dreams—that's what you've got. And I'm not the only one who thinks so. It's the consensus of this entire family that you're a romantic flake and that marriage to a nice, stable, down-to-earth boy like Stanley Drabkin is exactly what you need."

"Well, I hope the family is happy being married to Stanley. Because I don't intend to marry him myself."

"Just get out of the tub and get ready," she said as she turned to go, "if you know what's good for you . . ." The walls buckled from the force of her slamming the door.

Shit, she's not for real, that mother of mine! Doesn't she know that her way of thinking went out with poodle skirts and Gidget movies? Hasn't she heard that this is the age of the Cosmo Girl? Hell, I don't know. Is it so farfetched to think that I, Shayna Pearl Fine, could be like those women I'm forever reading about in magazines? Those independent career women with their chic penthouse apartments, titillating love affairs and multiple orgasms? Is it so absurd to think that I could have my own life? My own money? My own place? A place where I could do what I want, whenever I want and with whomever I want? Where I could have love affairs with men of my own choosing . . . bearded, sexy men . . . men who wear inviting smiles on their faces and towels around their waists . . . or better still, nothing at all?

Oh, brother, who am I kidding anyway? Even a romantic flake like me who has no conception of reality knows that it takes money, loads of money, to have your own place and the kind of life that goes with it. And the fact of the matter is—I don't have enough money to keep me in dimes should I want to live in a pay toilet. Hell, even if I saved every penny of my pitiful salary it would be a year, maybe two, before I could even get *that* far.

Trapped. That's what I am. Trapped! Trapped if I do marry Stanley. Trapped if I don't.

Chapter 2

MA WAS FIT to be tied as the doorbell was ringing and I was just stepping out of the tub.

"For crying out loud, Shayna Pearl!" she cried, practically pulling my arm out of its socket as she stuffed it into the sleeve of my bathrobe. "Stanley's here and you're not even ready!"

"My, but you're observant."

"Never mind your sarcasm. Just hurry up and make yourself beautiful while I stall your fiancé-to-be. . . ."

"Don't ever call him that, Goddammit!" I yelled after her as she ran off to answer the door. *"I'm not going to marry him, do you hear? I'm going to be a free woman even if it means spending the rest of my life in this bathroom!"*

My threats fell upon deaf ears. Not only did she let Stanley into the house but she fussed over him like he was Pierre Elliott Trudeau or Frank Sinatra. I stood at the top of the stairs and eavesdropped.

"Stanley, dear!" I could hear her voice squealing with delight. "It's so good to see you . . . come in . . . come

17

in . . . Shayna Pearl's dressing but she'll be down short-ly."

"'Evening, Mrs. F.," Stanley said. He always calls her "Mrs. F." It drives me crazy. "You sure are looking beautiful tonight, Mrs. F."

"Oh, Stanley,"—she giggled,—"flattery will get you everywhere!"

"It's sure not hard to see where Shayna Pearl gets her good looks from."

"Well, you know what they say, don't you?" She giggled again. "The apple never falls far from the tree."

A shudder ran right through me. That had to be the most depressing thing I ever heard!

"I mean, they just don't make 'em cuter than Shayna Pearl, you know?" Stanley went on, sounding delirious. "I mean, those shimmering light brown curls! Those big brown doe eyes! That perfect little nose! That peaches and cream complexion! That petite but volup—,I mean, curv—, I mean *gorgeous* figure! Hell, she may only be five foot nothing, but what a package!"

"You really love her, don't you?" Ma said, making one of her more astute observations. "You love her a lot."

"I can't tell you how much, Mrs. F.," he said, as he proceeded to tell her anyway. "I know Shayna Pearl, she, well, she doesn't exactly feel the same way about me just yet; but she will—especially when I give her this. . . ."

"*Oh, Stanley! It's . . . it's . . .*"

"Shshshsh . . . not so loud, Mrs. F.!" he shushed her. "I don't want Shayna Pearl to know about this until the right moment."

"Oh, don't worry about her, she can't hear us," Ma reassured him. "She's up in her room getting dressed and if I know her, she's got that horrid rock music blasting in her ears. . . . Oh, Stanley . . . it's . . . it's . . ."

". . . a rock, isn't it?"

"It's a boulder!"

"It's a three-point-five marquise diamond to be exact—and that's not including the baguettes. I'm going to take

Shayna Pearl to this real swanky place tonight and spring it on her. Now you know what I meant before on the phone when I said tonight's going to be the first night of the rest of her life, eh?"

"Boy, do I ever!" Ma cried. "Shayna Pearl's going to flip when she sees this. It's exquisite!"

"You . . . you really think she'll flip over it?"

"I don't think, Stanley. I *know*. Why, no woman in her right mind would turn down a magnificent ring like this. And if she does, she belongs in the booby hatch!"

Another shudder ran through me. I had visions of Ma standing on our front steps shouting: "Don't forget the shock treatments . . . she needs LOTS of shock treatments!" as two burly men in white coats hauled me off, kicking and screaming, to that infamous Montreal mental institution known as "Verdun."

"I don't know," Stanley said, sounding worried, "Shayna Pearl's been getting some pretty crazy ideas lately. Sometimes I . . . well, sometimes I get the feeling that she fancies herself as one of those independent, career-type women. You know, like the ones in *Cosmopolitan* magazine?"

"Shayna Pearl is always fancying herself as something, Stanley," Ma sneered. "Tomorrow she'll be fancying herself as the Queen of England."

"Are you saying I shouldn't take her seriously when she talks, you know, *that* way?"

"Oh, please, Stanley," she laughed. "You just put that ring on her finger tonight and it'll be like she never even heard of her precious *Cosmopolitan!*"

"Yeah, you're right, I guess. I sure hope so. I mean, it's a known fact that diamonds are considered a girl's best friend. Especially—if I may borrow that inimitable expression from south of the border—girls of the Jewish American Princess persuasion."

I couldn't believe my ears. I mean, they were talking about me like I was some kind of diamond-crazy J.A.P. who would sell her soul for a couple of carats!

"Yeah, I don't know what I was so worried about," Stanley went on. "No woman in her right mind could turn this down. Yeah . . . these women of today, this so-called New Breed, they may call guys like me Male Chauvinist Pigs and they may complain how they need to have their own lives and their own space and their own room to grow and expand as self-supporting, self-respecting individuals and all that crap . . . but when you come right down to it, they're really no different than women were twenty—or even a hundred years ago. Just slip a diamond ring on their fingers and they'll follow you anywhere!"

They both shrieked with laughter. I couldn't bring myself to join in all the merriment, however. I was too busy sitting on my hands to keep from tearing my hair out.

"Oh, Stanley, this is the happiest night of my life!" Ma gushed. "I couldn't ask for a nicer son-in-law. And I just know my daughter's going to be in good hands."

"Thanks, Mrs. F., I won't disappoint you."

"Why don't you call me Ma? All my children do!"

A tidal wave of nausea swept through me. I thought for sure I was going to throw up.

Stanley let out a gleeful laugh. "I thought you'd never ask!"

That did it. I threw up.

I was still throwing up when there was a knock at the bathroom door.

"Shayna Pearl?" It was Ma. "Don't tell me you're *still* in the bathroom?!"

"Go away," I retched, "I'm sick!"

"Sick?" Stanley was there too. "Did I hear her say she's sick?"

"Yeah," Ma sneered, "sick in her head!"

"She's not STILL taking a bath, is she?" he groaned.

"*Oh, go away!*" I shrieked.

"Aren't you happy to see me, Shayna Pearl?" he asked.

I retched twice more and then I flushed the toilet. Two retches plus one flush, I figured, would be worth a thousand words.

"Shayna Pearl, are you all right in there?" Ma cried. "Was that vomiting I heard just a minute ago?"

"No," I took a swig of Lavoris and spit it into the sink, "that was my Sid Vicious imitation!"

"Jeez, what's with her tonight?" Stanley said. "Is it, uh, you know, *that* time of the month again or something?"

"Oh, fuck a duck . . . I don't believe this!" I cried.

"Shayna Pearl!" Ma gasped.

"Hey, Shayna Pearl, I'll bet you'll feel much better when you hear what I've got planned for us tonight," Stanley said. "I'm going to take you to this real swanky place in Old Montreal where they have soft, romantic music and candlelight and I'm going to order some champagne and . . ."

"No, please!"

"Okay," he cried. I could just picture him flinching. "Okay . . . if you don't want to go there we can go somewhere else."

"No, YOU have to go somewhere else," I told him. I couldn't believe that he was just standing there and being so totally unaware of how I was feeling.

"We can go wherever you want to go, Shayna Pearl," he told me. "C'mon, you can't stay in the bathroom forever you know."

The window, I thought. I could always jump out the window! I leaped up and tried to pry it open. It wouldn't budge. I yanked and pulled. Pulled and yanked. Pounded on it with my fists. Attacked it repeatedly with a toilet plunger. But it was no use. It was stuck. And so was I.

"Will somebody please tell me what's going on around here?" Stanley wailed.

"I'll tell you what's going on around here, Stanley," Ma said. "My daughter is nuttier than a fruit cake, that's what's going on around here."

"Yeah, well you ought to know, Mother. You *baked* me what I am today!"

"Oooo, you're just lucky your father was called out to deliver a baby a few minutes ago, let me tell you," she seethed, "because if he were here I'd have him go in there and *throttle* you!"

"Ha! Don't make me laugh. You know damned well Daddy's never laid a hand on me!"

"Well, it's time he started. Maybe if he'd have given you a couple of good swats a day for the past twenty-three years instead of letting you get away with murder, you wouldn't be acting like the spoiled-rotten brat you are today!"

"Maybe if you'd get off my back and stop trying to run my life for me, I wouldn't be locked in the goddamned bathroom like I am today!"

"Ha!" she cried. "If you think I'm on your back now, just keep this up and I'll make your life so miserable, you'll be sorry you were born!"

That did it. I had just about all I could take.

"All right!" I unlocked the door and flung it open, emerging damp and dismal-looking in my terry cloth robe. "You win. I give up. But you'll be sorry!" I glared at her. "I think I'll go to my room to get dressed now. I wonder if I have anything black to wear. . . ."

"How about something black and blue?" She shook her fist at me. "Like a bruise?"

"You just put on something real pretty, Shayna Pearl." Stanley grabbed me and hugged me. "I'm going to take you to the swankiest joint in this city."

"Do we have to go somewhere swanky?" I wriggled out of his grasp. "I'm not in a swanky mood."

He looked at me and shrugged. "Whatever makes you happy, m'dear. How about the Cock 'n' Bull? I told Peter we'd probably be dropping by later anyway."

"Peter?" I said. "Who's Peter?"

"Peter Simon Freeman of Peter Simon Freeman and the Extinct Species Band.

"Extinct Species Band?" Ma gagged. "Why, are they a bunch of dodo birds?"

"Actually, they're Canada's answer to the Eagles," he shot back. "They sing like canaries and look like wild animals. And talk about wild animals, you have to see this guy Peter. He looks just like the last American shaggy buffalo."

Suddenly I felt a glimmering of hope. "A shaggy buffalo?" I could hardly conceal my excitement. "You . . . you mean, he's one of those long-haired, bearded types?" Stanley thinks all long-haired, bearded types, from Jesus Christ to Kris Kristofferson, look like shaggy buffaloes.

"Boy, is he ever!" Stanley rolled his eyes around in his head. "But who cares what the guy looks like as long as he can sing, right? And this guy can sing, let me tell you. It's only a matter of time before one of the biggest record companies out in L.A. signs him up."

"Peter Simon Freeman,"—I scratched my head—"have I ever heard of him before?"

"Probably not," Stanley said. "The Extinct Species is not exactly a household word around Montreal yet. They've been out on the road all year—playing the small towns from Chien de Bow Wow, Quebec, to Ruchasville, Ontario."

"How come you know so much about them?" I asked.

"Peter and I went to law school at McGill together before he dropped out to form the Extinct Species."

"Hmph." Ma made a sour face. Like she had swallowed a spoonful of sour yogurt or something. "If he were my son, I'd break his neck!"

"Anyway," Stanley went on, "he came by my office this afternoon for some legal advice, and he told me he was opening tonight at the Cock 'n' Bull and why don't I come down to catch his act?"

Peter Simon Freeman. Peter Simon Freeman. I chanted his name over and over again in my mind. I loved the way it sounded. Like a breath of fresh air. So unlike Stanley Charles Drabkin. *Peter Simon Freeman.*

"So what do you say, Shayna Pearl?" Stanley nudged my arm. "Does the Cock 'n' Bull strike your fancy?"

"Eh?" I started. "Oh, yeah, sure," I said, wandering off to my room to get dressed. "The Cock 'n' Bull strikes my fancy just fine. . . ."

PART II

Knight Rider

Chapter 3

IT WAS LOVE at first sight.

The moment Peter Simon Freeman walked out onto the stage in his faded jean shirt and skin-tight beige Levis, I fell head over heels in love with him. I mean, the guy was a vision. A tall, lean and bearded vision with a soft, mellow voice that sharply contrasted with his rugged appearance. He seemed to be a unique combination of sensitive human being and wild animal. And his songs, mostly of the "Girl, Why Did You Leave Me?" variety, spoke of vulnerability and loneliness.

"Please, God," I prayed as the house lights went on after the first set, "please let him spot Stanley so that he'll come over here to say hello and I can meet him, *please!*" I prayed like I never prayed before. "If You do me this one little favor, God," I told Him, "I promise, I swear I'll become a better Jew. Just let me meet Peter and I'll never touch another bite of pork for as long as I live. Not even the ribs at the Bar-B-Barn."

Apparently God knows a good sacrifice when He hears

one, because the next thing I knew, I looked up and Peter Simon Freeman was standing there in the flesh and shaking hands with Stanley.

"Stanley, how ya doin', man?" he said. "Glad you could make it down tonight. Did you hear anything new on that recording contract business out in L.A. yet?"

"No, and I'm not here to talk business either," Stanley said, wrapping his arm around my shoulder and making lovey-dovey eyes at me. "This visit is strictly pleasure."

"So I just noticed," Peter looked at me and grinned. "Is this your old lady or what?"

"This is my fian—, I mean, my girlfriend, Shayna P—"

"*Shay!*" I blurted. "My name is Shay." I never felt so strange in my entire life. My tongue felt too thick for my mouth, my skin too tight for my body. And my heart, my heart—it was ticking away a mile a minute, like a taxi meter or something.

"Shay, huh?" He sat down beside me. "Ya, I like it. It kinda suits you, you know? You look like a Shay." His eyes were riveted to mine. "Shay what?"

"Fine." I squirmed in my seat. No man had ever gazed into my eyes like that before. Except for maybe the Man of My Dreams. "Shay Fine."

"Fine like the bakery?"

"Fine like the gynecologist."

"No shit?" He laughed.

"No shit." I laughed too, though I wasn't quite sure what the joke was. And anyway, who cared?

He was attracted to me, I could tell. He couldn't seem to take his eyes off me. Which was okay by me because I couldn't take my eyes off him either. In fact, if he hadn't been called back to the stage to prepare for his second act, I think we might have spent the rest of the night just staring at each other.

Stanley was incensed. "Let's get out of this Cock 'n' Bull dump!" he told me as soon as Peter got up from the table. "This place gives me the willies!"

I refused to budge. Peter had said he was coming back to join us for a drink after his last set, and nothing short of a four-alarm fire was going to get me to leave the place beforehand.

"Please, Shayna Pearl," he pleaded, "I have something important I want to discuss with you. A matter of life and death!"

"Later, Stanley, later," I told him. I was too busy watching Peter's ass wiggling around in those tight beige Levis of his as he headed back toward the stage. "Much later. . . ." It wasn't so much that I meant to be deliberately cruel to Stanley. It's just that once I laid eyes on Peter I couldn't seem to concentrate on anybody or anything but Peter. I was like a woman possessed. "Much much later."

"I want to discuss it *now!*"

"So discuss, Stanley, I'm listening," I said, my eyes riveted to Peter's behind. He had a very cute ass, I thought.

"I can't discuss this with you while you're making goo-goo eyes at another guy, dammit," he fumed. "What the hell is there to look at, anyway? He's nothing but a shaggy buffalo."

"He's the goddamn sexiest shaggy buffalo I ever saw!"

"Hmph, I ought to go over there and punch his lights out. Don't think I didn't notice the way he was staring down your cleavage while he was sitting here."

"He was?" I couldn't help but smile. "And all along I thought he was merely gazing into my eyes!"

"What the hell did you have to go and dress so sexy for anyway?" he cried. "I mean, just look at you—you're half naked, for crying out loud! Can't you at least put on a bra when you wear those see-through blouses of yours? You ask for trouble when you dress like that." He grabbed my blazer from the back of my chair and draped it around my shoulders. "There now, that's much better."

Peter looked at me and grinned. I smiled back, my insides melting like mozzarella cheese on toast. "Pheeuuw, it sure is hot in here!" I shrugged the blazer off.

"Christ," Stanley put the blazer back around my shoulders again, "if your mother knew what you were wearing —or rather what you weren't wearing under this blazer tonight—she'd never have let you out of the house."

"Who do you think bought this blouse for me in the first place, Stanley?" I shrugged the blazer off my shoulders again. "Anyway, what do you expect me to wear in the middle of July? A turtleneck and my raccoon coat?"

"Okay, okay, let's not make a big deal over this," he said. "I didn't bring you down here to discuss your clothes. I brought you down here to talk about us, about our future togeth— Shayna Pearl, are you listening to me?"

"Uh-huh," I said, though my attention was on Peter. He was standing up on the stage and talking to his drummer, a strange-in-a-wonderful-sort-of-way character whose head was as bald as a baby's tush, save for a bright orange fringe of hair. Like Bozo the Clown. "What's on your mind, Stanley?" As if I didn't know. As if I cared. Up on the stage Peter and Bozo the Clown were being joined by the rest of the Extinct Species Band, a menagerie of exotic creatures not unlike that which you see at Parc Safari Africain. There was the tall, thin keyboardist who looked like a giraffe and the short, squat bass guitarist with the pushed-in face who looked like a gorilla in blue jeans and last, but certainly not least, there was the stout, hairy lead guitarist who easily resembled a wildebeest. It was a whole other world up there. I felt myself being drawn toward it.

"Shayna Pearl," Stanley nudged my arm. "Would it be too much to ask that you look at me when I'm talking to you?"

"I'm looking," I said while continuing to stare at Peter's magnificent jean-clad body. He must look très sexy in a towel, I thought with a smile, très sexy indeed.

"Dammit, Shayna Pearl, look at me, will you?!"

Reluctantly, oh-so-reluctantly, I tore my eyes away from Peter and I looked at Stanley. Stanley with his three-piece Pierre Cardin suit and patent leather shoes.

Stanley with his Pierre Cardin tortoise shell glasses and pinstriped tie. Stanley with his belly hanging ten pounds over his belt with the gold *C* on the buckle. Stanley with his thick Mick Jagger lips that are framed by a thin light blond mustache which looks more like a third eyebrow. Stanley with his round Pillsbury Dough Boy cheeks and his short, dirty blond hair that is rapidly disappearing at the temples.

"Couldn't we discuss this later, Stanley?" I said, my eyes roaming back to the stage. "There's just too many distractions around here to get into a heavy discussion." Up on the stage they were passing around a brown bottle of something. Whisky maybe. Whatever it was it sure looked potent. Peter took a swig, grimaced and then passed it on to The Giraffe, who took a swig, grimaced and passed it on to The Wildebeest, who took two swigs and didn't grimace. "What do you suppose they're drinking up there?" I asked Stanley, who was sipping on a fluorescent orange Planter's Punch with two cherries and an umbrella. "It sure looks strong."

"I hope it's hemlock," he sneered, spearing a cherry with his umbrella and popping it into his mouth. "Maybe if they all keel over and die up there you'll pay some attention to me."

Peter got up in front of his microphone and started tuning his guitar. My eyes followed his fingers as they slid down the long, slender neck toward the hole. There was something about the way his fingers glided over the frets. Something sensual. I could almost feel them on my skin. Gliding down my neck. Caressing my shoulders. My breasts. My nipples. My belly. My vagina. An intensely pleasurable shudder ran right through me.

"Why don't you put your eyes back into your head, Shayna Pearl," Stanley said. "He's not your type."

"Is that a fact?"

"Do you honestly think I'd have brought you down here tonight if I ever thought, for one minute, that Peter was your type?"

31

"We all make mistakes."

"Oh, for crying out loud, you wouldn't want to fall for a guy like that. He just happens to be Super Lech himself."

"Super Lech?"

"Yeah, he likes women and he likes 'em in bed."

"Is *that* a fact?"

"Yeah, well, you just happen to be Super Virgin, in case you've forgotten? I know I haven't."

"So?"

"So, you two don't have a single thing in common. He's a guy who's obsessed with sex, and you're a woman who avoids it like the plague. That's hardly the basis for a meaningful relationship, would you say?"

"Whatever you say, Stanley." I looked up at Peter and smiled. He winked back to me. I felt something stirring up inside me. Between my legs.

"Do you honestly think a guy like that's going to take cold showers for months and months, like I've been doing?"

"I never asked you to wait around for me, Stanley. That was your idea, not mine."

"I'm an old-fashioned guy. I respect your virtue. I always thought you were worth waiting for. I still do. Besides, I haven't minded the wait. If anything, it's made me want you that much more."

If anything, it's made me want you that much *less*, I thought.

"Do you honestly think a guy like Peter's going to respect your virtue?"

God, I hope not, I muttered under my breath.

"All he's going to want to do is get you into bed, you know?"

The lights went down and Peter started singing this beautiful song about a shattered love affair:

> Even as I watched you leavin'
> I never stopped believin'
> Girl, I knew you'd come around

And as I sat there watching him, listening to him, experiencing him, I thought about what Stanley had said—about Peter wanting to get me into bed and all.

In fact, I couldn't get it off my mind.

Peter Simon Freeman was the first real live guy I ever met whom I could picture going to bed with.

No, that's not quite true. He was the first real live guy I ever met whom I was dying to go to bed with.

And the longer I sat there watching him, the more I was dying to go to bed with him. Hell, I think I would have gone up there and done it on the stage in front of the entire Cock 'n' Bull if he'd have asked me to—that's how much I wanted him.

When he finished playing and came back to our table, I forgot everything Ma ever taught me about being a lady, and I did everything short of grabbing his balls to let him know exactly how I felt.

I complimented him on his music.

I told him how much I dig guys with beards.

I fingered the gold earring that was dangling from his left earlobe and told him how sexy I thought it was.

I leaned over as far as I could to give him a bird's eye view of the braless interior of my strategically unbuttoned shirt.

Stanley kept kicking me under the table and muttering things like "Let's go home!" and "You're drunk!" and "You're making a complete ass of yourself!" into my ear.

I ignored him though.

Peter was the only one whose opinion I was interested in, and he didn't seem to think I was making a complete ass of myself.

On the contrary.

He just kept offering me sips of whatever it was in that big brown bottle of his—"fire water" he kept calling it—and telling me how "fucking adorable" I was and how funny I was and what a "breath of fresh air" I was.

I really had him where I wanted him, I thought.

And after a few sips of "fire water" I even got up the

nerve to proposition him. Well, I sort of propositioned him. It was the only way I knew how.

He was in the middle of telling me how rotten it is being a musician in Canada, how the Canadian public and the Canadian press ignore you until you've made it big in the States "where it counts," when I stumbled on the perfect excuse to see him again.

"Hey, I work for a newspaper!" I blurted. "Why don't I do a feature story on you and your band?"

Bingo! Peter's face lit up and he told me to go on.

"I could do a piece on what it's like being a musician playing the clubs across Canada for a living," I said. "I could write about the hassles, the dreams—hey, I could call it 'The American Dream of a Canadian Band'!"

I didn't know if I was going about it the right way. All those "How to Proposition Men" articles I'd read in *Cosmopolitan* and the like suddenly escaped me, so I was really relying on my instincts. But I guessed I was doing something right because Peter was obviously impressed.

"Christ, that's good," he grinned, "you must be one hell of a journalist to think all that up on the spur of the moment!"

"Yeah, she's really a terrific journalist," Stanley interjected. "You should have read her last article. A masterpiece! What was it called, Shayna Pearl? 'What's New at the Y' or something?" ·

"Shut up, Stanley!" I muttered.

"What's with the journalist bit, anyway? You're a journalist like I'm Guy Lafleur of the Montréal Canadiens! And how could you even call the *Cote Saint Luc Weekly Register* a newspaper? Most people use it as *shmata* paper to line their birdcages and housebreak their puppies . . . and that's *before* they read it."

"Whoa there!" Peter cried. "I know the *Cote Saint Luc Weekly Register* ain't *Time* magazine, but publicity is publicity."

Stanley gave him an incredulous look. "You . . . you mean you're actually going to do it with her?"

"Oh, yeah," Peter looked at me and winked. "I can't think of anybody I'd rather do it with."

"If you've got the place," I smiled back at him, feeling bolstered by the fire water in my veins, "I've got the time."

Peter threw his head back and laughed that wonderful, crazy, hoarse laugh of his. "You're really something else," he told me. "I have a feeling this is gonna be one hell of an interview."

"Me too." I thought I was going to burst.

"How does tomorrow sound? Say, around noon? The band and I will be rehearsing here at the Cock 'n' Bull, and you can come down and get a feel for what we're all about. Or better still, why don't I pick you up on my Norton and take you out for breakfast first?"

"Your Norton?" I looked at him like he was nuts. "You call your car 'Norton'?"

This time Stanley threw his head back and laughed. He laughed and laughed and laughed. Snorting like a contented horse; acting like a horse's ass.

"What's so damned funny?" I fumed.

"You call your car 'Norton'?" he mimicked me. "Oh, brother, what a Woman of the World you are! Everybody knows that a Norton is a motorcycle . . . not a car! Ha, ha, snort, snort!"

"Well, how the hell should I know that a Norton is a motorcycle?" I snapped. "I've never been on a motorcycle in my entire life!" Ugh, I could have kicked myself for saying that. It sounded so unworldly. So unsophisticated.

"Well, you're about to," Peter grinned at me. "What time should I pick you up for breakfast?"

"Oh, no!" I cried. "I mean, yes, I'll have breakfast with you, but whatever you do—*don't* pick me up on a motorcycle!"

"Why not?"

"Because first you'd have to run over my mother and then you'd have to run over my father," I babbled. "They're always saying, 'Over our dead bodies will you ride on a motorcycle!'"

Peter and Stanley both collapsed in laughter.

It was all pretty unnerving since I wasn't even trying to be funny. I was dead serious.

"Look, why don't I just meet you here?" I said to Peter.

"Christ, you really are fucking adorable!" he hooted.

"How about ten?"

"Sure," he said, "sure thing. Hey, look, I've gotta go." He jumped up from the table. "I have some people waiting."

"You won't forget? Ten o'clock?"

"Are you kidding?" He took hold of a lock of my hair and gave it a twirl with his finger. "I wouldn't miss it for the world." And then he left.

Stanley whisked me into his Trans Am and drove back to Hampstead as fast as the car could carry us. Faster even. Only he didn't dump me on the curb in front of the house and screech off into the night, never to be seen again, like I expected he would. Instead he drove right past the house and pulled up in front of the big gray stone cottage that's for sale down the street. Number 8683 Blossom Road. Three doors down from where my wonderful twin brothers and their respective families live in semidetached splendor.

"What are you doing, Stanley?" I cried. "I don't live here!"

"You're not going to that 'interview' tomorrow." He spoke for the first time since we left the Cock 'n' Bull.

"See what I mean, Stanley?" I cringed. "That's why we haven't been getting along lately. You're always telling me what to do—like I have no mind of my own. I *do* have a mind of my own, you know?"

"Boy, do you ever! And it's always getting you into hot water. That's why you need a guy like me around—to take care of you."

"I can take care of myself!"

"You need somebody to look after you," he insisted, "and I'm applying for the job." He whipped out a boulder-sized diamond ring and shoved it under my nose. "Here's my credentials."

"God," I gasped, forgetting myself for a moment, "it *is* a rock!"

"Yeah," he smiled, "so put it on and own a piece of the rock, ha, ha."

"Oh, Stanley . . . I . . . I . . ." All of a sudden I was at a rare loss for words. It's funny, you know. Despite everything, I felt kind of torn up inside. This little voice inside my head (which sounded amazingly like Ma's) kept saying: "C'mon, Shayna Pearl, put the ring on your finger already. Stanley is a wonderful boy. He's going to take care of you. And God*knows*, if anybody needs taking care of, it's you. You just don't have what it takes to survive Out There on your own." But then there was this other little voice that said: "What, are you crazy or something? Are you going to settle for Gefilte Fish when you can have Shaggy Buffalo?"

"C'mon, Shayna Pearl, put the ring on your finger already!" Stanley cried, pressing it close to my nose. For a moment there I thought he was going to hook it right through my nostrils. "I'm asking you to be my wife. I'm offering you a lifetime of security. With me you'll have no worries, no cares, no struggles."

Just like dead people, I thought.

"What's the matter? Don't you like it? Isn't it big enough?"

"Oh, of course it's big enough." It sure was a beauty. "In fact, it's so big, it would probably give me a hernia."

"Could you think of a better way to get a hernia?"

"It's a beautiful ring, Stanley, really it is . . ."

"Are you afraid I can't take care of you, is that it? Are you worried that I'm going to hurt you? 'Cause if you are, let me set your mind at rest right now. If you marry me, I promise, I swear I'll take good care of you. As long as I'm around, nothing will ever happen to you!"

Well, *he* said it, I didn't. "I'm sorry, Stanley." I handed the ring back to him. "It'll never work."

"See this house?" He pointed to the big gray stone. "I'm going to buy it for you. For us."

"God, Stanley, I don't want to live on the same street

as all my family. The way I feel right now, I don't even want to live on the same planet!"

"You can furnish it any way you like," he went on, ignoring me, "Chinese, Modern, Antique. I'll take you over to Fraser Brothers and you can buy out the whole place if you want."

"Fraser Brothers?" I found myself swallowing hard. He was really hitting below the belt. It's not every day that a girl is given carte blanche at the most exclusive furniture store in Montreal—a vast wonderland of everything from the dining room of your dreams to the bedroom of your fantasies. It took a moment for me to come back to my senses. Try though I did, the bedroom of my fantasies just did not include Stanley in it. "But I don't love you . . ."

"We'll park our matching 'His' and 'Hers' silver Mercedes 450SLs in the driveway," he continued, oblivious. "And we'll plant tomatoes and zucchini in the backyard. And kids! We'll have at least two, one boy, one girl . . ."

"But I'm not ready for kids yet!"

"And wait'll you see the inside,"—he whistled—"fifteen rooms! Five bedrooms, maid's quarters in the basement, a fully equipped kitchen and laundry room for you, a play room for the kids, a den for me."

"Look, Stanley . . ."

"And I'm going to put one of those vibrating E-Z chairs in there, you know, one of those twenty-four position numbers like your father has? And every night, when I come home after a hard day's work, I can lie back in my chair and relax while you, my loving wife, fetch me my slippers and my newspaper. . . ."

"God, Stanley, you don't want a wife, you want a golden retriever!"

He took my hand and brought it up to his lips. "I want you,"—he kissed the tips of my fingers—"you and only you."

"Yeah, well, what about what I want?" I pulled my

hand away and put it in my pocket. "Has it ever occurred to you that maybe *I* don't want to live in Hampstead all my life?"

"Dammit, Shayna Pearl!" He banged his fist against the steering wheel. "When we first started seeing each other, you wanted the same things I did—at least, that's what you said."

"I thought I did—back then." I shrugged.

"So what made you change your mind? One day you just woke up and decided you'd rather be a Woman of the World instead of a Hampstead housewife?"

"Yeah, I guess you could say I woke up one day."

"What day?"

"I don't know, I guess it was one day this past March. I was sitting on the steps in front of my house, watching the snow melt on the lawns of Hampstead, and all of a sudden I found myself holding my breath and screaming inside: *shit*—is this all there is to life? Is Hampstead all there is to life? Is there life in Hampstead?"

"That's ridiculous!" he scoffed. "Hampstead is the ultimate!"

I knew better. According to my boss, Mrs. Finkelberg, I didn't have the street smarts she had while growing up poor and hungry in the old Jewish ghetto in East End Montreal, but I was well aware of what was happening on the hoity-toity west end streets of Hampstead. I had the whole tableau etched into my mind. In March the snow melted. Dog shit appeared layer by layer. Swarms of Italian gardeners swooped down from atop their bright red trucks to clean up the dog shit and replace it with expensive sheep shit. Thousands of dollars worth of plants, shrubs, flowers and imported rocks were planted. Built-in lawn sprinklers were turned on. Signs went up saying:

Lawn Landscaping by Don Giovanni

&
Sons

New cars bloomed in driveways. Flashy blue and show-offy orange Corvettes or brassy gold and midnight black Trans Ams with obscene spread eagles painted on the hoods sprang up beside your basic Caddy and/or Mercedes. Sons of Hampstead came out to wash and wax their cars; fathers went off to play golf; daughters headed for the hairdresser's to get the latest in perms, dyes, and blow jobs; mothers shipped the kids and their designer jeans off to camp or Europe or Out West. Mothers went off to play tennis and/or golf. Kids came home to bomb around the streets on their ten-speed bikes, Yamaha Chappys and fiberglass skateboards. Leaves fell. Gardeners swooped down from atop their red trucks to rake them up. Brand-new four-wheel drives replaced Corvettes sent into hibernation for the winter. Snow fell. Gardeners shovelled. . . .

"It's just not for me," I tried to explain.

"So what do you want?" he asked me. "What exactly is it?"

I shrugged. "I only know what I don't want. I don't want the same old shit. Now could you take me home? Please!"

"Okay," he said, putting the car in reverse and backing up to the house. "But as far as the marriage thing goes, I won't take no for an answer."

"It'll never work, Stanley. We want different things out of life."

"I don't believe that for one minute! You're just going through some kind of phase or something."

"You can believe what you want to believe. You always do anyway." I opened the door and got out of the car. "Bye, Stanley."

"No, not good-bye, uh-uh, no," he said, "'cause you're going to feel differently after a good night's sleep. I just know you will."

"Don't hold your breath!" I slammed the car door behind me.

"That's exactly what I'm going to do." He popped up

through the sun roof. "I'm going to hold my breath until you say 'yes'!"

"That's a bad idea, Stanley."

"You can give me your answer when I pick you up for breakfast tomorrow, say around nine?"

"Damn you, Stanley, you've got to be the most exasperating person I know! You're even worse than my mother!"

"See you in the morning, Shayna Pearl . . . I love you!!!" He waved good-bye and drove off.

"The hell you will!" I muttered as I watched his car disappear around the corner. "Tomorrow I'm having breakfast with a shaggy buffalo."

Chapter 4

THE MORNING started off with a roar.

A deafening roar that shook my entire room.

An earthquake, I thought, sitting bolt upright in bed. Montreal is having its first major earthquake and this is it!

I held my breath and braced myself for The End to come. Only, The End never came. Just three more deafening roars. Then silence. Then Ma's anguished cry:

"Oh, my God, Arnie, it's the Hell's Angels!"

I jumped out of bed and ran to the window.

"Oh, my God is right!" I moaned as I peeked out from behind my curtains. Parked over by the curb in front of the house was the biggest, blackest motorcycle I ever did see. And perched on top, complete with silver-flecked helmet and mirror sunglasses, was one Peter Simon Freeman. "I'll kill him!" I cried. I was furious. For about half a second. Then I found myself smiling with delight. I just couldn't help it. I mean, he looked so wonderful sitting there on his motorcycle. Like a knight on a giant steed.

Nobody else seemed to think so though.

Ma, Dad, and Giovanni the Gardener, who just happened to be standing out front at the time, didn't seem to think he looked wonderful at all.

In fact, they didn't seem to be thinking much of anything.

They appeared to be in a state of shock.

Over by the rock garden Ma was standing so still you'd have thought Giovanni had planted her there. And Dad, who was in the midst of loading his golf stuff into the trunk of his Mercedes, stood stock still, golf club in hand, as though considering its potential as a weapon.

Even Giovanni the Gardener had stopped gardening.

An eternity passed before anybody moved or spoke.

And then it was Peter who broke the silence.

"Hey there," he said, removing his helmet and sunglasses as he got off his bike and onto his feet. "Shay home?"

Nobody answered.

They all just stood there, bug-eyed, as if trying to convince themselves that they were really seeing Peter.

And after the initial shock wore off, they just stood there, mouths agape, as if trying to figure out which part of him they found hardest to believe.

His gleaming black Norton Commando and accessories?

His unruly mop of curly light brown hair and his closely cropped reddish blond beard?

The gold earring that was dangling from his left earlobe and glittering in the morning sunlight?

The way his khaki army pants were tucked into his knee-high Frye boots?

The way he was naked from the waist up, save for a faded jean jacket that was hacked off at the sleeves and unsnapped at the snaps?

The fact that at six foot something, he was a Gulliver among Lilliputians (the tallest of whom was Dad, who barely reaches five foot six in his cleated golf shoes)?

All of the above?

"Shay Fine *does* live here, doesn't she?" he asked. He sure cut a formidable figure standing there. "At least that's what it says in the telephone book." He waved a crumpled piece of paper in the air. "Page 697, to be exact."

"Good grief, Arnie," Ma suddenly snapped out of her trance, "I think he wants Shayna Pearl!"

"Yeah," Peter nodded, "that's who I want."

"Oh, God," I cried, "what the hell am I standing here for?" I threw on a tank top and a pair of jeans and after making the world's quickest pit stop at the bathroom to wash up, I flew out the front door and, as it happened, right into Peter's arms.

"Whoa, there," he said, "where's the fire?"

"What are you doing here?" I blurted.

"I came to ring the doorbell to see if you were home," he shrugged. "Nobody down there would tell me if you were or you weren't."

"No, I mean, what are you doing HERE . . . at my house?"

He just looked at me and laughed. "You know, I bet that wasn't easy."

"What wasn't?"

"Getting toothpaste on your nose like that." He rubbed the tip of my nose with his finger. "Either you've got bad aim or you get cavities in some pretty weird places."

"I was in a hurry."

"Mmmm . . ."—he licked his finger—"Crest?"

"It's Aim and you haven't answered my question yet!"

"About what I'm doing here, you mean?"

"We were supposed to meet downtown at ten. You weren't supposed to come here and pick me up at eight. Especially not on your motorcycle!"

"I just had to find out if we'd really have to ride out of here over your parents' dead bodies," he grinned.

"You're crazy!"

"No, just curious."

"You're freaking my parents out."

"And you love it!"

45

I glanced over at Ma and Dad. There was smoke coming out of their respective ears. I swear there was. I didn't exactly love it. But I didn't exactly hate it either. Actually, it was all kind of exciting. "I don't think they like you."

"So I noticed!" He laughed that wonderful, crazy, hoarse laugh of his. It sent shivers right through me. "And somehow I think the fun has just begun—'cause here comes your old lady and she looks mean. Real meeeaaannn."

I turned around and sure enough there she was.

Mrs. Arnie Fine, M.D., Ob., Gyn.

Née *Yenta Buttinski.*

And she looked mean. Real meeeeaaannn. Her hands were firmly planted on her hips, her nostrils were flaring in and out, in and out; her eyes were ablaze with anger and her lips were all curled up in one of her notorious "I'm Going to Eat You Alive" smiles. "Shayna Pearl, may I speak to you for a second—*alone?*" She grabbed my arm and pulled me aside.

"What is it, Ma?"

"Funny, I was just going to ask you that very same question!" She looked from me to Peter and then from Peter to me. "What, in God'sNAME, is it?"

"This is Peter Simon Freeman, Ma."

"Where did you find him? At Granby Zoo?"

"Maaaa . . ."

"Times sure have changed. In my day we used to go to the zoo to visit the animals. The animals never came to visit us!"

"Very funny! It just so happens that I met him at the Cock 'n' Bull. If you weren't so busy yelling at me last night for turning down Stanley's proposal, I might have told you about the interview."

"Interview?"

"First we're going to have breakfast and then I'm going to interview him for the *Register*. He's a singer. You know, the one Stanley was telling us about last night?"

"Oh," she breathed a sigh of relief. "It's only an interview. . . ."

"I have to be going now, Ma."

"Be going?"

"Yeah, downtown."

"On that thing?!" She pointed to Peter's motorcycle.

"Ma, please!"

"Please nothing!" She went up to Peter and shook her finger at him. "Young man,"—she blasted him—"I did not spend twenty-three years of my life raising a daughter so she should go out and get herself maimed, or God-FORBID killed, on one of those . . . those things!"

"Ma, puleeese!" It's a good thing embarrassment isn't fatal.

"Over my dead body will you go on that thing with him!"

I looked up at Peter and gave him a helpless shrug. I wouldn't have blamed him if he took off right then and there.

But he didn't.

He just stood there with his arms folded and he looked down at the puny little woman who was screaming blue murder into his belly button and he laughed that wonderful laugh of his. "You don't have to worry about Shay getting killed or maimed while riding on my thing," he told her. He told her but good. "Ain't never been a woman yet who's been killed or maimed while riding on my thing!" He winked at me.

We both cracked up laughing.

I laughed so hard I almost peed in my pants.

"I don't think this is a laughing matter." Ma was really rattled. "Those things are dangerous!"

"I'm not even gonna touch that one," Peter muttered.

"It sure is a beautiful motorcycle," I told him. "I can't wait to go on it." I looked at Ma and gave her one of what she calls my smart-aleck smirks. I couldn't get over how puny and ineffective she looked next to Peter. "I just can't wait."

"You're not going!" Ma said between clenched teeth.

"Oh, yes I am, Mother," I said, suddenly feeling ten feet tall. "I'm over twenty-one, in case you've forgotten."

"C'mon, let's split." Peter took my hand and pulled me toward his bike.

Ma was fit to be tied. "Arnie! Don't just stand there like a dope, do something!"

Dad, forever lurking in the background, forever silent, finally spoke his mind. "When are you going to learn to stop making a big issue, Sylvia?" he growled. "The minute you make a big issue these kids today go and do something out of spite. Christ, when are you going to learn?"

"Arnie," she pleaded, "do something. Stop her!"

"I'm late for my starting time, Sylvia." He slipped into his car and backed out of the driveway, giving me a stern look as he rolled by.

I got the message loud and clear. It meant: "Stop aggravating your mother, will you? Can't you see she's driving me crazy?"

I blew him a kiss as he took off down the street and raced toward the peace and quiet of his beloved Elmsdale Golf and Country Club.

"Oooooo, that man!" Ma cried out in frustration.

"Well, see you around, Ma." I waved good-bye to her.

"You stay away from that thing!"

"There's nothing to worry about, really," Peter reassured her. "Hell, I take my five-year-old son for rides all the time and he just loves it."

Son, I thought, my heart sinking to my feet. It hadn't occurred to me my wild buffalo might be married.

"Don't listen to her!" He pulled me by the arm. "C'mon, you're gonna love riding on my bike. It'll blow your mind!"

"She'll blow nothing of the kind!" Ma grabbed my other arm and pulled me in the opposite direction. For a moment there I thought they were going to split me right in two. Like a wishbone.

"Ma, leggo of my arm!" I pleaded. "You're pulling it out of the socket!"

She loosened her grip and I fell right into Peter's arms.

"How could you go with him?" she glared at me. "What will people think when they see you riding around on a motorcycle with a married man? What about his wife?"

"What about my wife?" Peter shrugged.

"What will she think if she finds out that you're riding around with another woman?"

"She couldn't care less."

"Ha! What kind of wife would have an attitude like that?"

"An ex-one. I'm divorced."

"Divorced?" Her whole face puckered. Like she'd just sucked a lemon or eaten a sour grape.

"Two years already."

Thank God, I thought to myself. He's free! I was so ecstatic even my forehead was smiling.

Suddenly Ma noticed my tits jiggling around happily beneath my tank top and she pulled me aside. "Get into the house this minute and put on a bra before those bazooms of yours give you two black eyes!" she muttered into my ear. She should have only known that I got dressed in such a hurry, I wasn't wearing any underpants either. I ignored her. What she had to say was the same old thing. The same old shit. I was much more interested in what Peter had to say, and besides, he didn't seem to mind the way my tits were jiggling around or the way my nipples were jutting out of my rather skimpy tank top. He didn't seem to mind one bit. From the way he was eyeing them and grinning, I could tell he was getting really turned on. So was I for that matter.

"C'mon," he said, slapping a motorcycle helmet on my head, "let's get going. I have to stop by my apartment on the way. There's something I just gotta do there before I could even *think* of having breakfast!"

"Sure, anything you say," I found myself telling him.

"You're not taking her on that thing!" Ma warned him.

Peter ignored her and proceeded to do up the chin strap on my helmet.

"God, you're amazing," I whispered into his ear. "I

never met anyone who wasn't afraid of my mother before."

"Just stick with me, kid,"—he winked—"and I'll liberate you from all this shit in no time!"

"In that case, you must be the Knight in Shining Armor I've been waiting for!" I giggled. "The one my mother said didn't exist."

"Oh, she said that, did she now?" He grinned. There was a devilish gleam in his eye. "Well, we're just gonna have to show her!" He stripped off his faded jean jacket with the hacked-off sleeves, and he smoothed it out on the ground next to his bike. "Sir Galahad, your Knight in Shining Armor, at your service, m'lady." He took a deep bow. "My steed is awaiting." And then, much to my delight—and Ma's horror—he scooped me up into his arms and hoisted me onto the back of his bike.

"Put her down!" Ma yelled at him. "Put her down this instant, you—you Svengali you! Shayna Pearl!"

"Bye, Ma!" I yelled as Peter climbed aboard his bike and revved up the engine. "Have a nice day!" I wrapped my arms around his waist and we sped off, with Peter half-naked, through the superclean streets of Hampstead.

"SHAYNA PEARL, COME BACKKKKKKKKKKKK!"

Poor Ma.

Poor hysterical Ma.

No doubt she spent the whole day worrying about what was going to happen to me while I was on the motorcycle with Peter. And it was all for no good reason too. I mean, she had nothing to worry about while I was on the motorcycle with Peter.

It was when I got off the motorcycle that she should have started worrying.

I guess you could say Peter and I rushed into things, but once we got down to his apartment in the McGill Ghetto there was just no stopping us.

We wanted each other so badly it hurt.

Anyway, it all happened so naturally—so beautifully—that it didn't feel cheap or anything like that.

It felt right.

Especially after we shared a couple of big, fat joints—Colombia's finest, Peter called them.

Especially after he put the raw, pulsing reggae music of Black Uhuru on the stereo and he pulled me down to the rug on his den floor, kissing me like I'd never been kissed before.

God, he stirred up feelings inside me I never knew I had. I didn't even know where they came from or why—all I knew was that there just seemed to be no end to them. They just kept getting stronger and stronger until I thought I was going to burst.

And then he pulled off my top, and he started caressing my breasts.

Touching them.

Feeling them.

Kissing them.

Licking them.

Sucking and biting them.

My whole body seemed to come alive. Like there was an electric charge going through it.

And then Peter undid my jeans and slipped them off.

And then he did the same with his.

And then we started rolling around on the rug—so excited; so naked. Like a scene right out of *A Star Is Born* with Streisand and Kristofferson. It was all so perfect. So incredibly perfect. Especially when Peter's hand started caressing me, and God, it felt good. Insanely good. I had to bite my tongue to keep from screaming out with excitement or whatever it was that was turning my body into an ever-tightening knot.

And then his mouth started traveling downwards.

Down.

Down.

Down.

And his fingers spread me wide.

And his tongue started sliding up and down; up and down.

Exploring me. Kissing me. Licking me. Sucking me.

"Oh, God," I found myself moaning, "Ohhhh, Godddd . . ."

And then we rolled around some more and I found myself reaching out for Peter's penis.

His hardened, pulsing penis.

My first.

I wasn't quite sure what to do with it. So I just let my hands explore it. Caress it. Fondle it. The way my best—and far more experienced—friend Jo Ann Pecker showed me how it was done on "Fluffy" the stuffed elephant's trunk, one night in Camp Hiawatha many moons ago. The way I'd been doing it ever since—in all those fantasies about the bearded Man of My Dreams. Anyway, I must have been doing something right because Peter started writhing and moaning and groaning. Like he was really enjoying it.

And then I got on top of him and I started kissing my way down his body.

Down.

Down.

Down.

Until I came face to face with his penis. Boy, it sure did look big. Enormous even. For a moment I was filled with panic. It just didn't seem possible that such a huge thing could fit into my tiny little mouth.

And then I remembered something Jo Ann once told me.

"Giving a blow job is very much like eating a popsicle," I could just hear her singsongy voice saying. "You plunge it in and out of your mouth like you would a popsicle . . . you lick it, suck it and slurp it like you would a popsicle . . . you try to make it last as long as possible like a popsicle . . . you do everything you'd do with a popsicle except . . ."

My mind went blank.

I couldn't for the life of me remember what came after "except." It was only after my teeth sort of clamped down on Peter's penis and he sort of cried out in pain that it came back to me.

". . . You do everything you'd do with a popsicle," I could hear Jo Ann's voice loud and clear, "except take a bite out of it, of course."

Of course. After I remembered that vital tidbit of information it was smooth sailing. I followed Jo Ann's instructions to a T (I guess you could almost have called it a blow job by numbers), and I just couldn't believe the effect my mouth was having on Peter's penis. On his entire body for that matter.

God, I was driving him berserk.

I couldn't believe the things a woman's mouth can do to a man twice her size!

The pleasure she can bring him.

The ecstasy.

I never dreamed.

I just never dreamed!

It was a whole new feeling for me. A whole new world.

I just kept licking, sucking and slurping away until Peter gently withdrew himself from my mouth and pulled me up toward him so that we were face-to-face, mouth-to-mouth and crotch-to-crotch.

And then the most wonderful thing of all began to happen.

The Moment of Moments.

The icing on the cake, if you will.

Peter rolled over on top of me and he started poking his penis up in between my legs.

Poking and prodding.

Prodding and poking.

"You on the Pill or something?" he whispered. His voice was hoarse, strained. There was a kind of breathless urgency about it. An urgency not unlike that of the throbbing penis that was poking its way up into my vagina.

For a second there I froze, tensed up.

I wondered if it was the right time to tell him I was a virgin. With his being twenty-seven and a father, I wasn't sure how he'd react if he knew he was about to take the first plunge into No Man's Land.

"Are you?" he whispered again.

Poking and prodding.

Prodding and poking.

"Yes!" I cried out. *"Oh, God . . . yes!!!"* I knew it was a risk, lying the way I did. I knew it yet I lied anyway. I just didn't want to spoil something so beautiful—something so natural—with a pain-in-the-ass technicality. I wanted Peter to concentrate on all of me, on us. I didn't want him to be preoccupied with a technicality.

And then he reached down and guided himself inside me.

And then he was inside me.

And then it was definitely too late to scream: *"Stop! I'm a virgin!"*

Because I wasn't one anymore.

And I was glad. Not to mention amazed. I mean, it didn't even hurt. And it just slid in so easily, so naturally, so painlessly!

It felt as if it belonged there.

I *liked* having it there.

And that amazed me no end.

I'd heard you weren't even supposed to like your first time. Jo Ann didn't. A lot of the other girls I know didn't either. Time after time I can remember sitting over coffee and strawberry cheesecake at Nuddick's Restaurant and listening to my friends recount their first-time horror stories. Each would take turns describing their first time.

"The pain," one would grimace.

"The bloody mess," another would shudder.

"The guilt," a third would wince.

"The fear and the awkwardness," they'd all agree. "That's the worst!"

But I felt none of those things.

I felt wonderful. Lying there with Peter inside me—it felt right.

I started moving to his rhythm.

I caught on pretty fast too. Hell, it was as natural as trotting a horse. He pushed up; I pushed down. He pushed down; I pushed up. We really went well together, I thought. In fact we were downright perfect.

Even the music was perfect.

Amid throbbing guitars and pounding drums, Black Uhuru was singing something about how you rock over here and bounce over there and bum somewhere else.

Urging us onward.

Forward.

Upward.

It was like having our own cheering section.

God, how sweet it was, how exciting it was to feel a man's body—Peter's body—so entangled with mine. So entwined. Like two pieces of rope bound together and knotted as one.

And then the knot got tighter and tighter and tighter until we reached the point where we just had to unravel.

And we did.

Boy, did we ever.

Chapter 5

"MAN, AM I STARVED," Peter said as he dug into a plateful of eggs at Beauty's, a cramped noisy little greasy spoon that serves the best brunch in town. "There's nothing like one of Beauty's famed 'Mish-Mash' omelettes for the after-sex, after-grass munchies, wouldn't you say?"

"Uh-huh," I replied, picking at my food.

"What's the matter? Aren't you hungry? I thought you'd be starved after this morning. Christ, you must have had *ten* orgasms!"

"Peter?" I blurted. "There's something I think you should know." I had to tell him. I felt so dishonest. "I've never been, you know, with a man before."

"You what?" I thought his face was going to crumble up and fall on his plate. "You mean . . . you mean you're a virgin?"

"Not anymore, I'm not." I glanced nervously out the window. The streets were jam-packed with Saturday morning shoppers combing the Mount Royal and St.

Lawrence Street discount stores for bargains. I wished I could disappear among them. "I'm sorry. I guess I should have told you before. It's just that, well, I was afraid. I thought it might, you know, spoil things . . . the mood . . . I . . ."

"A fucking virgin!"

"I—I guess you could put it that way."

"But . . . but there was no pain . . . no blood . . . no mess . . . it was so clean!"

I let out a nervous giggle. "You sound like a Tide commercial!"

"But how?" he marveled.

I shrugged. "I guess I hurt more than my pride when I fell off my brother's bike ten years ago."

He shook his head in disbelief. "God, I thought you were kind of innocent, but I never dreamed . . . nobody's *that* innocent anymore!"

"It wasn't like I was saving myself for marriage or anything corny like that," I explained. "It's just that I never met anyone before who I wanted to be *that* close to."

"But you knew what you were doing. I mean, your mouth, your hands, your body—hell, you sure seemed to know what you were doing!" I guess he forgot that I almost bit the tip of his penis off. "How'd you know what to do?"

"Jo Ann Pecker."

"Whose pecker?"

"Not *whose* pecker! *Jo Ann* Pecker. My best friend."

He gave me a strange look. "You a dyke?"

"No, of course not! Jo Ann is married. To Dr. Richard Pecker. He's a shrink. Or at least he will be as soon as he finishes his residency in psychiatry at the Jewish General."

He shook his head, as if he was trying to clear it. "What has *that* got to do with anything?"

"Well, you see, it's like this," I explained. "Jo Ann and I have lunch a few times a week at Nuddick's—their strawberry cheesecake is out of this world—and she tells me, amongst other things, all about her sex life with her husband—that is, whenever she has something new and improved to report—though lately all she seems to talk about is being pregnant—which is what she is. Oh, and I read *Cosmopolitan*, of course."

"Jesus!" He rolled his eyes around in his head.

"What's wrong? Did I go too fast for you? Sometimes I talk fast when I'm nervous—and right now I think I'm nervous."

"Pheeeuuuwwww," he sighed, tugging at his beard and shaking his head over and over. For the longest time he didn't say anything else. He just sat there stabbing his omelette repeatedly with his fork while I sat there wincing and biting my lower lip. "Why didn't you tell me before?" he said finally.

"You didn't ask."

"I asked you if you were on The Pi— Oh, my God, you're not on The Pill, are you?"

"Uh-uh."

"You're not on anything?"

"Just Femirons and the occasional Pamprin."

"Holy shit!" He smacked himself on the head with the palm of his hand. "Jesus Christ on crutches!"

"I'm sorry." Tears welled up in my eyes. I felt awful. Like a criminal or something. "Really I am." I tried to blink back the tears, but they wouldn't stay put. They streamed down my face and splashed onto my Mish-Mash omelette.

Which was just as well. As it turned out, Peter just happens to be one of those men who hates to see a woman cry.

"Aw, hey, c'mon, don't bawl." He reached over and wiped a tear away with his finger. "C'mon now, it's not the end of the world . . . I hope."

"It's not?" I brightened.

"Nawww,"—he smiled at me—"just don't do it again, okay?"

"You must think I'm the world's biggest idiot," I winced.

"Naw," he reached out and stroked my hair. "Let's just say you got carried away in a moment of great passion."

"That's just what happened. Really. No shit."

"Okay, but from now on just be honest with me, okay? Lies have a way of catching up with you—especially when you lie about being on the Pill."

"It was really stupid of me, wasn't it? God, I could end up pregnant!" I shuddered at the thought.

"It's too late to worry about that now. C'mon." He grabbed my hand and pulled me to my feet, "let's go. We have things to do today."

"Like what?"

"Like going to the drugstore to buy some safes for one thing. Not that I'm crazy about using safes, mind you, but they'll have to do for now."

"Are we going back to your apartment to do it again?" I cried, unable to conceal my excitement.

"Later," he laughed, "much later. Right now I have a rehearsal to get to. And then we're going to spend the afternoon with my kid. And then I have a show to do tonight. Think you could hold out till then?"

"I'll try." I gave him a look out of the corner of my eye. "But it won't be easy."

"Cripes, I've created a monster!"

"What are you going to do about it?"

"Just this." He wrapped his arm around me and kissed me in front of the entire restaurant. "There now," he grinned sheepishly. "That ought to hold you till tonight."

"I don't have a choice, do I?"

"Nope. Anyway, you've got a story to do, remember?"

"A story?"

"Yeah, the one you're supposed to do on my band?"

"Oh, that story!" It had kind of slipped my mind.

"Yeah, *that* story. It was the reason why we arranged to meet today, wasn't it?"

"Yeah, but that was before I lost my Reporter's Impartiality—if you get my drift."

"Oh, I get your drift, all right, Babe," he laughed, "and it's knocking me right on my ass!"

Talk about knocking someone right on their ass.

Everything Peter and I did knocked me right on mine. His rehearsal in the morning, his son in the afternoon, his body at night, the way he kept calling me "Babe," the fact that he didn't laugh in my face when I told him I wanted to be a Hollywood screenwriter—it all just knocked me for a loop.

Peter Simon Freeman was the most incredible thing that ever happened to me.

And if there is such a thing as a "moment" when you realize that you're really in love with someone, I think my "moment" came in the middle of the afternoon. In the toy department at Eaton's. The thing that really grabbed me was the sight of Peter standing there amongst the Big Birds and the Cookie Monsters with his little son, Nicky, propped high atop his shoulders. I actually got goose bumps from watching them together—the way Peter kept letting Nicky dip backwards and hang upside down; the way Nicky would then shriek with laughter and drool all over Peter's backside; the way father and son were getting off on each other. It was all I could do to keep from running up and pinching them every minute to make sure they weren't just something that stepped out of a dream or a fantasy or a Coke Adds Life commercial.

And Nicky! Nicky with his curly mop of reddish blond hair, pouting eyes, button nose and Pepsodent smile; with his Miami Dolphin's football shirt, faded blue jean overalls and little Adidas running shoes; with his tendency to mimic Peter's every gesture and every word— including some of the bluer words, like schmuck, cocksucker and fuckin' bitch (which was apparently considerably less charming to several passers-by, who turned red-faced with embarrassment) . . . I mean, he was just too cute for words!

He was, in Peter's own words, a "gas."

"If I ever have a kid I want one just like him," I kept telling Peter—much to his delight.

And I meant it.

I was head-over-heels in love with father and son. I could already picture the three of us playing touch football on Mount Royal or skiing in the Laurentians or vacationing in a secluded little island beach house off the coast of Maine.

I made up my mind right then and there: I wanted in. In for keeps. And you can't get in much deeper than I did when I went back home with Peter at the end of the night.

After we smoked some more grass and made love for a second incredible time, Peter asked me to stay over.

"The whole entire night?" I cried.

"Yeah, the whole entire night," he laughed. "What'd you think I meant?"

I bit my lip. "I don't know."

"What's the matter. Don't you want to stay?"

"Oh, I do! More than anything. It's just that . . ."

"Your mother again, huh?" he frowned.

"If I stay out all night, she'll send the entire M.U.C. police force after me. Maybe even the R.C.M.P. Quite possibly the C.I.A. If she hasn't already!"

"What do you mean—if she hasn't already?" he asked. "I thought you called her earlier this evening to let her know you were still alive or something?"

"No, I said I tried to reach her but there was no answer. She must be up at the club with my father. They have a big deal up there every Saturday night."

He glanced at the clock. "It's pretty late. I'm sure they must be home by now. Why don't you try again?" He put on a robe and headed out the bedroom door. "I'm going to the kitchen to get some munchies."

"What the hell am I going to tell her?" I yelled after him.

"I'm sure you'll think of something! It'll be good practice for your screenwriting career!"

"Thanks a heap!" I lay there panic-stricken. I knew I

had to call Ma and tell her something. But what? That I'd just become a woman and she should wish me *mazel tov?* That I broke my hymen and couldn't be moved for twenty-four hours in case of hemorrhage? Or maybe I was supposed to ask her, woman to woman, if she wouldn't mind my sleeping through the night with the guy I'd already slept with? I could almost hear the conversation:

"You lost your *whaaaaaatttt?*"

"My virginity, Ma. My maidenhead."

"To that—that animal?"

"Don't worry about it, Ma. He didn't tear me in half, if that's what you mean."

"Oh, God, Shayna Pearl, I think you lost your head, never mind your maidenhead!"

"Ma, I'm a woman now, be happy for me."

"That Svengali—I ought to have him arrested!"

"For what? Breaking and entering? I mean, really, Ma, I'm twenty-three years old!"

"Kurveh!" Click.

So much for that approach, I decided. I knew I'd have to come up with something a lot better than the truth if I wanted everything to work out happily ever after. If I wanted there to *be* an "ever after." And then it came to me. Jo Ann! If anybody would know what to do, I thought, she would. She always has an answer for everything. I picked up the phone and called her. She answered on the first ring.

"Jo, it's me, Shay," I blurted. "Did I wake you?"

"Uh-uh," she replied, "Richard and I just got home from the club. It was 'Country and Western' night. How come you and Stanley weren't there?"

"It's a long story. Listen, Jo, I . . ."

"You should have been there, Shay. Everybody was there."

"Ya, well . . ."

"Marsha Slutsky came with her *A*-rab boyfriend. Some nerve, huh? Showing up at a Jewish golf club like Elmsdale with an *A*-rab? Everybody was talking about what a nerve it was. Oh, yeah, and you had to see Marcie Karpman. She was walking around with her tits hanging out from here to tomorrow. Flaunting them at everything in pants. Including the bartender. Oh, yeah, and this is the best! You've just gotta hear this. She kept ordering piña coladas and calling them *penis* coladas— especially when there were men around. That girl's really been hot-to-trot since her divorce, don't you think? Actually, that's probably why she's divorced. Oh, and by the way, I also saw your parents there tonight. Your mother was really packing in those penis coladas, if I do say so myself. . . ."

"My mother?" I was taken aback. "But she doesn't drink. She pops Valium!"

"Yeah, well, if you think that's weird, wait till you hear the rest of it. When I went over and asked her where you were tonight, she got this funny look in her eye, and she started rattling on and on about what a lucky woman *my* mother is to have a wonderful daughter like me—you know, because I'm married to a doctor who looks like Warren Beatty if Warren Beatty had a Jewish nose and because I live in a brand-new two-hundred-thousand-dollar home in Cote Saint Luc and because I'm going to have a baby and all that. . . . is there something going on that I don't know about?"

"Jo, I need your help!" I could hardly conceal my desperation. "The most wonderful guy in the world has asked me to spend the night with him and I need an alibi—you know, for my mother."

She tittered. "So you and Stanley are finally going to do It after all these months, eh? Well, what do you know?"

"It's not Stanley, Jo," I blurted.

"What?" she cried. "Who then? When? Where? What?"

"I can't get into all the details right now. He's waiting for me in the next room. I'll tell you all about it tomorrow. Right now, you've got to help me, please!"

"Okay, but at least tell me his name so I don't spend the whole night dying of curiosity."

"It's Peter. Peter Simon Freeman."

"Hey, that sounds familiar. Is his mother Bessie Freeman of Westmount? Does he have a sister Nancy who lives in Calgary? If he does then I know who he is. My mother plays canasta with his mother every week . . ."

I thought I was going to blow a fuse. "Jo Ann, this is no time to be playing Jewish Geography, for crying out loud!" Sometimes she can be so exasperating. "This is an emergency."

"Okay, okay, just tell me one more thing. What does he do?"

"He's a rock singer."

"No, I mean, what does he do for a *living?*"

"I just told you, he's a rock singer."

"Eeeuw! Isn't that an unusual occupation? For a Jewish guy, I mean?" There was a short pause. "He *is* Jewish, isn't he?"

"I dunno . . . I guess . . . he never said he wasn't."

"You sleep with a guy and you don't know if he's Jewish or what?"

"Who cares? He's gorgeous!"

"Who cares? Your parents would— Oh, God he's not an A-rab, is he?"

"JO ANN, PLEASE!" I wailed. "I have to call my mother yet!"

"Okay, okay. How about Plan A?"

"Plan A?"

"Yeah, you remember? Whenever I used to spend the night at Richard's before we were married, I'd tell my mother I was sleeping at your house. And then if she needed to get in touch with me, she'd call you and you'd tell her I was in the middle of taking a shower or something. Then you'd call me at Richard's and I'd call her back."

"Oh, yeah." My head was reeling. "That Plan A."

"It worked every time, didn't it?"

"Yeah, yeah, it's perfect, Jo. Let's do it!"

"Okay then. Give me the number where you are and

then call your mother and tell her you're sleeping here tonight."

I gave her the number. "There's just one problem though. How do I come to be sleeping at your house all of a sudden? My mother knows I wasn't with you tonight. She saw you at the club."

She stopped to think for a moment. "No problem. Tell her we just bumped into each other at Nuddick's and I asked you to sleep over because . . . because Richard was called out to the hospital on an all-night emergency and I was too petrified to stay alone in my new house. How's that?"

"God, you have the most devious mind of anyone I know!" I marveled.

"Thank you. And speaking of my new house, you've got to come over and see my new living room furniture. It's for fainting!"

"I will. Soon. Oh, and Jo?"

"Yeah?"

"You sure she's going to buy it, eh?"

"Take my word for it. She'd much rather believe that you were sleeping at my house than spending the night with a man. There isn't a mother alive who wants to know from her daughter's sex life. It says so right in that book I lent you a while back. What was it called—*My Mother/My Self* or something? Anyway, it says right there in black and white that mothers hate to think of their daughters as sexual beings. They don't want to know that we're doing It and they especially don't want to know that we're enjoying It. So just tell it to her the way we agreed and everything will be smooth sailing. You'll see."

Jo Ann was right of course, as usual.

Everything was smooth sailing as far as my phone call to Ma was concerned.

Sure she gave me a good blasting for going on that "monstrous thing" with "that hoodlum" and she was pissed off as all hell that I didn't bother to phone her all day to let her know that I was alive and well and still in one piece, but when I told her that I was spending the night at Jo Ann's, she was delighted.

"That's fine with me," she said. "Jo Ann's always been a good influence on you. Maybe she can talk some sense into you!"

And that was the end of that.

I felt a couple of twinges of guilt (accompanied by palpitations, sweating and appendicitislike stomach cramps) after I put the phone down, but then Peter got into bed with a cartonful of Kahlúa and milk and a bag of Oreo cookies and pretty soon I was feeling no pain.

It's kind of hard to feel pain when you're having Kahlúa and milk and cookies in bed with a naked man.

Especially when you're lying there, licking away at the cream center of an Oreo, just like you always do whenever you eat Oreos, and he turns to you and says:

"Christ, did anyone ever tell you you're a very seductive eater?"

From that moment on I forgot I even had a mother, let alone that I had just told her the first major lie of my life.

"A seductive eater? Who me?" I giggled. The nicest thing anybody ever said about me and food was that I eat like a bird. "Really?"

"It must be the way you're lying there and licking away at that cream center," he said. "It's almost as if you're giving head to that cookie."

"In that case," I gave him a look out of the corner of my eye, "do I swallow it or spit it out?"

"Swallow it,"—he grinned—"*definitely* swallow it!"

"Really?" Suddenly the curiosity—or something—got the better of me. "Funny, I could have sworn you were Jewish!"

"I am. Why? Does it make a difference?"

"I dunno. I guess not. I just didn't think Jewish guys expected Jewish girls to actually swallow it. Only *shiksas* . . ."

"Who the fuck told you that?" he cried.

"My friend Jo Ann . . ."

"I don't think your friend knows her ass from her elbow!"

"Where do you think I learned how to eat Oreos?"

He laughed. "Well, on second thought . . ."

"There's a real art to eating these things, you know?" I don't know what came over me but I was really getting turned on by the kinkiness of the whole conversation. "A real art." I kicked off the covers so that we were both lying there stark naked and then slowly, oh-so-slowly, I raised a cookie to my lips and set my mouth upon that cream center in the most cock-teasing way I knew how—gliding my tongue over the smooth surface; making exaggerated sucking noises; smacking my lips suggestively; smiling seductively.

Peter went absolutely bananas. He was literally panting —drooling even. His entire body seemed to be rippling with appreciation. Applauding my performance. Urging me on.

Even his penis sprang up to give me a standing ovation.

I couldn't believe the effect I was having on him.

I mean, the things a woman can do to a man just by eating an Oreo cookie!

The things she could do to his penis without even touching it.

The power she can have over it.

The awesome power.

The mystical snake charmer's power.

I never dreamed.

I just never dreamed!

"Jesus," Peter whispered hoarsely as he lunged at me, "sweet Je-*zus!*"

What a night! Peter taught me to screw in places I didn't even know you could screw. Like the beanbag chair in his den. Like the shower. I never felt so free in my whole life. So guilt free. So problem free. So absolutely and completely free. I was floating so high I didn't think I would ever come down!

Which just goes to show how little I knew about life.

Not to mention the law of gravity.

Because if I knew anything about either, I'd have known that nothing floats freely forever.

That whatever goes up has got to come down sooner or later.

And that if you're the only daughter of Sylvia and Arnie Fine, M.D., Ob., Gyn., chances are you're going to come down a lot sooner than later.

Splashdown to planet Earth came at approximately 11:00 A.M. on The Morning After.

Actually, it was more like a crash landing.

Or a scene from a Gidget movie.

When I pulled up to the house in a taxi, I found the whole damn family sitting there on the front steps and waiting for me: two brothers, two sisters-in-law, four nieces, one grandmother, one father, one mother—plus Stanley, and all of them on the verge of mass hysteria.

"Where were you?" they all screeched in perfect unison, as if they'd been rehearsing all morning long.

"And don't tell me you were at the Peckers'!" Ma shook her finger at me. Like I was a naughty puppy that had just disgraced itself on the living room rug. Apparently she failed to notice that I was a New Woman—footloose and fancy free. "It just so happens that I called the Peckers' first thing this morning and Jo Ann's husband told me that you weren't there. In fact, he hasn't seen hide nor hair of you in weeks!"

My blood ran cold. "What were you doing calling the Peckers' anyway? Checking up on me?"

"Noooo, I wasn't checking up on youuuu!" she sneered. "It just so happens that I called there because I wanted you and the Peckers to join us for brunch. Your father, God*bless* him, went out to the Brown Derby this morning and bought enough bagels, cream cheese and lox to feed an army."

"I already ate!" I glared at her.

"I told you she probably already had breakfast!" my not-too-bright sister-in-law Arlene said to my wonderful brother Terry. "Everybody was worried for nothing. I knew she wasn't going to starve to death just because she didn't come home for breakfast."

"We weren't worried because of that, you pea brain!" my wonderful brother Terry laced into her. "Honestly, Arl, you're not just getting older, you're getting dumber!"

"Shayna Pearl's gonna get a spanking, Shayna Pearl's gonna get a spanking!" my little nieces gleefully chanted in the background. "Grandma's gonna give her such a smack on the seat, she won't be able to sit down for a week!"

"You think maybe she spent the night with that Hell's Angels character Ma was telling us about?" I heard my other wonderful brother David say to his incredibly pregnant wife Eva, who was busy chomping on a bagel that was oozing cream cheese from all ends.

"Ohhhhhh!" Not-Too-Bright Arlene suddenly experienced a rare surge of brain activity. "Is *that* why we were worried?"

"Mmmmmm . . ." said Incredibly Pregnant Eva as she demolished the last remnants of her bagel and licked the cream cheese off her fingers, "all this talk about food is making me hungry. I think I'll go inside and get something to eat."

"And speaking of breakfast, Shayna Pearl," Stanley had to throw in his two cents worth, "we had a date for breakfast yesterday to discuss some very important matters. I don't appreciate being stood up, you know."

"You're hungry, Mameleh?" gurgled Bobbeh Fine, who, owing to the fact that she's as deaf as a post, was totally oblivious to the goings-on around her. Lucky duck. "You want I should make you something to eat?"

"Look, I'm sure this is nothing but a big misunderstanding." Ma forced a smile to her lips. "I'm sure Shayna Pearl has a perfectly reasonable explanation, don't you, dear?"

"Ya," Bobbeh Fine nodded enthusiastically, "*zi ist a shayna maideleh.* . . ."

"Don't you, dear?"

"Such a *nice* girl . . . such a *good* girl."

"Well, young lady," Dad fumed, "we're waiting for an explanation. What do you have to say for yourself?"

"*You all drive me insane!*" I burst into tears and ran upstairs to my room.

"Jeez, there's just no talking to you these days without you getting all hysterical!" Dad yelled after me. "What the hell is wrong with you anyway? Is it *that* time of the month again or what?"

Chapter 6

MA SHOOK ME so hard my teeth rattled.

"Wake up, Shayna Pearl," she said, "we have to talk."

"Go away!" I buried my head under my pillow. "Christ, can't a person get any privacy around this place?" Stupid question. A person can get more privacy living in a toll booth on the Laurentian Autoroute. "Just leave me alone!"

"No, I will not!" She yanked me into a sitting position and propped me up against the wall. "I'm worried to death about you. First you take off on that motorcycle yesterday morning with that . . . that hairy hoodlum! Then you spend the entire night God*knows* where doing God*knows* what. Then you come home this morning—looking like the Wreck of the Hesperus, I might add—and what do you do? You crawl into bed and go to sleep until . . . until . . . what time is it now?" She glanced at her watch. "Until five o'clock in the afternoon! This just isn't like you."

"Oh, give me a break, will you?" I groaned. I didn't feel

so hot. My thigh and stomach muscles ached something awful. My vagina felt raw—like the time I had slipped off the seat of Terry's ten-speed bike and landed on the metal bar. My head was throbbing. Even my tongue hurt. But then I thought about last night and I couldn't help but smile. It was definitely worth every ache and every pain, I decided.

"You know,"—she plunked herself down on the bed with a heavy sigh—"I don't even know who you are anymore. I look at you and I see a stranger." She shook her head. "A stranger."

"Yeah? Well, when I look at me, I see a woman!" I glanced in the mirror and smiled at my reflection. "And I like what I see. For the first time in ages I *like* what I see."

"And just what, exactly, is *that* supposed to mean?"

"You know," I glanced around my room with its baby pink walls and its frilly pink curtains and its fluffy pink and white carpet and its bright white furniture with the gold trim, "this room sucks!"

"What? What's wrong with it?"

"It's decorated in Early Barbie Doll, that's what's wrong with it!" My blood was boiling. Stupid woman, why couldn't she understand? "I outgrew it ages ago! But you—you've got this dumb hangup about letting me redecorate it. Putting natural stain on the furniture was out of the question, you said, because brown furniture is for offices. Painting the walls white or blue was a no-no because pink is for girls; blue is for boys and white is for hospitals, you claimed. And those stuffed animals!" I pointed to the top shelf of my bookcase with its menagerie of Snoopy dogs and teddy bears. "Every time I put them away in the basement, you haul them out and put them back on the shelf!" I picked up my pillow and flung it at the bookcase. One of the Snoopy dogs careened off its shelf and landed on the floor with a thud. "I'm the only twenty-three-year-old woman I know who lays herself down to sleep each night with a giant Snoopy dog at her feet!"

"Are you quite through now?" she said, her eyes narrowing.

"No! I've only just begun!"

She took a deep breath and let it out slowly. "I spoke to Jo Ann awhile ago. She said her husband was mistaken about your not being there when I called this morning. It seems he had just come home from an all-night emergency at the hospital and he wasn't aware of the fact that you were asleep in his guest room." She gave me a piercing look. "He *was* mistaken, wasn't he?"

"And what if he wasn't?" I glared back at her.

"What?" She stared at me in disbelief. Poor Ma. Poor prehistoric Ma. Her whole body seemed to cave in. Like a deflated balloon. God, she looked so pitiful sitting there. So terribly distraught. I almost wanted to run and throw my arms around her and promise her that I'd remain her little girl for ever and ever, amen. But of course, there was no turning back now. My days of playing Mother May I Take a Step had run on too long as it was.

"Peter and I are in love," I blurted.

"In love?" she scoffed.

"Well, we are! And there's nothing wrong with two people spending the night together if they're in love."

"Is that a fact, Ms. Know-It-All-With-The-Five-Year-Subscription-To-*Cosmopolitan*-Magazine?" She looked at me with pure disgust in her eyes. Like she'd just found out I was "Ilsa—She-Wolf of the SS" or something.

"Don't look at me like that, Ma!" I wanted to dig a hole and crawl inside. My God, didn't she realize what a sexual retard I was? "Maybe if you'd read *Cosmopolitan* once in a while you'd realize what a Pope's dream you have for a daughter. Hell, most of the women my age are already into penicillin shots and D&Cs!"

She threw her hands up in the air. "As if that's supposed to console me?"

I began to rack my brain for excuses. As if I really owed it to her to console her for my behavior. But then I stopped to think about what I was doing, and I just wanted to kick myself. "Why the hell am I getting the third degree like this anyway? You never gave my brothers such a hard time when they spent whole nights . . . or whole weekends . . . or even whole vacations with their girlfriends before they got married. Why are people still clinging to the double standard in this day and age? It's not fair!"

"Nobody ever said life is fair."

"Oh, forget it." It was like talking to a wall. "I can't talk to you. You don't understand."

"You're right!" she exploded. "I don't understand. There's a perfectly wonderful boy out there who's dying to marry you, a boy who can give you a good home and a good name and a good life, and you just want to throw it all away! And for what? So you can tramp around with that rude, arrogant, vulgar no-goodnik who's got nothing to offer you except a heap of trouble?"

"How the hell do you know what he has to offer me?" I cried. "What do you even know about him anyway?"

She grabbed me by the shoulders and shook me. "Why are you so intent on ruining your life. Why?"

"I'm not ruining my life, for crying out loud! I just think there ought to be something in between Snoopy dogs and holy matrimony, that's all. I need time to find out what I want out of life. I'd like to move out on my own and learn how to take care of myself. I want to try my hand at becoming a screenwriter. . . ." I looked up at her with tear-filled eyes. "Don't you understand? I just want to *be* somebody before I think about becoming somebody's *wife!*"

"Yeah, well, I've got twenty-three years invested in your life, and I'll be damned if I'm going to stand idly by and watch you throw it down the toilet!" She turned around and stormed out of my room.

"And just what is that supposed to mean?" I yelled after her.

I got my answer about two seconds later.

"Look, Shayna Pearl," she said, returning hand-in-hand with Stanley himself, no less, "look who I found watching the baseball game in the den with your father!"

"Well, well, well," he smiled at me, "I see Sleeping Beauty is awake at last."

"I don't believe this!" I almost hit the ceiling.

"Now, why don't I leave you two lovebirds alone? I'm sure you have plenty to talk about." And with that my two-timing mother rushed out and closed the door behind her.

"Shayna Pearl." Stanley moved toward me. "I can't tell you how much this means to me. . . ."

"Get out of here, Stanley." I backed away. "I have nothing to say to you."

"But your mother . . ."

"My mother's full of shit!"

"I want you." He backed me into a corner. "I want you more than I've ever wanted anything."

"The whole world's gone crazy!" I cried. "I'm getting out of here!" But before I could even move he whipped out his engagement ring and shoved it onto my finger. He almost succeeded too except that it got stuck on my knuckle.

"Owwwwwww!" I yanked my hand away. "Just what the hell do you think you're doing?"

"I'm proposing, what do you think? Here,"—he reached for my hand again—"let me fix it for you. Once you see it all the way on, I just know you won't ever want to take it off."

"Are you crazy?!" I pushed him away. "Now look what you've done." I tried to pull the ring off but it wouldn't budge. "It's stuck!"

"I see you woke up on the wrong side of the bed, for a change," he flinched.

"As far as I'm concerned, I woke up on the wrong side of the world!" I seethed.

"You know, you're so cute when you're bitchy," he sighed. "I just love the way your little nostrils flare in and out. It kind of reminds me of Ali MacGraw in *Love Story*."

"Oh, God, tell me this isn't happening!" I sobbed as I tried in vain to twist the ever-tightening ring off my swelling knuckle. "Shit!"

"C'mon, stop fighting it. You know you love me."

"Is that so? And how do you figure that?"

"You're wearing my engagement ring, aren't you?"

I grabbed hold of the ring and yanked at it until I saw stars.

"Why don't you just leave it alone? It belongs there. Deep inside you know it does."

Deep inside I knew I'd rather have cut my finger off first.

"It really is smashing."

"Soap," I muttered, "I'll get it off with soap!" I made a beeline for the bathroom.

"You know what they say, don't you?" He followed me into the bathroom and stood there smiling smugly as I drowned my finger in Ivory Liquid. "They say diamonds are forever."

"Not this one." I slid the ring off forcibly and it flew up into the air.

"Jesus, Shayna Pearl!" He scrambled to catch it. "That's not a piece of used Kleenex you're throwing around there!"

I glanced down at my knuckle. It looked like I felt. Inflamed. "You . . . you . . ."

"Oh, give me a break, will you? I've been waiting all day to talk to you. The least thing you can do is listen."

I turned my back on him.

"You're not going to get rid of me that easily." He plunked himself down on the toilet. "If I'm anything at all, I'm a good lawyer. And being the good lawyer that I am, I never, ever give up on a case until I've exhausted every last round of appeal."

"I'm not a case, Stanley," I cringed. "And in *case* you haven't noticed, this isn't the Palais de Justice!" I went over to the tub and turned on the water. "Now if you don't mind, I'd like to take a long soak in a hot tub and think about the incredible time Peter and I had yesterday."

He jumped up to turn the water off. "And just what is that supposed to mean?"

"Peter and I are in love!" I blurted.

"In love?" he gulped, looking positively stricken.

"It's not something we planned . . . it just happened," I tried to explain. Funny, I had kind of mixed feelings about telling him the whole thing. Part of me was relieved because now he would know the truth (or most of it, anyway) and with any luck, he'd be out of my life for good. Yet hurting him that way didn't give me nearly as much pleasure as I thought it might. "It just happened. . . ."

He shook his head. "You don't honestly believe you're in love with that long-haired, bearded *schmuck*, do you?"

"Are you kidding? I love everything about him!" I cried defensively. "And that includes his long hair and beard. I've always wanted to go out with a bearded guy. Everybody in Hampstead shaves!"

"I don't believe it." He threw his hands up in the air. "I'm in love with a girl who thinks she's in love with a *beard?*"

"We're just not meant for each other, Stanley. . . ."

He reached over and ran his hand over my shoulder, down across my breast. "How do you know you don't like something if you don't try it out?"

I froze in my tracks, not knowing how to react. He repelled and infuriated me, but he was also so pathetic. I stood speechless, wordless.

He gave me a strange look, and then he turned around and hurried out of the house.

Shaking with a mixture of outrage and disgust after my confrontation with Stanley, I picked up the phone and called Peter.

I knew I'd feel much better once I'd heard his voice.

And I was right, of course. The moment I heard his voice I was on Cloud Nine.

But then I heard what he had to say, and I came down to Earth rapidly.

"Hey, Babe, this must be ESP or something! I was just about to call you."

"You were?"

"Yeah, I wanted to say good-bye. I have to go out of town for a couple of weeks."

"Out of town?" My heart sunk right to my feet.

"That's the life of a rock musician, I'm afraid. Here today, gone tomorrow."

"For a couple of weeks?" It might as well have been a couple of years.

"At least. Me and the band are flying out to L.A. to lay down the tracks for our debut album. Isn't that something else?"

"It's terrific, really. I'm thrilled for you. I know how much you wanted it."

"Do I detect a *but* in there somewhere?"

"I just wish I was going with you, that's all."

"Believe me, I'd like nothing more myself. But this trip is strictly business. I wouldn't have a second to spend with you. Maybe next time, huh?"

"Sure." I knew he was making sense and everything, but that didn't stop me from feeling like it was the end of the world. "I wish you were back already."

"I haven't left yet!" he laughed.

"Peter? Do you think I'm a wanton woman?"

"A wanton woman?" he laughed again. "I didn't even know there was such a thing in this day and age!"

"My mother, she found out about last night. She suspects what we . . . well, you know what she's like?"

"She giving you a rough time?" He sounded truly sympathetic.

"Do you suppose there are Jewish nuns?" I was feeling truly sorry for myself.

"I don't know. I doubt it. Why?"

"I think she's going to put me in a convent!"

"Christ, what do you need that shit for?" he cried.

"Why don't you just tell SMother Superior to stuff it, and move out?"

"I can't afford it."

"What about a place around here—in the McGill Ghetto? It's not exactly the height of luxury but at least it's affordable."

"I don't have very much money in the bank yet. I've only been working a few months."

"Oh? Well, maybe we can put our heads together and come up with something when I get back, huh? Right now I've got to get going."

"I'll . . . I'll miss you." I muffled a sob.

"Me too, Babe. See you in a couple of weeks, huh?" *Click.*

They say desperate people do desperate things.

So I went to talk to Dad about a loan.

I should have known better.

"What?" he cried. "You want me to give you money so that you can move into an apartment in the McGill Ghetto?" He dropped his newspaper and shut off the vibrating Magic Fingers on his twenty-four position E-Z chair and glared at me. "Have you flipped your lid?"

"It's just a loan, Daddy!" I tried to explain. "I'll pay you back when I start making more money."

"But why would you want to move into a student ghetto? You're not a student anymore."

"You don't have to be a student to live there. The Ghetto's full of young people like me who just need some space, you know?"

"Fourteen rooms in this house and you don't have enough space?" he laughed.

"That's not the kind of space I was referring to," I said between clenched teeth. "I just think I need to get out on my own. It's time."

"Out of the question! It's dangerous for a girl to live alone. And besides—why should you pay rent and throw away good money when you can live in this beautiful house for free? Meals, laundry and maid service included? Anyway, I thought what's his name wants to marry you?"

I gave him an incredulous look. Good old oblivious Dad. He didn't have a clue as to what was going on around him—as usual. "His name is Stanley, Daddy. And I don't want to marry him. Look, all I want to do is stand on my own two feet. Is that so terrible?"

"No, that's very admirable."

"So can't you just help me out a little? Just to give me a head start?"

"But that doesn't make sense!" he laughed. "In one breath you're telling me how you want to stand on your own two feet, and in the next you're asking me to support you. Besides, you need a lot more than a *little* help. I mean, you're completely dependent on me. You make next to peanuts at that job of yours. You buy all your clothes and whatnots on *my* MasterCard. You use *my* Texaco card to fill up the car that *I* bought for you. . . . If you can't afford to pay your own way, you don't move out. And that's all there is to it!"

"Hmph, I'll bet if I were a boy instead of a girl you wouldn't be saying that. You'd be proud of me for wanting to stand on my own two feet. You're just a male chauvinist, that's your problem!"

He gave me a stern look over his reading glasses, which were teetering on the tip of his nose and then he pointed to the couch and ordered me to sit on it. "Shayna Pearl," he said, "have I ever told you how poor I was when I grew up on St. Urbain Street—in the heart of the Jewish ghetto—the one Mordecai Richler immortalized in his novel *The Apprenticeship of Duddy Kravitz?*"

"Oh, no, Daddy, not again!" I groaned. "Not the story of the 'Apprenticeship of Arnie Fine' again!"

He just ignored me and went on about his rough and tough days at Baron Byng High (". . . the very same Baron Byng High that Mordecai Richler . . ."). He told me all about how poor little Arnie went to school all day (walked six miles, even in snow storms) and toiled all night in his father's shoelace factory for a dollar a week—just so he could put himself through McGill Medical School. "And do you know *why* I worked myself to the bone, Shayna Pearl?"

"Because you had a dream," I moaned, "a dream about being a successful doctor who could afford to buy a nice piece of land in a beautiful place like Hampstead, so you could build your dream house and bring up your dream family . . . *but what has all this got to do with me wanting to move to the McGill Ghetto-oooooo?!*"

To which he replied:

"Because I'll be goddamned if I finally made it to the richest suburb in Montreal only to have *my* daughter run off to live in a goddamned ghetto-oooo!"

"Does that mean you're definitely not going to lend me the money?"

"Bingo!"

"I'll go anyway!" I threatened.

"Good-bye," he chuckled, "let your mother know when you're leaving and she'll pack you a sandwich."

"Oh, Christ on crutches!" I couldn't believe he had said that.

"That's what your mother used to do whenever you used to threaten to run away from home as a little girl, you know? She'd pack you lunch. And you, you were so cute the way you used to sit on your little suitcase and wait for her to spread peanut butter and jam on the bread and cut off the crust. . . ."

"Stop it, Daddy!"

"And then she'd cut it in quarters and put it in a little baggie and off you'd go!" He shook his head and smiled. "Of course you never went further than the back porch next door and you always came home just as soon as your sandwich was finished. Yes, sir, even then you knew where your bread was buttered!"

"You really think I'll starve to death on my own? Is that what you think?"

"Do women have ovaries?"

And that was the end of that.

Down went the vibrating twenty-four position E-Z

chair; up went the newspaper over his face; on went the
Magic Fingers switch and that was the end of that.

Click! Case dismissed. I couldn't believe it.

"You're gonna be sorry!" I cried. "Because I'm moving
out no matter what. *Even if I have to sell my body down
by the harbor to pay the rent!*" I shrieked so loud I'm sure
all of Hampstead and half of neighboring Cote Saint Luc
heard me. But not Dad. Not dear old Dad. He never even
heard a word I said. He just lay there reading and
vibrating, vibrating and reading . . . totally oblivious of
everybody and everything except that damned newspaper over his face.

"So long, Daddy-o!" I stomped off to my room, pulled
my tote bag out of my cupboard and started packing. Not
that I knew where I was going, mind you. But even the
Old Brewery Mission seemed better than home.

"What's all the commotion about, Shayna Pearl?" Ma
came running. "I could hear you screaming all the way
down in the laundry room." She glanced down at my tote
bag. "What on earth are you up to now?"

"I'm packing. What does it look like I'm up to?"

"Why? Where are you going?"

"I don't know. Somewhere. Anywhere!"

"Somewhere, Anywhere? Is that in Canada or the
U.S.?"

"I'm moving out, Mother!" I threw some underwear
into my bag. "And if you dare say 'Good-bye, I'll pack you
a sandwich,' I'll . . . I'll . . ."

"Oh, dear, you're not thinking of going to *him*, are
you?" she looked positively mortified.

"No, I'm not going to *him!*" I mimicked her. "You'll be
happy to know, I'm sure, that *him* had to leave town."

"For good?" she perked up.

"You should be so lucky. Now, if you don't mind, I have
to pack."

She shook her head. "What happened to us, Shayna
Pearl?" she said in a grave voice. "We used to be able to
talk to each other."

"Sure we used to be able to talk to each other. As long as you did all the talking and I did all the listening!"

She took a deep breath and let it out slowly. "I always thought we'd grow closer as you got older. That we'd become good friends. Do things together."

"Become friends?" I didn't know whether to laugh or cry or what. "Do things together? How many times in the past couple of years have I asked you—no, begged you—to go to New York with me so we could see some plays and do some shopping and just have a plain good time? Dozens, that's how many. Hundreds! But you were always too busy. Or too tired. Or too something!"

"All right then, how about now?"

"What?"

"Why don't we take that trip to New York now? Just the two of us? I can make the arrangements right away. We could leave tomorrow."

I kept on packing. "Don't you think it's a little late for New York?"

"Don't you want us to be friends?"

I looked up at her. "Are you kidding? Do you think I like being enemies with my own mother?"

"So? This could be the perfect chance for us to get closer, don't you think?"

I sat down on the bed beside her. "I don't know."

"We could try."

"It sure would be nice if we could be friends for a change." The whole idea was becoming more and more appealing by the minute. God, I thought, wouldn't it really be something if this trip could actually bring us closer together? Maybe we could even establish one of those intimate mother-daughter relationships where I could tell her personal stuff without worrying that she's going to have a stroke or something? And then maybe, just maybe, she wouldn't hassle me about my relationship with Peter? "Yeah, it sure would be nice." And besides, I reassured myself, if things didn't work out for the best in

New York, the Old Brewery Mission would still be here when I got back.

"So what do you say?" she nudged my arm. "Is it a date?"

I looked at her and smiled. "Let's do it!"

"Oh, Shayna Pearl!" she hugged me. "We're going to have a ball, you wait and see!"

"Things at the paper are kind of slow now anyway. Mrs. Finkelberg probably won't even mind giving me the time off."

"See how it all works out?" She folded up a pair of underpants and tucked it neatly into the corner of my bag. "You go ahead and finish packing now," she said as she got up and headed out the door. "I'll go call the airline."

Chapter 7

THE UNTHINKABLE HAPPENED.

Ma and I actually had a good time in New York.

In fact, we had a ball.

We were just like two girlfriends buying everything in sight that we could eat or wear.

And laugh, God, did we ever laugh! We laughed at the people, we laughed at the Broadway shows, we laughed at the price tags on all the designer clothes we bought and we laughed at the thought of Dad's face going into contortions when we presented him with all the Master-Card bills at the end of the trip.

"Christ, Ma," I'd tell her, "when Daddy sees how much money we've spent, he'll have heartburn for an entire year!"

"So?" She'd giggle. "We'll buy him a year's supply of baking soda!"

And then we'd go off to Fifth Avenue and shop like there was no tomorrow.

The best was the last night though.

"We ought to do something really special before we go

home tomorrow," Ma told me. "We ought to have a last fling."

So we went out and got snockered with a capital *S*. God, I'll never forget it as long as I live. We had a blast. After a six-course meal at Mamma Leone's that started with Dubonnet on the rocks, progressed to champagne and ended with Harvey Wallbangers, Ma suggested that we head over to Times Square (". . . to take a peek at all those perverts who dress up like women," she said).

It was right in the middle of Times Square that we laughed so hard we both peed right in our pants.

We were standing in front of the Eros Theatre, watching all the transvestites go by, when some poor old bum staggered up to Ma and asked her for a dime for a cup of coffee. The next thing I knew, she was grabbing me by the elbow and dragging me down the street screaming:

"Police! Help, poliiiiiiiiccccccce!"

I couldn't understand, for the life of me, why she was throwing such conniptions. I mean, the poor guy was so decrepit, he could hardly walk. When she finally stopped to catch her breath, I asked her why she was so afraid of some poor wino who was so out of it he still thought coffee only costs a dime.

"A dime? Money for coffee? Is that all he wanted?" She seemed almost disappointed. "I thought he was trying to pick me up!"

"Pick you up?" I giggled.

"I thought he said—'Lady, do you have *time* for a cup of coffee'?"

Right then and there we sat down on the sidewalk and peed a river. God, it was wonderful. Just the kind of stuff intimate mother-daughter relationships are made of.

But the most wonderful part of all was yet to come after we got back to our hotel room at the Plaza.

"I'm having a fabulous time, Ma," I told her as we stood over the bathroom sink rinsing out our underwear. "In fact, this is one of the best times I've ever had in my whole life!"

"It sure has been wonderful, hasn't it?" she smiled. She was bursting with joy. "It's nice when a mother and daughter can be friends, isn't it?"

"Yeah, I kinda like it, you know?" I laughed.

"Shayna Pearl, I have something I want to give you," she blurted. "Something special. I was going to save it for your birthday, but I want to give it to you right now. This very minute!" She ran to her purse and whipped out the exquisite watch with the thin black face and the gold mesh bracelet I had been drooling over at Cartier's earlier in the week.

"Ma!" I couldn't believe my eyes. "That watch cost almost *three* thousand dollars!"

"Three thousand, two hundred and eighty-nine—and seventy-five cents, to be exact," she said as she strapped it onto my wrist.

I looked at her as if she had flipped her lid or something.

"What's the matter? A mother can't spend three thousand, two hundred and eighty-nine bucks—and seventy-five cents on her own daughter if she wants to?"

"Oh, Ma, I love you!" I gushed, suddenly overcome by an overwhelming feeling of love for this woman I hadn't much liked lately. "I really do!"

"I love you too!" she cried. "And don't you ever forget it!"

"I won't, Ma."

"I'm only sorry we didn't take this trip ages ago. Before things got so bad."

"Ma, I . . . ." I wanted to talk to her about Peter and me.

"It's amazing what can happen between a mother and daughter in just ten days, isn't it? Before we left we were on the verge of World War III and now look at us. We're actually friends!"

"Ma . . . I . . . ." I wanted to try and make her understand how I felt about Peter. How important this relationship was to me.

"Let's not let anything ever come between us again, never!"

"Ma, there's something . . ."

"What is it, dear?" She gave me an anxious look. "Is there something troubling you?"

"Ma, I, oh, never mind, forget it. It's nothing." My instincts told me that this was not a good time to talk about Peter. This was something that had to be handled with care, I decided. One step at a time. "It's nothing."

"Are you sure?"

"I'm sure." I hugged her.

"Oh, Shayna Pearl, I'm so happy I could cry!"

And then she burst out crying. And I burst out crying. And we both stood there in the bathroom sobbing in each other's arms and blowing our respective noses into wads of soggy toilet paper.

God, it was wonderful.

From the looks of things, Ma and I were going to be friends for life.

Nothing was ever going to come between us again.

Wouldn't you just know it.

The moment we got home from that trip to end all trips, I found a telegram waiting for me on the hall table.

"I hope it's not bad news," Ma said as I tore it open. "The last time I got a telegram was when Aunty Gertie dropped dead while peddling one of those giant tricycles around Century Village."

"Oh, Mother, you're always such a pessimist!" I pulled it out of the envelope and read it to myself.

SHAY: TAKE A CHANCE. COME LIVE WITH ME. I'LL BE IN MONTREAL SAT. TO CLOSE UP MY APARTMENT. THEN I WANT TO TAKE YOU BACK TO L.A. WITH ME IN 10 DAYS OR SO. THINK YOU COULD WRITE SCREENPLAYS IN A BEACH HOUSE OVERLOOKING THE PACIFIC? SO WHAT DO YOU SAY, BABE? I NEED YOU. LOVE, PETER. P.S. ARRIVE DORVAL 10 A.M. AIR CAN. FL. 124 FROM L.A. SEE YOU THEN.

"Oh, my God!" I cried, slumping into a chair. My knees were like water.

"What is it?" Ma gasped. "You're as white as a sheet, for crying out loud! Is it bad news? What?"

"Oh, my God . . ."

"At least tell me who it's from!"

I gave her an anxious look.

She frowned. "It's from *him,* isn't it? The Svengali!"

"Ma, don't call Peter that! He's really very . . ."

"I knew it was bad news! Telegrams are always bad news!"

"But you don't even know what it says!"

"Anything that has to do with him is bad news as far as I'm concerned."

"Ma, I really think we should sit down and talk about this. He's coming home the day after tomorrow and . . ."

"You can talk until you're blue in the face, but you won't change my mind about him. He's bad news."

"At least let me try and make you understand how I feel about him. . . ."

"I really thought things were going to be different after New York. I thought surely you'd come back with a fresh perspective on things."

"You don't understand. I love him!"

She laughed. "Don't be absurd. You hardly know him!"

"I know enough!"

"I think you should stop seeing him before he gets you into *real* trouble," she said. "And if you care anything about what I think . . ."

"Of course I do. But I have to live my own life too."

She massaged her temples. "I don't want to talk about this anymore. I'm getting one of my headaches." She reached into her purse and pulled out her bottle of Valium. "I think I'll take a couple of these and go upstairs to lie down for a while."

"You're copping out on me!"

"I already told you how I feel."

"I thought things were going to be different after New York!"

"And they are, Shayna Pearl," she reassured me, "and they will be. As long as you stay away from that boy." She went up to her bedroom and closed the door behind her.

Oh, swell, I thought, sitting there in the hallway, unable to move—just perfect! I want to go to California with Peter more than anything else in the world, but what am I supposed to do about Ma? She hates him. She hates everything about him. And if I move in with him she'll hate me too. Hell, even if she were crazy about him, she'd hate me for moving in with him. We could take a million trips to New York, she and I, but she'd never approve of my Living In Sin. No matter who the man was or what he did. Why, just the month before, she'd told me quite eloquently her opinion of her friend Shirley Babushkin's daughter, Mimi, who had moved in with her boyfriend.

"If that were *my* daughter," she wailed, "I'd run out to Fleet Road and throw myself in front of the first 161 bus that came by!"

And Dad. He was disgusted. Not to mention incensed and outraged.

"That's the thanks Bernie Babushkin gets for working his tail off so his kids could have the best of everything—" he fumed, "a kick in the teeth! If you ever pull a stunt like that, Shayna Pearl, I'll disown you so fast you won't know what hit you!"

Of course, Mimi Babushkin's boyfriend was as poor as a pauper and as black as Sidney Poitier—but still. The thinking around here is that twenty-three-year-old Jewish Princesses from suburban Hampstead marry Professionals and have security, not to mention babies. They don't gallivant off to California with (God*forbid*) rock musicians, even Jewish rock musicians.

Damn, damn, damn. Why does everything always have to be so bloody complicated? I don't want to alienate my family, but I have to get on with my life. Going to California with Peter . . . writing screenplays in a beach house overlooking the Pacific . . . it's like a dream come true. I'd have to be crazy to say no. It's the chance of a lifetime. Maybe my only chance.

Oh, God, what the hell am I going to do now?

A plan, a course of action—that's what I need. Something logical. Sensible. Direct. Something somewhere in between committing mass murder and stealing away in the middle of the night.

A plan. . . .

PART III

Chicken Suitor

Chapter 8

WHAT CAN YOU SAY about a Friday that starts off with a 7 A.M. phone call from Stanley Charles Drabkin?

Just that it's got to get better.

I'd been up all night thinking about the telegram. Worrying about Ma and Dad. Dreaming about Peter and California. Trying to put the two into perspective. Coming up with nothing more illuminating than a migraine headache. But the Gravol suppository I had to take for the accompanying nausea was mild compared to the pain in the ass I got from Stanley. I know it's bitchy of me to say this, but it's true. God, is it ever the truth!

He called to tell me how much he missed me the ten days I was in New York with Ma, that he hadn't been able to sleep a wink since I left, and that he may never be able to close his eyes again as long as something was missing from his bed. That something, which he proceeded to describe in graphic detail from mole to beauty mark, was my body. Not that he'd ever seen my body, mind you, but did that matter?

"Why don't you just call up and breathe heavy, Stanley?" I cried. "That's what most perverts do!"

You'd have thought he'd hang up after that, but no, not Stanley. Not good old Stanley. Speaking of disaster movies, how was New York, he wanted to know.

"New York?" I felt a twinge in my gut just thinking about it. The fun. The laughter. The closeness. "New York was . . ." I got another twinge as I recalled the final night of our trip, in our suite at the Plaza, when my mother had presented me with my eighteen-carat gold Cartier watch. How we'd hugged and kissed and tearfully declared undying friendship—never to let anything come between us again. "New York was . . ." I glanced down at the telegram in my hand—"Shay: Take a chance. Come live with me." God, I felt so torn up inside. How could I go with Peter and hurt Ma now that we'd finally got so close and everything? How could I not go with Peter? And how could I deal with any of it when Stanley was always breathing down my neck? "Goddammit, Stanley!" My head felt like it was going to explode. "Why do you always have to stir up trouble?"

Him, stir up trouble? No, no, that's not what he wanted to do at all. He only wanted to know if I'd come to my senses about his proposal now that I'd had all that time in New York to mull it over.

"You've got to be kidding? I'm in love with another man!" I croaked.

To which he responded by declaring his undying love for me.

"This is a nightmare, right?" I said.

He reassured me that this was indeed for real. Crazy as it sounded, he wanted me now more than ever before. So I was a little confused, so what? I'd get over it.

"You've got bats in the belfry, Stanley, do you know that?"

To which he responded by promising not to give me up without a fight. From now on I was going to see a side of him I'd never even known existed.

He then told me not to underestimate him.

"And just what is that supposed to mean?"

That was for him to know and for me to find out.

He informed me that he'd changed a lot since I'd left for New York. All I had to do was give him a chance to prove it.

"Oh, for crying out loud!" I slapped an ice bag over the left side of my head, which was throbbing something fierce. "Nobody changes that much in ten days!"

To which he responded by inviting himself over for dinner tonight so I could see the new Stanley for myself—first hand.

"Forget it!"

But there was just no getting through to him. He reminded me that this was Friday Night Supper—to which he'd had a standing invitation for the past eight months—issued by none other than my very own mother.

"But that was before," I protested. "Surely you don't think . . . not after everything that's happened . . . I withdraw the invitation!"

To which he replied that it wasn't mine to withdraw and that he'd see me tonight at six sharp—eleven hours and counting. . . .

"*You make me crazy!*" I slammed the phone down and made a beeline for the bathroom. The thought of Stanley —old or new—coming for dinner tonight sent me running for a second dose of Gravol.

Should a genie have appeared to me then and granted me one wish, I'd have asked him to cancel the rest of the day until further notice.

This was definitely not my day.

As if I didn't have enough problems already, that second dose of Gravol I took knocked me out, and I ended up getting to work an hour late.

And it was just my luck too, that I got caught trying to sneak into the office through a rear exit by none other than Mrs. Yetta Finkelberg Herself, the owner, publisher, managing editor, editor-in-chief and chief delivery boy of the *Cote Saint Luc Weekly Register*—affectionately known amongst her employees as the "Wicked Witch of West End Montreal."

"Just what do you think you're doing, Shayna?" she snarled after I practically smacked right into her on the way to my desk. "Just what the hell do you think you're doing?"

I gave her a startled look. God, I didn't know what the hell I thought I was doing. I guess I just figured that nobody would notice I was late if I came in through the back way. Wishful thinking, I suppose. Pure stupidity, more likely.

"J.A.P.s!" she screamed in front of the whole office. "I don't know why I hire J.A.P.s! Not only do they take off for New York for almost two weeks on a moment's notice, but then they have the unmitigated *chutzpa* to think they can get away with showing up an hour late on their first day back!" Whenever she gets mad at me, which is often, she tends to refer to me in the plural. It's as if she holds me personally responsible for the sins of my entire generation. "What happened? Did you fall off your clogs and sprain an ankle? Lose a false eyelash? Stop off for a nose job along the way?"

"I . . . I'm sorry." I wanted to dig a hole and crawl inside. God, did she have to make such a public spectacle of me? "I'm really very sorry. It's just been one of those mornings, you know?"

"One of those mornings? And what was it, exactly, that held you up, Your Majesty?" she cackled facetiously as she looked me up and down, up and down. "You couldn't find a Gucci belt to go with your Gucci outfit?"

Some of my co-workers tittered.

"What the hell are you laughing at?" she yelled at them. "Do you think I pay you to stand around and laugh?" She waited until they all went back to work, which took about one split second, and then she started in on me again. "And as for you, young lady,"—she glared at me—"if you must get all Guccied up for the office, try getting out of bed an hour earlier!"

I LOST IT ALL IN MONTREAL

"I'm not all Guccied up!" I said between clenched teeth. It was all I could do to keep from reaching out and tearing every bleach blonde hair out of her head. "I don't even own a Gucci outfit."

"Oh? Well, excuse me. My mistake." She reached for the Givenchy reading glasses that were hanging around her neck and she placed them on the tip of her nose. "Hmmm"—she sneered as she inspected the designer labels on my clothes—"so that's why you were so late this morning. You had to call *Vogue* magazine to see if it was okay to mix 'n' match your Calvins with a Geoffrey Beene top!"

"I'm late because I had a headache," I winced. For some reason she always gets off on making fun of my clothes. I don't know. I guess maybe it's because she's jealous. It'll be a snowy day on the equator before she fits into a pair of size twenty-seven Calvin Klein jeans and a Geoffrey Beene halter top. "A migraine . . ."

"Hmph, a likely story!" She waddled into her office and slammed the door behind her. Obviously she liked her version much better. She always does.

"Stupid fucking bitch," I muttered under my breath. "Who the hell does she think she is anyway?" I exchanged disgusted looks with everybody in the copy department and then I wandered over to my desk and sat down. "That bleach blonde hippo! I don't have to take this shit from her." I pulled Peter's telegram out of my purse and I reread it for the zillionth time, relishing every word and every line, especially the part where it says, "Think you could write screenplays in a beach house overlooking the Pacific?" Imagine, I thought, writing screenplays by the ocean every day. Making love with Peter on a different stretch of sand each night. No Mrs. Finkelberg to make me feel like two cents. No parents to make me crazy with guilt. No Stanley. Just me and Peter and a beach house in Los Angeles, California. Imagine . . . I closed my eyes and smiled. Imagine . . . Freeways. Freedom. Freeman. Mine. All mine!

I could just picture it.

I could see myself soaring down the Pacific Coast Highway on the back of Peter's gleaming black Norton Commando . . . hugging his black leather jacket . . . the wind whipping our faces . . . the sun beating down on us . . . the powerful roar of the bike's engine vibrating through our bodies.

Just like *Easy Rider*.

Just like Kawasaki Let the Good Times Roll.

And then I could see us pulling up to this fabulous beach house in the middle of nowhere and tearing into each other like a couple of starving animals . . . right there on the beach . . . right under the setting sun . . . with the roar of the waves for mood music and miles and miles of warm, golden sand on which to roll around.

"Are you daydreaming on my time?!" a voice came screeching into my ear, scaring the living daylights out of me.

"Huh? What!" I sat bolt upright in my chair. "Who, me?"

"No, Princess Grace! Who do you think?" It was Mrs. Finkelberg. "Am I paying you to sit at that desk and work or am I paying you to stare out the window and daydream?"

I glanced out the huge storefront window, forlornly, as the golden sands and roaring waves of L.A. gave way before the reality of the busy, noisy mall that houses the *Register*. Shoppers coming and going. Going and coming. Hauling groceries. Pushing babies. Trying on makeup in the store across the way. Some place for a newspaper!

"Well?"

"Work," I muttered, folding up Peter's telegram and stuffing it back into my purse. So much for California Dreamin'. "Work!"

"You haven't even taken the cover off your typewriter yet!"

I whipped off the cover and stuck a piece of paper in the carriage.

"Boy, are you ever out to lunch!" she snarled. "More than usual."

I looked at her and shrugged. She wasn't telling me anything I didn't already know.

"The Mayor of Cote Saint Luc is in my office," she said. "I want you to go in there and interview him."

"Me? Interview the mayor?" I perked up. "Really?" I had never interviewed a mayor before. "Me?" Sensing that this might be a big story, maybe even the biggest of my career, I grabbed my note pad and a pen and I headed toward her office, my head dancing with visions of bold, flashy, front-page headlines:

REPORTER'S EXPOSÉ OF PAYOLA SCHEME TOPPLES ADMINISTRATION

WATERGATE COMES TO COTE SAINT LUC

MAYOR ROTSTEIN RESIGNS OVER LURID SEX SCANDAL

"Hold your horses,"—she grabbed me by the elbow as I whizzed past her—"you don't even know what it's about yet!"

"Oh, yeah, right!" I could hardly conceal my excitement.

"Do you remember when my Herb went jogging in Wentworth Park with our two sons a few weeks ago and he slipped in a pile of dog poop and ended up with a sprained ankle and a concussion?"

"Yeah," I groaned, "I remember." How could I forget? She bumped one of my best articles, an interview with one of the only women symphony orchestra conductors in the world, and replaced it with one of her infamous "Kvetch and Retch" editorials, entitled "We Must Get Rid of Dog Droppings in Our Parks NOW!" "What about it?"

"The mayor is finally going to do something about it,

thanks to me," she smiled proudly. "By next week, Cote Saint Luc is going to have the stiffest 'Poop 'n' Scoop' laws of any suburb in Montreal!"

"You want me to interview the mayor about 'Poop and Scoop' laws?" I stared at her in disbelief.

"It's about time people started cleaning up after their dogs!" She banged her fist on the desk, her voice filled with the same passion as that of Oral Roberts when he talks about being Born Again. "If I can clean up after my Ziggy, the rest of Cote Saint Luc can deal with their dogs!" At the sound of his name, Ziggy, her overweight, ill-tempered pug-dog, to whom she bears an uncanny resemblance, waddled over and plunked himself down at her feet. "Dog poop poses a major hazard to this community, and it is our duty as this community's only newspaper to do something about it!"

I thought I was going to be sick. What are you doing here, Shay, you idiot you? a voice screamed inside my head. You should be home packing for California. Why the hell are you standing here and taking all this crap from her? Dog shit she wants you to write about! Go on. Tell her you don't need this crummy job anymore. Tell her to go screw herself. Tell everybody to go screw themselves. Do it, damn you, why don't you just do it and get it over with, you wishy-washy little wimp, you despicable little *nebbish*. Can't you make a decision for once in your life?

"Nu shoin?" She nudged my arm. "You think the mayor has nothing else to do while you stand around with your head in the clouds? He's a busy man, you know?"

Just then the mayor came out of her office to remind her of a pressing engagement.

"What's taking so long, Yetta?" he asked her. "We have a brunch date with Harry Wasserman at Nuddick's in about fifteen minutes, remember? And you know how I like to get there early—before the pickles and cole slaw dry out."

"Oh, don't ask, Irv," she glared at me, "these kids today give me a royal pain-in-the-you-know-what!"

"Tell me about it," he sighed. "Do you know where I have to go after brunch today? I have to go over to Harold Cummings' to order my daughter a Corvette for her eighteenth birthday. All the kids are driving 'em, Daddy, she says. *Everybody* gets a Corvette for their eighteenth birthday, Daddy!"

"Yeah, well we're not doing them any favors—spoiling them rotten the way we do, believe you me." She clucked her tongue in disgust. "By handing them everything on a silver platter, we've turned them into a generation of vegetables!"

"How true," he nodded. "How t-rue!"

For a moment there I thought they were going to spout top hats and canes and burst into a song and dance rendition of "Kids—What's the Matter with Kids Today?"

"I don't know, Irv," she went on, "these kids are definitely missing something. They just don't have our drive and ambition."

"They're not hungry like we were when we grew up on St. Urbain Street. They're used to being spoon-fed."

"A spoon-fed, overfed generation, that's what they are!"

My mouth dropped open to my knees. I mean, I just couldn't believe what I was hearing. I weigh a whole ninety-seven pounds soaking wet and they had the nerve to stand there—a collective five hundred pounds of unsightly fat—and call *me* overfed?

"What a waste!" Mrs. Finkelberg looked me straight in the eye. "Some of them have such potential, and they just don't know what to do with it."

They both shook their heads and then they took their fat selves off to Nuddick's, no doubt to sit over a five-course Fresser's Special and reminisce about the Good Old Days of the Good Old Jewish Neighborhood where Poverty reigned supreme and Suffering was aplenty.

"Well, folks, it's finally happened," Meryl the receptionist said in her nasal, singsongy voice, "the old witch has finally flipped her lid!"

"You know," I fumed, "she and my father would make a terrific pair. They ought to get together and form the Duddy Kravitz to Pepsi Generation Lecture Circuit. They'd make millions!"

"I think it's disgusting the way she talks to you, you know?" Christine Desjardins, our token *shiksa* said. "I'd die if she talked to me like that, you know?"

"You don't have to worry, Chris," I told her. "She likes you. You don't know how lucky you were to be born poor."

"Yeah, it's true, you know? She's always bending over backwards to help me. Do you know I've had three raises in the past two months?"

"Three? I've had one in ten! And when I asked her why, she said I didn't need it!"

"God, she's even harder on you than she was on me when I was Chief *Schlock* Processor and Drivel Writer lo these many moons ago." Karen Biskin, who now holds the positions of political reporter and supplement editor, gave me a sympathetic look. "But cheer up, kiddo,"—she winked—"sooner or later the old witch has got to promote you to feature writer and then she'll find herself a new *schlock* processor to pick on."

"I won't hold my breath," I said. "I mean, let's face facts—she thinks I'm nothing but a good-for-nothing J.A.P."

"Don't you believe it!" Elaine Popkin, the life styles writer, reassured me. "The old witch may be a lot of things, but she knows talent when she sees it."

"Yeah, and you've got loads of talent, kiddo," Karen added. "You're a natural."

"God, what would I ever do without you guys?" I couldn't help but smile. Good old Elaine and Karen. They'd been rooting for me since my very first day on the job. And having them in my corner has meant a lot to me. I've always kind of looked up to them. They're both so together, so self-assured. Karen is twenty-seven, attractive, independent and gutsy. Very gutsy. Once she even told Mrs. Finkelberg to fuck off right to her face—and Mrs. Finkelberg was the one who ended up apologizing! And Elaine, she's pretty special too. Besides being a damned good feature writer, she's a striking woman of forty with a husband, three kids and a brown belt in karate. The kind you read about in women's magazines. "I'd really miss you if I decided to leave this place."

Elaine raised an eyebrow. "Leave? You're not thinking of quitting, are you?"

"I almost did it this morning." I sighed. "I almost did it, but I just couldn't seem to spit the words out. I'm afraid of my own shadow, that's my problem. I've always been that way. Hell, I even slept with a Donald Duck night light by my bed until I was thirteen. And Huey, Dewey, and Louie were placed in various strategic areas around the house just in case, God*forbid*, I should meet the Boogey Man on the way to the can in the middle of the night."

"Ah, c'mon, Shay,"—Elaine laughed—"this is your first job, and you've only been at it a few months. You're hardly broken in yet. Just give it more time. Mrs. F's bound to let up on you eventually. She can be pretty decent at times, you know? I mean, she hires women for all the key positions."

"Yeah," Karen said, "and she especially likes to hire Jewish Princesses and whip them into shape. That's how she gets her jollies. She'll let up on you soon."

"Ha, don't you believe it!" Dora Litman, our copy editor, sneered from the far corner of the room where she was hunched over her desk, editing copy with her ever-present squeaky red magic marker. "I've been here, what, five years now, and the old witch *still* sends me home in tears every night!"

"That's becuase you *let* her walk all over you," Karen told her. "You and Shay both."

"What you guys need is a course in self-defense!" Elaine chopped at the air with her hands. "Ever since I got my brown belt, the old witch hasn't said 'boo' to me."

"Or better still, sign up for the Assertiveness Training

program I took at the Women's Center," Karen said. "Guaranteed nobody will push you around after that. They teach you to stand up for your rights."

"Or even better still—join the Wolf Pack at the Y," Meryl the receptionist piped in, referring to that infamous group of fanatics who jog daily among the unlikely mixture of lush greenery, horseshit, broken Labatt beer bottles and perverts of Mount Royal—sort of the Central Park of Montreal. "Ever since I started running with them on my lunch hours, I've been like a new person. I feel like I could conquer the world. The old witch can yell at me until she's blue in the face, and I don't even bat an eyelash anymore!"

"Oh, you people and your stupid courses," Dora sneered, "you think they're the answer to everything!"

"Don't knock it till you've tried it," Karen retorted. "Assertiveness Training changed my whole life. Thanks to A.T., I have the guts to do things I could never do before. Like going to Mrs. Finkelberg to demand a raise. Or telling my parents that my new roommate's name is actually Frank—not Francine. The unassertive me would have lied to them, that's for sure."

My eyes almost popped out of my head. "You moved in with a man?"

"That's right. You've been away the past couple of weeks, I guess you haven't heard."

I shook my head.

"You remember I told you about that terrific guy I met while playing racquetball at the Cavendish Club last month?" she said, referring to the suburban Cote Saint Luc health club where we Jewish girls tend to hang out when we're not out to lunch at Nuddick's. "Frank Shapiro? Well, last week he asked me to move in with him. And that's just what I did."

"Just like that?" I snapped my fingers.

"Like that." She snapped hers.

"Hey, I know Frank Shapiro—he has his office in Cavendish Mall!" Meryl cried, referring to the gigantic shopping plaza in the heart of Cote Saint Luc where we

Jewish girls tend to hang out when we're not at the other two places. "He's an orthopedic surgeon. Gorgeous. Divorced. No kids. Drives a BMW 733i . . ."

"God, Meryl," Karen laughed, "do you know his prick size too?"

"You want it in inches or centimeters?" Meryl shot back.

"I thought you never kiss and tell, Meryl!" I cracked, and we all shrieked with laughter.

"Christ, this place is beginning to sound worse than a men's locker room!" Karen cried.

"I know,"—Elaine chortled—"don't you just love it?"

"It's gotten so it's the only thing I *do* love about this job," I said wistfully.

"Job, oh, God!" Meryl jumped up and scurried off to the advertising department. "I have a ton of filing to do!"

"Yeah, I have to get going myself." Elaine glanced at her watch. "I'm late for an interview and it's way the hell out east!" She grabbed her purse and her French dictionary—a necessary tool for the not-completely-bilingual who venture out to the predominantly French half of Montreal—and she flew out the door.

"I have to go too," Karen said. "I'm covering a fashion show at Holt Renfrew for the fall supplement. They're showing all the American designer fashions that give all us Jewish Canadian Princesses our unique identity."

"Karen," I said, "can I ask you something?"

"Sure, kiddo, just hang on a sec while I call a cab. Would you believe I actually got the old witch to spring for one?" She made a quick call to Diamond Taxi. "Now," she said as she hung up, "what is it you wanted to know?"

"Your parents—how'd they take it when you moved in with your boyfriend?"

"Well, they didn't exactly do a *hora*, that's for sure. But they're coming around. I think I've finally convinced them that I'm a grown woman and that I have the right to live my own life the way I see fit. And it's all thanks to Assertiveness Training."

"Do they have a crash program?"

"Nope, the introductory course is about ten weeks. Why? You thinking of moving in with a guy?"

"I guess you could say that." I showed her Peter's telegram. "I met him a couple of weeks ago. It was love at first sight, you know?"

"Wow,"—she whistled as she read it—"no wonder you've been so preoccupied this morning. This is some telegram!"

"I want to go with him, Karen," I told her, "but how am I going to break it to my parents? They'll have grand mal seizures. I know them. They're going to feel rejected, dejected and *far* from objective. When they hear that I want to go and Live In Sin with Peter, they're liable to have me kidnapped and brought to the Jewish Institute of Brides and Grooms for deprogramming—ten free lectures by various esteemed rabbis and psychologists and hopefully I'll be cured of my *mishegaas*."

"Are you sure it's your parents you're afraid of?" she shrugged. "Sounds to me like you're more afraid of yourself."

"Huh?"

"Just a few minutes ago you were telling us how afraid you were of your own shadow, remember?"

"Yeah, but my parents, they . . ."

"Listen, kiddo, it's very easy to blame other people for your problems, but that's a dead end. Believe me, I know. I've been there. You'll never get anywhere if you don't start taking responsibility for your own life."

"Yeah, but nobody let's me!"

"It's not something anybody can help you with. It's something you've got to do for yourself. . . . Shit, there's my taxi! Listen, kiddo, I'll see you later, huh? In the meantime, if the old witch comes back and starts hassling you, stand up to her. Let her know she can't push you around. Let her know you're a person too! If you can stand up to her, you can stand up to *any*one! You got that, kiddo?"

"Person . . . stand up . . . *any*one! Yeah, I think so," I said, savoring these crystal words of wisdom and desperately hoping that eventually they might even come to make sense.

"Nobody's as formidable as they want you to think," she said as she headed out the door. "Even Mrs. Finkelberg has a heart somewhere under all that blubber."

"Formidable . . . heart . . . blubber! Gottcha!" *Oy veh!*

Mrs. Finkelberg was in a rotten mood when she got back from Nuddick's—or "Nudnick's" as she prefers to call it.

"Why the hell do I eat at that crummy restaurant? That zoo?" she grumbled to no one in particular. "The noise gives me a headache, the food gives me heartburn . . ."

"One Cow Brand Cocktail coming up!" Meryl zipped off to the kitchenette as fast as her high-heeled clogs could carry her and returned with a tall glassful of what looked like dirty bathwater. "Here," she said, handing the concoction to Mrs. Finkelberg, "I put in two heaping spoonfuls of baking soda, just the way you like it."

"Damned heartburn,"—Mrs. Finkelberg grimaced—"it's going to be the death of me yet!" She drained the glass dry and banged it down on the reception desk. "And speaking of heartburn,"—she squinted in my direction—"where's Shayna?"

"Right here at my desk," I cringed. *Formidable. Heart. Blubber.*

"Hmmmm,"—she put on her glasses and gave me a piercing look—"what are you doing there? Daydreaming for a change?"

"Proofreading!" I waved a stack of freshly typeset articles in the air.

"Hmph," she snarled, "just make sure you catch all the typos this time. There were far too many in the paper last week."

Person. Stand up. Anyone. "I wasn't even here last week!"

"I don't care who's to blame. I'm just stating facts. And now, if it's not too much trouble, kindly get on the phone with the mayor's office and set up an interview for this afternoon."

I made a sour face. I was hoping she'd forgotten all about that stupid "Poop and Scoop" business.

"Well, do it already! Before you forget!"

I reached for the phone. *Person. Stand up. Anyone.*

"My God, you move slowly!" she blasted me. "I've seen turtles that move faster than you do! What does it take to get a rise out of you, anyway? A lit firecracker up your ass?"

That did it. *"I'm a person too, you know!"* I exploded.

"I beg your pardon?" She gave me a startled look.

"She said—she's a person too, you know!" Meryl cried ecstatically, giving me a clench-fisted salute behind Mrs. Finkelberg's back.

"That's what I thought she said." Mrs. Finkelberg scratched her head. "Hold my calls, will you Meryl? Shayna and I are going into my office to have a little talk."

"Oh-oh," Meryl said, giving me an exaggeratedly mortified look.

"Listen, Ms. Yenta Telebende, if I want commentary, I'll turn on Howard Cosell!" Mrs. Finkelberg glared at her. "C'mon, Shayna,"—she nudged me—"let's get this over with." We went into her office and she closed the door. I got the feeling that my career with the *Register* was about to come to an abrupt end. And I was almost relieved. One less obstacle between me and a new life in California. One less decision to make. "Shayna, Shayna, Shayna . . ." She wearily plunked herself down at her desk and popped a Rolaid into her mouth. "What are we going to do with you, Shayna?"

C'mon, fire me already, you bitch, I thought, get it over with so we can all get on with our lives!

"Sit down, Shayna."

"I'd rather stand." I folded my arms defiantly across my chest.

"Suit yourself."

"It's about time I did."

"You know, you're beginning to sound more and more like our friend Karen Biskin every minute."

"Thank you." I smiled.

"Yes,"—she nodded—"I suppose that is a compliment. In the three years Karen's been working here, she's evolved into quite a young woman. You know, she's even had a couple of articles published in *Maclean's* recently? That's quite an accomplishment—getting published in Canada's answer to *Time*."

"I know. I read them."

"They were really quite good, you know. Karen's really going places. But she's worked hard to get where she is. She's paid her dues."

"So have I." I sniffed. "I went to McGill for five years. I got my B.A. in Communications."

"You know what a B.A. in Communications stands for in my books?" she hollered, the fat on her face jiggling like Jell-O. "It stands for knowing Balls All about Communications. Not to mention life! Look at me, Shayna, look at me. I'm a self-made woman. I built this paper up from scratch. I'm a pillar in this community!" She popped another Rolaid into her mouth. "And the only school I ever graduated from was the School of Hard Knocks."

I rolled my eyes around in my head. "I didn't ask to be born well off you know?"

"Yes, well, just because you were doesn't mean you're exempt from paying your dues like the rest of us. We all have to pay our dues if we're ever going to get anywhere."

"Yeah?" I cried, figuring I had nothing left to lose anyway. "Well, how am I ever supposed to get anywhere if I'm always doing jobs like proofreading or helping Dora with the copy editing or writing dumb little articles about things like dog shit?" I threw my hands up in the air. "Dog shit, yeesh!"

"But that's what paying your dues is all about, Shayna. You have to start at the bottom and work your way to the top. I told you that the very day I hired you, didn't I? And do you remember what you promised me in return?

You promised to be the best damn Chief *Schlock* Processor and Drivel Writer I ever had—even though the job was a far cry from what you expected after graduation."

"Yeah," I almost laughed aloud. "I remember." In fact, I'll never forget that day as long as I live. I was so grateful to her for hiring me that I'd have agreed to clean toilets if she'd have asked me to. Six months I'd been looking for a job! Six months of nothing but disappointments. I must have applied to every film company, radio and television station, and newspaper in the city. From the National Film Board to the CBC. From the *Montreal Gazette* to the *Midnight Globe*. Nobody had any openings for recent graduates in Communication Arts though. Mrs. Finkelberg was the only one who would give me a break. "Yeah, I remember," I muttered, suddenly feeling like a total *shtunk*. Especially when she went on to remind me that I don't always get the *schlock* jobs. Like the time she sent me out to interview that lady symphony conductor.

"Oh, I know I haven't run it yet," she told me, "but I will; it was too good an article not to. And how about those humorous articles of yours? I believe Dora told me that you write them in your spare time—sort of as a hobby? They were splendid, each and every one of them. Especially that last one you did—on that auto mechanics course for women you took? I laughed so hard I almost *crapeered!*" She shook her head and chuckled. "Ask my Herb. Herb, I told him, this kid could be Canada's answer to Art Buchwald!"

"Me, Art Buchwald?" I was astounded. A compliment from Mrs. Finkelberg is about as rare as a total eclipse of the sun, and here she was giving me a whole flood of them? Naw, it couldn't be, I thought, reaching down to pinch myself on the thigh, this must be a dream. I took too much Gravol this morning and slipped into a coma and now I'm having a weird dream.

"Don't look at me like that, Shayna! Plenty of writers got their start on small suburban newspapers like this one. Besides, not everyone can write humor, you know.

It takes a very special gift—and I believe you've got it. That certain something."

"You do?" I was floating two feet off the ground. I never realized how much that woman's approval meant to me. I just never realized! And to make matters more confusing, she went on to tell me about how she has friends in high places—including the wire services—and how, maybe, with her help, I could have my own syndicated column someday. "God!" I was really getting swept in.

"But!" Her eyes narrowed. "Before I lift so much as one pinky to help you, you've got to give me a sign, some kind of concrete sign that you're ready to go for it. Because talent is worth *borsht* unless you're willing to work your butt off. And that willingness can only come from within you. God,"—she sniffed haughtily as she leaned back in her chair—"only helps those who help themselves."

"You'd . . . you'd really help me?" I was in a state of awe. Moses at the burning bush.

"Just prove yourself first. Can you do that, Shayna? Can you prove to me—and more importantly to yourself—that you're not just another Guccied-up J.A.P. who's content to coast through life on Daddy's MasterCard?"

"I . . . I . . . I . . ."

"I have high hopes for you, Shayna. I hope you won't disappoint me."

"Oh, God." I slumped into a chair and buried my face in my hands. Shay, you turkey you, a familiar voice screamed inside my head, why are you letting her get to you like this? You don't want to be the next Art Buchwald, for crying out loud. You want to write movies—like Woody Allen. You want to go to L.A. with Peter. The man you love! That is what you want, isn't it? Isn't it?

"Shayna?" A hand touched my shoulder.

I looked up. It was her! Go away, I wanted to scream, go away and leave me alone. You're making me crazy with all these decisions. You were supposed to fire me and make things easier, not more complicated. The last thing I need is more complications, damn you! But the words got stuck in my throat.

"Are you all right?" she asked. "You're as white as a sheet."

"I—I don't know." My head was reeling. I was so confused. I didn't know if I was coming or going or what.

"You look awful." She touched my forehead with the back of her hand in one of those rare moments of tenderness I'd only heard about. Damn her, why now? "And you're warm too. Maybe you should see a doctor?"

"Yeah, a doctor." Jo Ann, I thought, I'll go over to Jo Ann's. She can help me sort things out. She always does. "I really think I should see a doctor."

"Go on then. I'll get somebody to cover for you. And don't worry about the interview with the mayor. You can do it first thing Monday morning."

"Yeah, first thing Monday." I was ready to agree to anything just to get out of there. "Thank you." I got up and rushed out before she could change her mind.

Chapter 9

Jo Ann, looking her usual exquisite, dressed-to-kill self, was walking out the front door just as I pulled up to her house.

"Hey, Pecker!" I honked my horn. "Where are you going?"

"Shay, it's you!" she cried as she ran down to the car to greet me. "Boy, are you ever a hard person to get a hold of. First I called your house and your mother said you were at work; then I called you at work and they said you'd left for the day."

"I got the rest of the day off."

"I've been dying to hear all about your trip to New York. Your mother says you had a fabulous time."

"Yeah,"—I sighed—"we sure did."

"Well, don't sound too thrilled about it or anything!" She grabbed my wrist. "So where's the watch? Your mother says she bought you a real beauty at Cartier's."

"It's at home." I pulled my hand away. "I'm, uh, saving it for special occasions, you know?" Actually I couldn't

117

bear to put it on this morning. It made me feel so guilty! "Jo, I've really got to talk to you," I blurted. "I've been dying to talk to you ever since I got in from New York last night. I must have called your house a thousand times!"

"We took my in-laws out to Ruby Foo's for their anniversary. Why, what's the big . . . ? Oh, I know. This has to do with the guy you spent the night with a couple of weeks ago, doesn't it?"

"I'm so mixed up." I rubbed my throbbing temples. "You've got to help me sort things out before I explode!"

She gave me a pained look. "I'm afraid this isn't a very good time." She glanced over at the house, which, along with her pregnancy, occupies most of her time these days.

I turned toward the imposing white marble cottage with its massive front pillars and lush green lawn—a standout even on this cul-de-sac full of better Cote Saint Luc homes and gardens. What now? I wondered. The plumber? The interior decorator? Maybe they were both there together, putting in designer pipes? God *forbid* the plumbing should be out of sync with the rest of the place. "Well, if you're busy with the house . . ."

"No, not the house this time," she said. "Take a peek in the driveway."

I did as directed. And there sat two girls I hadn't seen in ages, Sandy Kreisman and Brenda Frank, waiting in the back seat of the Peckers' banana yellow Cherokee jeep. They smiled and waved at me. I waved back.

"Be there in a sec!" Jo Ann yelled to them.

"Jesus, I haven't seen them since camp," I said.

"Me neither," she shrugged. "Ten years at least."

"So what are they doing in Richard's jeep?"

"Well, you didn't expect me to fit them into the back of my Firebird, did you? They're both in their eighth month!"

"Both of them?"

"Yeah, they still do everything together—just like they used to when we called them the 'Bobbsey Twins' way back then. Remember? They even used to go to the bathroom together!"

I strained to get a better look. They were pregnant all right. Very pregnant. They looked more like Tweedledum and Tweedledee than the Bobbsey Twins. "You having a baby shower on wheels or what?"

"They heard I was in my fourth month and they thought it would be fun if we 'pregos' got together and compared notes. So we're going to Nuddick's for lunch."

"Oh." Today was pregnancy day. I might have known. If not the house . . .

"Anyway, it's kinda nice to get together with people who are going through the same thing as you, you know?"

"Sure." Suddenly I felt like the only single person left on earth. "Well, see you." I started my car.

"Hey, wait a minute, where are you going?" She reached over and pulled the keys out of the ignition. "Don't you want to come?"

"I don't know . . ." The thought of sitting in that zoo of a restaurant all afternoon and talking "Baby Talk" with Tweedledee and Tweedledum made me ill. "I'm not much into diapers, you know?"

"C'mon, they have to leave for a doctor's appointment at two. Then we can sit and talk about whatever it is you want to talk about. C'mon, I really want you to come."

"Well, I guess . . . if they're leaving at two." I leaned over to take a look at myself in the rearview mirror.

"C'mon, you're gorgeous!"

"Just checking." I fluffed my hair and smoothed on some lipgloss. One can never look too good for Nuddick's. Every dressed-to-kill *yenta* and her *buttinski* mother-in-law goes there for lunch. And when you walk through the door, they all look up from their diet plates of cottage cheese and Melba toast to check you out. And if they don't approve of what you look like or what you're wearing or who you are, they set aside their diet plates of cottage cheese and Melba toast and devour *you* for lunch instead. "I look okay?" I asked her as I got out of the car.

"Perfect. Hey, look at her in the Geoffrey Beene halter

top and the Calvins!" she cried as she gave me the once-over. "Nice Louis Vuitton purse too! Part of your loot from New York?"

"Uh-huh." I winced. Sometimes I wonder if Jo Ann isn't getting to be as bad as those *yentas* in Nuddick's.

"God," she gave me an envious look, "you're so skinny, I hate you! Look at me." She patted her stomach, which had a tiny bulge in it. Sort of like a radial tire. "I'm beginning to show already. Would you believe I can't even fit into my Sasson jeans anymore?"

"Yeah, but you can still get into your Calvin Kleins I see."

"Yeah, but the Sassons are my favorite," she sighed.

"Christ, will you just listen to us!" I cried. I really hated this conversation. "Sassons, Calvin Klein, Geoffrey Beene! God, we sound like such J.A.P.s!"

"That's 'cause we are!" she laughed. "C'mon." She took my hand and pulled me toward the jeep. "Brenda and Sandy must be *plotzing* already."

Nuddick's was packed as usual.

It was just wall-to-wall-to-ceiling with the usual assortment of dressed-to-kill *yentas*, *buttinskis* and Jewish Princesses.

And Jo Ann, the Bobbsey Twins and I had to walk through the usual gauntlet of eyes to get to our table.

Shit—those eyes!

I don't think I'll ever get used to them. They made me so nervous that I kept checking my fly to make sure it was closed.

By the time we sat down at our table I was in a perfect sweat.

Not Jo Ann though. Jo Ann looked like she had just stepped out of one of those beautiful people Arrid Extra Dry commercials.

Jo Ann was cool, calm and collected.

And the Bobbsey Twins were basking in all the attention.

From the way they were sitting there, waving and

smiling at everyone, you'd have thought they were on a float at the Grey Cup Parade.

"What's the matter, Shay?" Jo Ann asked me. "You're all flushed."

"I just wish people would keep their eyes to themselves." My head was spinning. Even the gaudy red and gold decor was closing in on me. "Sometimes I think they can see right into my soul."

"You'd think you'd be used to it by now," she laughed. "I mean, looking people over at Nuddick's is practically a Jewish tradition, like having bagel and lox on Sunday morning or going to Miami for Christmas." She took a look around. "Though people do seem to be staring more than usual."

"It's because of us," Brenda said. "It's been this way ever since we started showing."

"That's right," Sandy agreed. "In this day and age when more and more people are living together, getting divorced or choosing careers over having children, it kinda renews everyone's faith in humanity when they see a young pregnant woman go by."

"Or two." Brenda patted her enormous stomach.

"Or three!" Jo Ann cried.

And they all cracked up laughing.

For the next hour and fifteen minutes and forty-five seconds the three of them sat there over their chef's salads, strawberry cheesecake and tall glasses of milk and talked nothing but Baby Talk. Everything you always wanted to know about pregnancy but were understandably afraid to ask. From Ultrasound (Jo Ann couldn't hold in the mandatory six glasses of water and peed on the table) to Internals (they kill). From Labor Pains (they kill more) to Episiotomies (they kill after the freezing wears off). From Epidurals (they're a blessing—if you have enough money to *shmear* the anesthetist so that he'll show up on time, if at all) to Enemas (so that you don't shit in the doctor's face when you're pushing the baby out). Brenda even described, in graphic detail, how her sister-in-law's best friend's sister's water broke while she was grocery shopping at Hypermarché, Montreal's biggest—and busiest—supermarket (it gushed all over a fellow shopper's brand new $600 handmade snakeskin cowboy boots and wiped out an entire shelf of Dare Chocolate Chip cookies before she even knew what hit her).

It was definitely not one of the more appetizing lunches I have ever attended.

And then, as if all that wasn't hard enough to take, there was the endless stream of well-wishers who kept stopping by.

"*Mazel tov*, dear!" a friend of Jo Ann's mother cried as she reached over to feel Jo Ann's stomach. "Your mother tells me you're carrying a little bundle of *nachas* in there. And when's your turn?" she said to me, apparently forgetting that I didn't have a husband yet.

"You're both going to have boys," a woman who knew Brenda and Sandy told them, "there's no doubt about it."

"You're both going to have girls," said another, "I'm willing to bet my life on it!"

"Keep on having those babies, ladies," a middle-aged man in a three-piece suit told them, "and for God*sakes*, don't let that *farbissener* separatist Parti Québecois scare you off to Toronto—like it has so many of our young people!"

And in between all that, there were the bits and pieces of conversations from surrounding tables that kept filtering in.

In the booth to our right, four middle-aged busybodies were busy discussing Ruth Somebody-or-Other's recently divorced daughter who goes down to Thursday's and all those other swingin' Crescent Street bars every night to pick up men. And to our left a couple of J.A.P.s were talking about some poor soul named Rhea Bibberman who got her boyfriend's safe stuck up her *knish* and had to be rushed to the hospital to have it removed with forceps. And in front of us a bunch of sixteen-year-olds (the kind Mrs. Finkelberg would call P.I.T.s, or Princesses in Training) were trying on each other's jewelry and discussing what they were going to wear to Patty Somebodyski's upcoming "Sweet" at the Hyatt.

It was enough to make a person want to get on the next plane to California and never come back.

By the time two o'clock rolled around and the Bobbsey Twins got up to leave for their doctor's appointment, I was in a stupor.

"Thank heavens!" I cried as they waddled off, waving and smiling, like two movie stars at a premiere.

"God," Jo Ann sighed, "I can't believe I'm going to look like that in a few months. They're so big!"

"They were heavy to begin with," I reminded her. "Now could we . . ."

"I'm happy I'm pregnant and everything," she rattled on. "I just wish I didn't have to get so goddamned fat! I mean, look at me . . . just look at me . . . my nose is swollen, my face is puffy, my tits are humongous, my middle is spreading . . . Did I tell you that I can't even fit into my Sassons anymore?"

"About an hour ago." I could feel my blood beginning to boil. "Now could we . . . ?"

"Richard keeps assuring me that I look more beautiful than ever, you know? He's especially thrilled with my humongous tits. But still," she winced, "I could cry every time I look at myself in the mirror, you know?" She picked up a knife and studied her reflection in it. "I could just cry." She gave her streaked blonde hair a quick fluff, resurrected a drooping eyelash with the help of one of her inch-long "Delightfully Red" fingernails, smoothed over her heavily glossed lips with an expert sweep of her pinky and then she set the knife back down on the table. "Miss Piggy, that's who I look like!"

That did it. "You're no help!" I fumed, throwing my share of the bill down on the table and getting up to leave.

"Hey." She suddenly noticed I was alive. "Where are you going?"

"You wanna know where I'm going?" I exploded. "I'll tell you where I'm going. To California to live with Peter, *that's* where I'm going!"

"You're what?"

About a dozen heads turned our way to check out the commotion. The four busybodies in the next booth shoved aside their diet plates of cottage cheese and Melba toast and began licking their chops. *"Gib a kik,* Frances!" they murmured in Yiddish as they poked each other with their elbows. *"Kik ihr uhn,* Zelda!"

Oh, no, I thought, staring at Frances, I know that woman from somewhere. But who is she? One of Ma's friends from Elmsdale? One of those distant relatives on Dad's side whom I only see at weddings, *bar mitzvahs* and funerals? Oh, no, what have I done?

"Sit down, will you?" Jo Ann said in a hoarse whisper. "Everybody's staring!"

"Oh, God!" I grabbed my purse and ran out.

Jo Ann caught up with me in the parking lot, demanding to know what was going on.

"I can't believe I just did that!" I wailed. "I mean, there are three surefire ways of spreading news around this city: Telephone, Television and Tell-It-At-Nuddick's. *And I just told it at Nuddick's!"*

"Calm down, will you?" she said. "Take it easy."

"Oh, sure, calm down! I just told half the world about something my parents know nothing about and you tell me to calm down? Shit, Jo Ann, I'd never have shouted it out that way if you hadn't been so wrapped up in your humongous tits and your fucking Sasson jeans!"

"I'm sorry, I had no idea it was that serious."

"I'm only on the verge of having a complete nervous breakdown, that's all! The Man of My Dreams wants me to come live with him in California; my mother wants me to forget he ever existed because she hates his guts—not to mention his looks, personality and occupation; Stanley wants to marry me and won't take no for an answer; and Mrs. Finkelberg . . . ! Mrs. Finkelberg wants to turn me into the next Art Buchwald! And my best friend won't even listen to me."

"Well, what do *you* want?"

"If I knew that,"—I threw my hands up to God—. "would I be on the verge of a nervous breakdown?"

"I just can't believe it." She shook her head. "He really asked you to move to California with him?"

"Yeah, he's there right now on business but he sent me this." I pulled the telegram out of my purse and handed it to her.

She sat down on a cement slab to read it. "God . . . Gawwwwdd!"

"What am I going to do, Jo?" I said, plunking myself down beside her. "I'm picking Peter up at the airport tomorrow morning and he's going to be expecting an answer. That means I'd have to break the news to my parents tonight—if some *yenta* from Nuddick's hasn't gotten to them first."

"God, your parents!" She gave me a horrified look. "They're going to *kill* you!"

"Thanks, Jo Ann,"—I winced—"I really needed that."

"Well, I'm just being realistic. I mean, I know your parents. They're just like my parents. They'd rather see you dead than Living in Sin!"

"Do you have to be so realistic?!"

"Look what happened to my cousin Rhonda when she moved in with her boyfriend. Her parents pronounced her D.W.A.—Dead While Alive. They actually sat *shiva* for her!"

"God!" A shudder ran right through me. I had visions of Ma getting dressed in black . . . of Dad having his tie snipped . . . of the men from Paperman & Sons Funeral Home setting down a bunch of those little brown *shiva* chairs in the far corner of the living room . . . of the family gathering around to mourn my "passing." "I'd just die if that happened to me!"

"That's the general idea, dummy!"

"You know what I meant!"

"I know, I'm sorry. And besides, my cousin's situation was a little bit more extreme. After all, the guy was Greek and her father was a big shot at the Shaar Hashomayim synagogue. But still, your parents are going to *kill* you!"

"Do you have to keep saying that?" I cried. "I came to you for advice—not potential headlines in the *National Enquirer!*"

"All the comfort in the world isn't going to change the facts. Your parents will never give you their blessing. They believe in marriage—a lot."

"Tell me about it." I groaned. "My mother truly believes that my life will have no meaning until I register my silverware pattern and dinner set at Kaplow's Gift Shop. Her dream has always been to see my little white card up against the display of "Bridal Selections":

Shayna Pearl Fine: Fiancée of
Mr. Blankety Blank. Royal Doulton
China. Moonlight Serenade—white
with gold trim. Service for 8.

"You know how it is? When your card goes up in that Bridal Selection corner, you're a Somebody. It's like seeing your name up in lights. People suddenly know you exist. You become legitimate. And my mother is dying for me to become legitimate. It's killing her, it's really killing her because all my friends are heavily into sheets, towels and wall-to-wall carpeting and I'm still not the fiancée of Mr. Blankety Blank."

"She's a typical mother. What do you expect? From the moment you were born she's probably been dreaming of the day she could make you a fancy-shmancy wedding at the Ritz—the whole *megillah*. Just like I had."

"Yeah, well, a fancy-shmancy wedding at the Ritz doesn't guarantee happiness, you know? Hell, look at Sandy Bloomfield and Marsha Slutsky. They waltzed out of their respective weddings at the Ritz and bunny-hopped into their respective divorces in record time—five months for Sandy; eight for Marsha." I shook my head. "And to think I once envied those girls. I mean, there they were, the Center of Attention. Center Stage. Their diamond rings were so huge that their bodies took a pronounced dip to the left when they walked. And bridal showers! Between them they must have had a dozen. Plant . . . bathroom . . . kitchen . . . Tupperware! I thought for sure they were set for life. So did they, for that matter. But look at them now—stuck with all the props and no leading men."

"I guess this means I won't be making you a bridal shower," she sighed. "I thought for sure you and Stanley were going to get married and I'd get to make you one in my new house."

"Well, you could always make me a 'Living In Sin' shower," I cracked.

She didn't answer.

"Ah, what's so great about bridal showers anyway? A bunch of well-dressed women sit around your living room sipping sherry and stuffing their faces with cheesecake from Ethel Potchkeh Caterers while you open their gifts and say truly profound things like, 'Ooooo, a spatula!' or 'Ahhhhh, an oven mitt!' or 'Wowwww, a toaster oven!' Things like that set women back fifty years."

"But don't you ever want to get married and have a family?"

"Someday, maybe. I'm just not ready for that whole scene now. Maybe I never will be."

"Didn't you tell me that Peter has a kid?"

"Yeah—Nicky. He's really adorable too. I'm crazy about him. But that's different. He lives with his mother. He's not my responsibility."

"Yeah, well what happens if his mother, say, gets killed in a car crash or something and he has to come live with you?"

"For Pete's sakes, Jo Ann!"

"I'm just being realistic."

"I don't know. I'll worry about it if the time comes. In

the meantime, it's just going to be me and Peter in our magnificent beach house overlooking the Pacific."

"God, you sound like something out of Harlequin Romances!"

"Well, Peter's a pretty romantic guy."

"I can't wait to meet this Mr. Wonderful."

"Yeah, he's kind of anxious to meet you too. He thinks you give great blow job instructions."

"Ooooh!" she squealed. "The old popsicle routine."

"It worked like a charm. By the end of the night I was practically a pro."

She smiled. "You're really crazy about him, aren't you? I can see it in your eyes, the way they light up when you talk about him. I've never seen you get this way over a guy before, that's for sure."

"I've never felt this way before. Shit, Jo Ann," I cried, "what do you think I should do? I mean, going to L.A. with him—it's such a big step. It's so scary."

"Hmmm . . ." She toyed with the ever-present diamond-studded *J* around her neck. "Well, if you want my advice, I don't think you should decide right now. I think you need more time to get to know him better. After all, you did only spend *one* night with the guy."

"You think he'd understand?"

"If he's as terrific as you say, he will. Look, you've got ten days before you're supposed to leave for L.A. Why don't you just wait and see how it goes before you decide anything? And for God*sakes*, don't tell your parents yet!"

"I guess that makes sense," I shrugged. "It's funny, you know—all your life you wait for your dreams to come true and just when they're finally about to, you become riddled with all kinds of doubts."

"I think it's only natural to have doubts," she reassured me. "After all, it says right here in the telegram—'Shay: Take a chance. Come live with me.' And that's exactly what you'd be doing. Taking a *big* chance."

I shivered. "And that's what's so scary about this whole thing. I mean, what chances have I ever had to take in my whole life? Not telling Peter I was a virgin that first time, letting that first time happen altogether—that was Shay Fine at her most daring!"

"I don't know about that." She laughed. "You told him you were on the Pill, which you weren't—now *that* was certainly taking a chance!"

We looked at each other and burst out laughing.

"I can't believe you did that!" she howled, her voice echoing across the parking lot.

"Neither could he!"

"God!" She got serious all of a sudden. "I hope you're not pregnant!"

"Naw, I got my period the day after I got to New York."

"Pheuw,"—she fanned herself—"that's a relief."

"You're not kidding," I agreed wholeheartedly. "I think it's part of the reason why I had such a good time in New York. I was just so relieved that I got my period. So was my mother, for that matter. I think it just confirmed her suspicions that my recent craziness was all because *that* time of the month was coming on."

"That's ridiculous," she scoffed.

"God, I sure hope so," I laughed. "I mean, I do get a *little* crazy before my period, but I'd sure hate to think I fell in love with Peter because my hormones were unbalanced!"

"Well, you have to admit the whole thing was a little crazy, for whatever reason. I mean, telling him you were on the Pill when you weren't!"

"He was pretty pissed off at first. But then he got over it and went out to buy some safes."

"Echchchchch! Safes are the pits!"

"Well, he wasn't too crazy about them, that's for sure. But what choice did we have?"

"C'mon." She grabbed me by the hand and pulled me toward her jeep. "You're coming with me."

"Where to?"

"To Dr. Yagod's to put in the Coil."

"Whoa!" I stopped dead in my tracks. "I don't know about that."

"Why not? It'll give you one less thing to worry about."

"I'm not crazy about having a piece of wire shoved up my *knish*, that's why."

"Don't be silly. It's a terrific gadget! They're not sure how it works, exactly, but it does. I used it for three years until I took it out to get pregnant. And the beauty of it is, you don't even know it's there. It just hurts a little when he inserts it and you get bad cramps during your period, but it's definitely the best of the bunch. You don't get fat like you do on the Pill and there's no *potchkeeing* around like there is with the other gizmos and doodads. And now's the perfect time to do it too. You're supposed to put it in right after your period."

"But I don't even have an appointment. I can't just walk into Dr. Yagod's office and ask him to shove a coil up me just like that. I mean, it's not like we're going to McDonald's to order a Big Mac!"

"You know his receptionist, Arnalee Gold?"

"Just from the few times I've gone there for checkups," I shrugged. "Why?"

"Well, I took her up to my father's factory for clothes a couple of times. She owes me. Maybe I can get her to squeeze you in some time this afternoon. Here,"—she handed me her car keys—"you wait in the jeep while I go and call her from the pay phone in Nuddick's."

Five minutes later we were on our way to the Medical Arts Building on Cote des Neiges, home of Yagod, Spitz and Klein, Ob. Gyns., Inc.

"Arnalee put you down for 3:45 but she thinks you might have to wait awhile," Jo Ann said, looking pretty pleased with herself. "Boy oh boy," she laughed, "having a father in the *shmata* business sure does come in handy sometimes, you know?"

I reached into her purse and pulled out a Rothman. My hand shook as I lit it.

"You're doing the right thing, you know," she told me.

"I just want to be sure," I said, blowing the smoke out slowly. "I mean, the Coil, it's risky, I've read things."

"Every contraceptive has its risks. Remember when I

took the Pill a few years ago? My tits got so huge I practically needed a shopping cart to lug them around."

I squirmed in my seat. Sometimes I feel more like Jo Ann's child than her best friend. She's always so on top of things. So sure of herself. "I know I sound like a little *kvetch* and everything but . . ."

"Look, I know this sounds primitive, but like it or not, contraception is still a woman's responsibility. If we had to depend on the men of this world to take precautions, our lives would be one loooooong pregnancy."

"That stinks!"

"Stinks, shminks, it's a fact of life, kiddo. Anyway"— she winked at me—"just think about how thrilled Peter's going to be when he comes home tomorrow and you surprise him with some 'No fuss/No mess' sex."

She had a good point there. I really did want everything to be perfect when Peter came home tomorrow. And besides, I decided, Karen Biskin had been right. It's about time I started taking responsibility for my own life.

"So what do you say?"

I looked at her and smiled. "I say—good-bye safes, hello 'No fuss/No mess' sex!"

Chapter 10

PUTTING IN the Coil was definitely a memorable experience.

I mean, it was right up there with two other of the most unforgettable experiences of my life: fracturing my pelvis and shattering my kneecap.

The moment I laid eyes on it I practically went into shock.

"That's it?!" I gasped as Dr. Yagod reached into a box and pulled out a double-looped gizmo with copper wiring protruding from its stem like insect antennas. "That's what you're going to put up inside me?"

"Yep, this is it," he said as he held it up to the light for inspection. "The Copper 7."

"It looks like a used car part!"

He laughed. "In a way, it does work like one of the parts in your car. You know what a catalytic converter is?"

"Yeah, sure, I learned all about it in my auto mechanics course. It cleans up the pollutants."

"Well then, just think of the Copper 7 as a catalytic converter for sperm, heh, heh."

"Heh, heh." Just what I'd always wanted.

"Okay, take a deep breath and relax." He smiled reassuringly as he prepared to zero the gizmo in for a landing. "You'll feel a cramp or two and it'll be all over."

Oh, God, I thought, wrapping my toes around the stirrups for dear life, that's exactly what I'm afraid of!

"Hey, c'mon now, just relax," he said in a kind, almost syrupy-sweet voice. "I've put in hundreds of these things and I haven't lost a patient yet."

"I . . . I'm sorry," I said, feeling like a total *nebbish*. I think that even my vagina was blushing. "I don't know what's gotten into me. Just give me a minute and I'll be all right."

"Sure thing, take your time," he said, glancing anxiously at his watch, as doctors often do whenever they tell you to take your time. "Take all the time you need."

Damn you, Shay, grow up, will you, I thought as I struggled to regain my composure, just grow the hell up! Do you always have to make such a big production out of everything? The guy says it's nothing. He's done hundreds. Millions of women go through it all the time. So grow up! "Okay, I'm ready." I took a deep breath.

"Okey dokey," he chirped cheerfully as he shoved it up and tore my *kishkas* out.

I passed out twice from the pain.

When I became conscious—and stayed that way—he presented me with a doggie bag full of painkillers stamped "Physician's Sample" and a pamphlet entitled "Everything You Always Wanted to Know About the Copper 7" and sent me on my way.

But not before he dropped a bomb on my head.

"You'll probably have some cramps and bleeding for the next few days," he said as he handed me over to Jo Ann, "so if I were you I'd take it easy until your symptoms subside."

I stared at him in disbelief. "You mean, like no sex?"

"That too."

But you can't do this to me, I thought. Peter's coming home tomorrow!

"Just take two of those painkillers every four hours when you need them, and I'm sure you'll be just fine," he reassured me in that syrupy voice of his. "But if the bleeding or the cramps get any more severe, call me immediately. Everything else you need to know is in that pamphlet I gave you."

"Jeez, nothing like that happened to me when I had the Coil put in," said a truly sympathetic Jo Ann on the way home. "Richard and I had sex that very night. The worst thing that happened was that he pricked himself on the tail a couple of times."

"Shit, and I wanted everything to be perfect when Peter comes home tomorrow," I said, trying to blink back the tears. "Perfectly awful, that's how it's going to be!"

"Look, I know you're disappointed and everything, but did you ever stop to think that maybe this is all for the best?"

"Nnnnngggggg . . ." I moaned as a Coil cramp tore through me. For the best? Was she nuts?

"It'll give you and Peter a chance to get to know each other better. You know, find out if you have more between you than just sex."

"Hnggggggggg . . ." If she was trying to console me, she was doing a rotten job.

"These things happen," she shrugged. "I'm sure he'll understand."

I gave her a pained look. Suddenly I wasn't so sure of everything she was always so sure of.

"Hey, don't look at me like that! I was only trying to help!"

"I know. I'm sorry," I said, recalling the promise I had made to myself earlier. The one about taking responsibility for my own life from now on. "It was my decision to put it in. Nobody stuck a gun to my head. It's just that . . ." I muffled a sob. "It's just that nothing seems to be going right. All I want to do is handle things like a mature adult and . . . and . . . and . . ."

"Aw, c'mon, don't be so hard on yourself," she handed me a Kleenex. "These things happen. It's not your fault."

"You know what I'm going to do the minute I get home?" I dabbed at my eyes with the Kleenex. "I'm going to crawl into bed and stay there until it's time to pick Peter up at the airport tomorrow morning. If I stay in bed I can't possibly get into any more trouble, right?"

"Well, whatever you do, don't say anything to your parents about the telegram until you've talked things over with Peter and you know what you're getting into. Now *that* would be a disaster!"

"Yeah, well maybe I'll save myself a lot of grief and not tell them at all," I decided. "Maybe I'll just run off with Peter and . . ."

"And what?" She gave me a disgusted look. "Do you really think running away will solve anything?"

"Maybe it'll solve *every*thing!" So much for being mature.

"Ah, you're just talking that way 'cause you're upset. If it's any consolation, things do have a way of working themselves out, you know. And they will . . . in time."

"Next thing I know, you'll be telling me that someday I'm going to look back on all this and laugh!"

"That was going to be my next line!" She laughed.

"I hope you're right," I said, feeling a little too queasy for comfort. "In the meantime, would you mind pulling over to the curb? I think I'm going to be sick . . ."

Ma was in the kitchen preparing Friday night's supper when I got home.

The smell of chickens roasting in the oven turned my stomach. So did the thought of facing Ma for that matter. I knew how disgusted she'd be if she ever found out about my coil. To her an unmarried woman who inserts a contraceptive device with intent to commit sex is, beyond a doubt, a *kurveh* of the cheapest kind. And besides, Jo

Ann had told me that I walked like I had a hot potato between my legs.

I took off my clogs and tried to sneak upstairs unnoticed.

I should have known better.

Hardly anything ever gets by Ma unnoticed.

Sometimes I think she has built-in radar or something.

"What's the matter?" she said as I started up the stairs. "Don't you say hello to your mother when you come in the house?"

"I, uh, I was just going upstairs to wash first," I said without turning around.

"Was it my imagination, or did I see you limping?"

Eyes like a pair of zoom-lenses.

"Limping?" My whole body stiffened. What the hell was I supposed to do? Tell her my catalytic converter for sperm was killing me? "I, uh, I, uh, pulled a muscle in my thigh," I sputtered, thanking God as I said it that mind-reading wasn't among her many talents.

"Well, how'd you do a thing like that?" she wanted to know.

"I, uh, I dunno, just one of those things, I guess."

"What? I can't hear what you're muttering there with your back turned to me." The persistence of a Jehovah's Witness on your doorstep.

I turned around to look at her. The Coil burned through me just as surely as if it had been a live wire. I had to sit down on the steps to keep from losing my balance. "I said it's just one of those things."

"Oh?"

"It's no big deal, really." I couldn't bear to look her in the face. All I could think about was that lousy coil imbedded within my innermost parts like some deep, dark secret. I never used to have secrets from her, I thought, feeling terribly guilty. And now I'm literally full of secrets. I'm just one big secret!

"Shayna Pearl?" A deep note of motherly concern. "Are you all right? You're acting awfully strange. . . ."

"I'm fine." I smiled so wide I thought my face was going to tear. "I think I'll go and take a shower." I got up and headed toward the bathroom. Anything to get away.

She followed me anyway. "You know, I haven't been able to stop thinking about New York all day long?" She plunked herself down on the toilet to pee. "We had quite a time, you and I, didn't we?"

"Yeah." I splashed some cold water on my face. "I kind of couldn't stop thinking about it myself."

"You know that Givenchy bag I got at Feiffer's on Grand Street in New York last Sunday? I saw it at Boutique Tilly today and it was double the price. Can you imagine? Now that's what I call a bargain!"

"Ma,"—I was almost doubled over from the pain in my belly—"could we talk about this later? I'd, uh, really like to take a shower now."

"What?" She snapped out of her trance. "A shower? Oh, yes, of course. I have to get back to my cooking anyway." She got up from the toilet and proceeded to pull up her girdle. "Darn thing!" she cried as she struggled to get it over her behind. "And they have the nerve to call this the 'I can't believe it's a girdle' girdle?!" She squirmed and wiggled, wiggled and squirmed. Her face turned deep purple. "Darn thing is going to be the death of me yet!"

"What the hell do you wear them for?" I lashed out at her. "They stop your circulation and give you varicose veins, not to mention the fact that they're downright uncomfortable!"

"I have unsightly bulges!" She grunted as she finally eased the girdle over her behind. "What would your father think if I walked around with unsightly bulges?"

I might have known she'd say that. Everything she does she does for him. Never for herself, always for him. Cooks and cleans for him. Lives and breathes for him. No doubt she'd even die for him. And umpteen times a day she wiggles in and out of that fucking girdle—just for him. And for what? He's always so wrapped up in his work or his golf or his real estate investments or his newspaper that he wouldn't notice if she dyed her pubic hair green and walked around stark naked! Doesn't she even know how trapped she is, I thought, shaking my head sadly, doesn't she even realize?

"Don't take too long in the shower now," she said as she turned to go. "The whole family will be here for supper in less than an hour."

"I can hardly wait." I grimaced as a cramp took my breath away.

"Are you sure you're all right? You've been making some of the strangest faces."

"I'm fine." I was seeing stars already. "Never felt better!"

"If you say so."

As soon as she left I popped a couple of the pain-killers Dr. Yagod gave me and crawled into bed—clothes and all. "Shit, what a day!" I moaned as I lay there writhing in pain. "I don't think it could get rottener if it tried!"

Which just goes to show how much I had yet to learn about life.

No sooner did those very words leave my mouth when the doorbell rang.

"Shayna Pearl!" I heard Ma beckon. "You've got to come downstairs and see this with your own eyes!"

From the way she was carrying on I thought maybe the Queen of England had dropped by for a visit— Princess Di, Prince Charles and all.

But what I saw when I got downstairs was not Bonny Prince Charlie, but two delivery men with "Bloom's Flower Shoppe" printed on their T-shirts going back and forth, back and forth, carting tons of droopy, blood red flowers into our living room.

"What's with all the flowers?" I cried. "Did somebody die?"

DONNA STEINBERG

"Aren't they just lovely?" Ma gasped.

"Who are they for?"

"The men said they're for you—from a Mr. Stanley Drabkin!"

"I might have known." I groaned.

"Did you ever see so many flowers in your life?"

"Not since we visited Annie the char's husband's body at Wray-Walton-Wray." I shivered. Maybe I was just being paranoid, I don't know, but as I gazed into the dense jungle of droopy red flowers that was once our *Architectural Digest* feature of the month Chinese Modern living room, I got the eerie feeling that I was witnessing the preparations for my own funeral. I mean, it was like something right out of the Twilight Zone.

"Aren't they just breathtaking?"

Oh, yeah, they definitely took my breath away.

"That Stanley!" she gushed. "That Stanley!"

"That Stanley!" I fumed. "That Stanley!"

The delivery men set down the last of the flowers and one of them handed me a card. "This was in one of the pots." He winked at me. "I'll bet it's one helluva love note."

"Yeah, I'll just bet." I snatched it out of his hand and went up to my room to read it.

What better way to commemorate
Tonight's meeting
Than with a truckload of flowers
Called "Love Lies Bleeding"?

See you at supper—
Love, Stanley

P.S. I know something you don't think I know.

Suddenly I got a sinking feeling in the pit of my stomach. Oh, God, I thought, it couldn't be! He couldn't possibly have found out about the telegram unless . . .

140

no, Jo Ann would never . . . naw, I'm just being paranoid again. There's no way he could possibly know that Peter's asked me to move to California with him.

I crumpled up the note and threw it in the garbage.

There's just no way he could know, I reassured myself. Could he?

Chapter 11

ALTHOUGH Sabbath dinner is by no means a religious occasion in our house, it is considered to be our most sacred family ritual.

Friday Night Supper is the bait Ma uses to bring the family together once a week. You don't dare miss one of her roast chicken and pickled brisket feasts unless you are gravely ill, out of town or dead—and even then you don't get off without feeling good and guilty.

We all know how Ma spends the entire day plucking capons, brewing chicken soup, chopping liver, simmering carrots in brown sugar, grating cole slaw and baking potato *knishes* and deep-dish apple pie.

From dawn to dusk she bakes for us, stews for us, rolls for us, steams and cooks for us. She slaves over a hot stove, ruins her manicure, kills her feet and wilts her hairdo.

Just for us.

She sets the table in the normally off limits dining room, where she lays out a dozen or so *House Beautiful* place settings upon a crisp, Chinese-laundered tablecloth. Each setting is an identical configuration of silverware, fine crystal wine glass, Val Saint Lambert crescent-shaped salad bowl, white and gold Royal Doulton fine china dishes and handwoven linen napkin. In front of Dad's place, at the foot of the table, is a bottle of Manischewitz red wine and a braided *Challah* bread. At the center of the table are the traditional pickles and cole slaw and at the head, Ma's place, is an immaculately polished silver tray with three sterling candlesticks and three white *Shabbes* candles—one for each child.

That's an elaborate spread for a family that couldn't care less about the religious import of the Sabbath, but go and tell that to Ma. To hear her tell it, the hard work is all worth it because the family that eats together "does a mother's heart good."

So when I tried to get out of joining the family for supper, it was like talking to a wall.

"But I don't feel good, Ma!" I insisted, even though I was feeling no pain thanks to the pain-killers I had taken earlier. "I think maybe I'm coming down with something." Actually I was just too paranoid to leave my room. I was convinced that the disaster to end all disasters was Out There just waiting for me to happen along. A perfect end to a perfect day. "Something contagious maybe."

"Oh, pooh, you don't even have a fever!" She pressed her cheek to my forehead. "You'll feel much better after you come down and eat something."

"Ma, I won't starve to death if I miss a meal, you know?"

"But this is Friday Night Supper!"

"If I go Out There it might be my *Last* Supper!"

"And just what is that supposed to mean?"

"Oh forget it, you don't understand."

"Stop your shenanigans, Shayna Pearl. The whole family is waiting for you."

"Is, uh, Stanley here yet?"

"Not yet."

"No?" I didn't know if it was a good sign or a bad one. "Hey,"—I brightened—"maybe he isn't coming?"

"He's coming. He called to say he was tied up at the office and that he'll be a little late is all."

"Oh." I shriveled.

"He said we should start without him—that he'll catch up when he gets here."

"I'm sure he will." I sneered. "He's got a mouth like a Cuisinart."

"Why do you say things like that?" She shook her head in disgust. "All that boy has ever done to you is love you."

"I don't want his love. I'm in love with Peter!"

"Oh, for crying out loud, I'm not going to stand here and get into *that* argument with you now—I've got a dozen hungry mouths waiting to be fed. Let's go!"

I didn't move.

"What are you waiting for?" she practically yelled. "An engraved invitation?"

"Couldn't I just eat up here in my room?"

"If you think I slaved over a hot stove all day so . . ."

I went down to the dining room and took my place at the table.

"There now, that's more like it." Ma beamed. She was in her glory. From her place at the head of the table, she could preside over her entire family and make sure everybody got enough of everything. At the foot of the table was her obstetrician-husband, making his regular Sabbath evening appearance (since no baby dares to be born during Friday Night Supper if it knows what's good for it). On either side of her sat her twin sons (her Pride and Joy respectively), her two daughters-in-law (one of whom was a week overdue in giving birth to grandchild number five), her four granddaughters (her little "Morning Stars"), and last, but certainly not least, her one and only daughter (her little "princess" for whom she held the highest hopes). "Now that everything is under control, we can begin," she declared by the authority vested in her.

And we began.

Things started off just as they always do. Dad made the ritual blessings over the wine and the bread, Ma made her ritual blessings over the candles, and the rest of us took this ritual time to discuss how well the Montreal Expos were doing this season.

Everybody except me that is.

My attention was upon Ma, who was lingering over my candlestick, the third, unmatched candlestick, which was bought when I was born and which sits behind my brothers' matching pair—the candlestick that was bought eight years after Birks Jewelers discontinued the pattern of the other two.

"Thank You, God," I heard her say through cupped hands, "thank You for letting Shayna Pearl and I have such a wonderful time in New York. Keep up the good work."

The flame on the candle let out a vicious crackle. I could swear I felt Peter's telegram burning a hole right through my back pocket. "Ma," I squirmed. "Could we eat already? I'm starved."

"Starved?" She looked at me like I was crackers for sure. "Two minutes ago you weren't even hungry."

"Well, I am now. So let's eat already!"

"Honestly, sometimes I just can't figure you out," she said as she began dishing out the soup.

"I gave up a long time ago," Dad grumbled.

"Hey everybody," Ma chirped, "did you notice the flowers Stanley sent Shayna Pearl this afternoon?"

"Ma, do you think they're blind?"

"Aren't they just lovely?"

Everybody "oooooed" and "ahhhhed" in agreement. Except me that is. "I think they suck!"

"Shayna Pearl!" Ma gasped. "*Must* you talk like that at the table? And in front of the children yet?"

"What's the matter, little sister?" David said. "Did you two have another lovers' spat for a change?"

"Ah, she just loves giving the poor slob a hard time, that's all," Terry laughed. "Our baby sister likes to keep her men dangling on a string. It's probably a technique she picked up in the latest issue of *Cosmopolitan*."

"I think Stanley's kind of sweet," David's wife, Eva, said. "I certainly wouldn't object to having him as my brother-in-law."

"Yeah, and isn't it a riot the way he chases after her while she plays hard to get?" my other sister-in-law, Arlene, giggled. "The two of them remind me of Kate Hepburn and Cary Grant in *The Philadelphia Story!*"

"Oh, yeah, he hangs in there all right," I cringed. "Just like a penicillin-resistant strain of V.D.!"

"Shayna Pearl!" Dad cried. "Christ, the things that come out of your mouth sometimes!"

"That's *your* daughter!" Ma clucked her tongue in disgust.

"Jeez, what's with her tonight anyway? Is it that time of the month again or what?"

"Oh, for crying out loud, Daddy!" I could have just spit blood. "Why is it that when a man is in a bad mood it's because he has real problems, but when a woman is moody it's automatically *that* time of the month?"

"Oh, I don't know, my wife hasn't had a *that* time of the month for nine months already and she *still* gets pretty moody!" David cracked as he patted Eva's enormous stomach.

Everybody burst out laughing.

"This place is a nuthouse!" I cried.

"That's enough, Shayna Pearl!" Dad warned me. "I've been doing 'C' sections and hysterectomies since six o'clock this morning, and I'm in no mood for your *shtik!*"

"*What she needs is a husband to put her in her place!*" Stanley's voice suddenly boomed from behind.

I could only groan as all heads turned toward the botanical gardens that used to be our living room, waiting for Himself to make an appearance. And I'd just begun to hope that he'd be tied up at the office until hell froze over.

"Yeeesh," he cried, brushing off his suit as he emerged

from the dense jungle of blood red flowers, "if I'd known that I'd sent this many flowers, I'd have brought along a machete!"

"And what lovely flowers they are!" Ma gushed. "And so unusual."

Once again everybody "ooooed" and "ahhhed" in agreement.

Everybody except me, that is. I was too busy counting to ten under my breath.

"Yeah, they really are exquisite, if I do say so myself," Stanley marveled. "And what a beautiful name too," he said, giving me a mournful look, "—'Love Lies Bleeding.'"

I made my eyes disappear inside my head. What a schmuck!

"Sit down, Stanley dear," Ma said as she served him up a bowl of chicken soup. "You're just in time for the first course."

"Mmmmmm . . ." he said, taking a whiff of the soup as he plunked himself down at the empty place beside me, "thanks Ma."

"Don't call her that." I hissed at him between clenched teeth. "She is *not* your mother—in any way, shape or form!"

"Fine and you, Shayna Pearl?" He kissed the top of my head. "You're looking as adorable as ever."

"How'd you get in here anyway?" I muttered. "Don't tell me they've given you a key to the house now?"

"Your mother left the front door unlocked so I wouldn't disturb anyone in the middle of supper by ringing the bell. Say, you never told me what you thought of my flowers?"

"Hmph!"

"And how about my little note, eh?" he whispered into my ear.

"I'd like to know what the hell you meant about your knowing something I don't think you know?" I whispered back. "That's what I'd like to know!"

He raised an eyebrow. "You'll find out soon enough."

"And just what is that supposed to mean?" I squirmed. If he was trying to worry me he was doing a superb job. "If you have something up your sleeve you'd better not . . ."

"Aunty Shay, Aunty Shay," my niece Erin tugged at my sleeve.

"What is it, sweety?" I scooped her up into my lap. "What's on your mind?"

"Could you take me and Victoria and Melissa and Andrea to the Dairy Queen for chocolate dips and Mister Mistys tomorrow?"

"Yeah!" Melissa cried. "We have the best time when we go with you!"

"Yeah," Victoria nodded, "you always let us have whatever we want, and you never yell at us."

"And you always make us laugh!" Andrea giggled. "Remember the last time we went and that strange man pinched you on the behind and you dumped a whole tutti-frutty sundae on his head?"

They all shrieked with laughter.

"You're the best aunt!" Erin hugged me.

"Careful girls," Stanley said, "you're spoiling her image!"

"Shut up, Stanley!" I muttered.

"Could we go tomorrow?" Erin pleaded. "Please, please, please?"

"Yeah, could we, could we?" the others chanted. "Puleeese?"

I put Erin back in her chair. "I'm sorry, I can't tomorrow," I said, hating myself for having to disappoint them. If only I could tell them about Peter coming home tomorrow and everything, I thought, but of course I can't now. Not unless I want the Stanley Drabkin Fan Club to pounce on me like a bunch of piranhas and eat me alive. "Some other time, okay?"

"Awwwwwwww . . ."

"I'm sorry."

"What are you so busy with tomorrow that you can't spare a few minutes to take them for ice cream?" Ma said.

"Yeah,"—Stanley butted in for a change—"what's so special about tomorrow that you can't take your little nieces for ice cream?"

"I'm busy."

"Just what *are* you doing tomorrow anyway?"

"Stuff!"

"Mysterious, aren't we?"

"Lay off, Stanley!" I muttered. There was something in his tone that was really getting me rattled.

"You wouldn't be trying to hide something from us, would you now?"

"And just what is *that* supposed to mean?"

"Hey, Stanley!" Arlene cried. "Is it my imagination or is there something different about you tonight?"

"At last!" He threw his hands up in the air. "*Somebody* noticed!"

"Wait, don't tell me," Terry cracked, "you're in love!"

"Naw, that's old news," not-too-bright Arlene shook her head.

Bad news is more like it, I thought. "He looks the same to me."

"Look more closely, Shayna Pearl." He stuck his face right into mine.

"Oh, for crying out loud!" I couldn't believe my eyes. There was a thin layer of wispy, whitish blond hair covering his face. It was a beard. Or a reasonable facsimile thereof. Actually it looked more like a cobweb.

"I grew it while you were away in New York. I thought I'd surprise you." He ran his hand over his face. "So what do you think of the old fuzz, eh?"

"I think you should kill it before it multiplies!" I muttered.

"I thought beards turned you on," he whispered.

"Just what are you trying to prove anyway?" I whispered back.

"Now, now, let's not get nasty."

"We are going to get a lot nastier if you don't tell me what that P.S. in your note meant! Just what *do* you know that I don't think you do?"

"Goodness, what are you two whispering about over there?" Ma wanted to know.

"Nothing!" I cried.

"Just like two lovebirds!" Arlene swooned.

"Shayna Pearl here was just telling me what she, uh, thinks of my beard," Stanley said. "What do you think, Ma? You think it suits me?"

"I think it looks very distinguished dear. Very lawyer-like."

I gave her an astonished look. "Distinguished? Lawyerlike? I thought you hated beards!"

"Not necessarily."

"But you . . ."

"It just depends on the man behind the beard." Stanley smiled like a Cheshire cat. "Isn't that right, Ma?"

"Stanley dear!" Ma came to his rescue, plunking down a plateful of food in front of him. "I baked your favorite tonight—potato *knishes!* Piping hot from the oven . . . eat, eat . . . before it gets cold."

He picked up a *knish* and took a bite. "Mmmmm . . ." He gave me the eye. "I just love piping hot *knish.*"

Something told me that the *knish* to which he was referring was not the potato kind. "You pig!" I muttered, kicking him under the table.

"I thought pigs were your favorite animals," he muttered back. A piece of *knish* got stuck on his lip and his tongue snaked out to lap it up. "Mmmm . . ." he smacked his lips, "love that *knish.* . . ."

Suddenly I got the feeling that he was having *me* for supper. "I'm getting out of here!" I cried, pushing my chair back.

"You're not going anywhere, young lady!" Dad gave me a dirty look. "Your mother spent all day slaving over a hot stove to make this meal for you, and you're not going to upset her!"

"Yeah, Shayna Pearl,"—Stanley pushed my chair back in—"you don't want to upset your mother now, do you? Or any other time,"—he went back to whispering—"like tomorrow?"

A shiver ran right through me. Did he know what Peter and I were planning?

"What's wrong, Shayna Pearl? Why, you're paler than the tablecloth. Did I say something to upset you?"

I gave him the coldest look I could muster.

"Ouch!" he winced. "I've seen some dirty looks in my time . . ."

"Hey, don't mind her," Dad told him, "she's just in one of her moods tonight. You know how women are?"

Stanley sat there winking and smiling, winking and smiling. It was like sitting beside a flashing Mr. Muffler neon sign. "Oh, yes, sir, I know exactly how women are."

"If you let 'em they can drive you crazy," said one World's Foremost Expert on Women to the other.

"Don't I know it!" said the other.

The rapport between them was uncanny. Not unlike that between ventriloquist and dummy.

Christ, I thought, is this meal *ever* going to end?

"All right, Shayna Pearl," Ma said, "everybody's been served except you. Which do you prefer tonight, chicken or brisket?"

"Huh? Oh, I'll just have a couple of wings."

"Two chicken wings?" she frowned. "What kind of supper is that?"

"I'm not very hungry."

"But two minutes ago you were starved!"

"Ah, she eats like a bird!" Dad said.

"Here." Ma handed me a big plate with two wings on it. "Don't overeat!"

"Maybe she plans on flying somewhere?" Stanley said.

I almost dropped the plate in my lap.

"God, you're as jumpy as a catfish tonight!" He shook his head. "Even jumpier than when my Aunt Frances saw you today."

"Your Aunt Frances?" What the hell is he leading up to now, I wondered. My T-shirt was soaked with sweat.

"Yeah, she said she recognized you but that you didn't seem to recognize her." He gave me an intense look.

"That was you she saw having lunch today at Nuddick's with a bunch of your pregnant friends, wasn't it?"

"Nuddick's?" I gulped. "Today?" Suddenly the whole room began to spin. Oh, no, I thought, oh, no . . . that, that woman . . . the one sitting in the booth beside us who I thought looked so familiar but couldn't place, the one who overheard me telling Jo Ann about the telegram —*gib a kik* Frances—that was Stanley's aunt!

"Tsk, tsk, tsk, Shayna Pearl," he whispered into my ear, "you should have known better than to discuss such personal stuff at Nuddick's. Someone you know or who knows you or your mother's sister's brother-in-law's great uncle might overhear!"

Oh, God, he really does know, I thought, my head reeling; he knows that Peter's asked me to go to California with him! That's why he sent me those Love Lies Bleeding flowers. That's what the P.S. in the note meant. That's why he's been tormenting me all night. He knows!

"It's funny, you know," he went on, still whispering, "I really busted my keester to get Peter that recording contract out in L.A."

"You?" I gave him an incredulous look.

"I really thought it would get him out of your life for good so that I could have you all to myself . . . you know, out of sight, out of mind?" He let out a heavy sigh. His breath was hot against my ear. "I never dreamed the jerk would ask you to go with him!"

"Do we have to talk about this now?" I glanced nervously around the table. Everybody was staring at us.

"What do you plan on doing anyway? Stealing away in the middle of the night with Peter and then dropping your family a postcard once you get to L.A.?"

I bit my lip.

"Jeez, will you look at those two?" Terry marveled. "One minute they're at each other's throats and the next they're whispering sweet nothings into each other's ears!"

"What do you suppose the big secret is?" Ma asked.

"If you'd just hear me out," Stanley whispered again. "I just know I can convince you that you're making a big mistake. We can go for a walk after supper. . . . It's for your own good, believe me."

"You mean for *your* own good!" I whispered back. The more sensible he sounded, the more outraged I became. "Damn you, Stanley!" My hand jerked and I knocked over a glass of wine.

"Oh, for crying out loud!" Ma fumed. "My good table-cloth! What is going on over there anyway?"

"Nothing!" I blotted up the mess with a napkin. "It was just an accident!"

"And you haven't touched your food yet! Everyone's almost finished and you haven't even started eating yet. What is with you tonight?"

"Nothing, I told you!" I could feel the rage welling up inside me. The outrage. "Just leave me alone, okay?" I got up from the table and stormed upstairs to my room.

It wasn't long before Ma and Dad came barging in after me—with Stanley bringing up the rear.

"What is this?" I cried. "The Mod Squad?"

"Something's going on," Dad fumed, "and we're going to get to the bottom of it. Right now!"

"Let's go for that walk," Stanley looked at me with pleading eyes.

"She's not going anywhere until we get to the bottom of this!" Ma said adamantly.

"When is everybody going to stop telling me what to do?" I burst out. "I'm old enough to take charge of my own life, for crying out loud! I'll do what *I* want."

"Not as long as you're living under *my* roof!" Dad informed me.

That did it. I had just about all I could take. "All right!" I cried. The rage inside me just took over. Nothing seemed to matter anymore. Not consequences, not feelings, not New York. All I could think of was how Living In Sin was going to be heaven on earth compared to this place. "You're so bloody anxious to know what's going on, I'll tell you!" I whipped Peter's telegram out of my pocket and waved it frantically in front of them. They all flinched, like I was threatening them with a loaded pistol or something. "You see this? It's from Peter. He's asked me to come live with him in a beach house in California. He's going to work on his music and I'm going to write screenplays!" There, it was out. It was out and I was glad. For a second.

I glanced over at Ma and winced. Her hand was raised to her mouth, only she couldn't seem to find its exact location. And Dad. He was standing there and glaring at me, his lips puckered so tightly they were practically white. He didn't say anything. He didn't have to. I could tell he was not thinking good thoughts. It was just as I had feared. They were not taking my news well.

"Oh, brother," Stanley groaned, shaking his head grimly.

"This child has lost her marbles!" Ma cried.

"I'm not a child, Ma," I cringed, "and I know perfectly well what I'm doing!"

"No, you don't," Stanley said. "Eight months ago I fell in love with a sweet, adorable, sensible girl who wanted the same things out of life as I do. I just can't believe . . ."

"People change, Stanley."

"If you'd just sit back and think for a moment. Think of what you'd be doing to your family. To me. To yourself! I mean, you're ready to turn your back on the people who really care about you to run off to a strange place full of strange people with a guy you hardly know!"

"Over my dead body she will!" Ma fumed.

"I'm over twenty-one, Ma!"

"I know how old you are. I gave birth to you, remember?"

"Please try and understand," I said, trying to get a hold of myself. "Peter and I are in love. We want to be together. And California is the place for a screenwriting career." It all made such perfect sense to me. Why couldn't they see it that way? "Can't you just wish us well?"

"Arnie, did you hear that? We should wish them well!"

"I heard her," Dad said between clenched teeth.

"Where did we go wrong with her anyway? All her friends are getting married, settling down and having babies and *she's* going to Hollywood with Mr. Rock and Roll?"

"Oh, c'mon, Mother," I bristled. "You make it sound like I'm doing something wrong. This is the nineteen eighties. Living together is as acceptable as blue jeans!"

"I don't care what other people are doing! No daughter of mine is going to live with a man she's not married to. It's unthinkable!"

"Yeah, well, I don't care what you think!" But if I didn't care what they thought, why was I standing there trying to get through to them? Damn parents anyway. They can be such a pain. "Look," I said, trying to regain my composure, "couldn't we just sit down and talk about this like mature, rational human beings?"

"Unfortunately, we're one mature, rational human being *short!*" Ma screeched in a frequency that must have opened electric garage doors for miles around.

"Listen to me, all of you, cool down and listen to me!" Stanley interceded. "You'll never get through to her this way! We've got to . . ."

"Get through to her?" Ma cut him off. "I'm going to break her neck! I'll *kill* her before I let her go and live with that . . . that singer!"

"Fine!" I yelled. "I'll call Paperman's right now and order the *shiva* chairs for you. Maybe they have something in Chinese Modern to go with the living room!"

She shook her finger at me. "I'll give you a *shiva* chair in a minute!"

"What is it you're afraid of? Are you afraid of what people will say? What? I mean, it's not as if he isn't Jewish. . . ."

"I don't care if he's a rock 'n' roll rabbi! You're not going and that's final!"

"Try and stop me!"

Her eyes narrowed into razor sharp pinpoints. "I don't understand you. A couple of days ago we were the best of friends. Didn't we have a good time in New York? Don't you like the things I bought you? The watch?"

She was really using cheap tactics. Which only made me angrier. "Oh, keep the goddamned watch!" I cried, losing what little control I had left. "I didn't know you bought it so you could hang it over my head for the rest of my life. It's not a gift. It's a guilt trip!" There was an audible gasp. It took a moment before I realized it was mine. "Oh, God . . ." I bit my lip. It was too late. The damage was done. I could see the hurt etched several layers deep in her face. "Ma, I . . ."

Just then David came bursting into the room. "Ma, Dad, come quick, it's Eva!"

We all ran downstairs to the dining room. Eva was standing there by the table and clutching her swollen belly, her face contorted in pain. "I think we'd better get me to the hospital," she gasped.

The next thing I knew, the whole house went into absolute chaos, and everybody was rushing out the front door and so was I.

"You're not going to the hospital!" Dad grabbed me by the arm at the top of the stairs.

"But that's my godchild!" I cried. "David and Eva promised that if it's a boy . . ."

"I don't give a damn!" His face turned *borsht* red, and the veins were bulging right out of the middle of his forehead. I don't think I'd ever seen him so angry. "I don't want to see your face again tonight. I want you to sit home and think about what I'm going to tell you right now: you are not going to California with that bum with the guitar, and if you ever pull a stunt like this again, I swear I'll hit you so hard you won't be able to see straight! And one more thing . . . it's either him or us.

Choose him and you are no longer a member of this family. If you can't live by the rules of this house, then get out—*tonight!*

I stared at him in disbelief. "Are you giving me an ultimatum?"

"That's exactly what I'm giving you," he said. "You can't have your cake and eat it too!"

"Fine!" I was incensed. "If that's the way you want it, then I choose *him*. At least he didn't laugh in my face when I told him I wanted to be a Hollywood screenwriter. At least he treats me like a person!"

I never even saw it coming. I just felt his hand whacking across my cheek, and it almost knocked me off my feet. "You—you hit me!" I gasped as I covered my burning cheek with my hand. "You hit me!" I just couldn't believe it. He had never laid a hand on me before. Not ever.

"Christ," he said numbly as he stood there staring at his hand. "Christ." His expression was not unlike that on Eva's face when she was seized by that labor pain back in the dining room.

A horn blew and we both jumped.

"I—I have to go now," he started to babble, "I have a *simcha* to get to. The birth of a child is a real joy—a cause for celebration. It's a pity,"—he winced—"it's so ironic that such joy never comes without pain and suffering!"

I looked at him like he was nuts for sure. From the way he was acting, you'd have thought *he* was the one who was going through childbirth!

The horn blew again. He shook his head and looked at me kind of blankly. As if I was someone he thought he recognized but couldn't quite place. And then, without saying another word, he turned around and rushed off.

I was really confused as I stood at the top of the stairs and watched them all drive away without me. So confused that I instinctively raised my hand to wave. All I managed was a pathetic little jerk of my wrist. Then I noticed out of the corner of my eye Peter's telegram, which I had been holding in my hand and completely forgotten, flapping up and down in the breeze.

I stood there at the top of the stairs for what seemed like an eternity.

And then, suddenly, something yanked at my hand and I heard a tearing sound.

I turned around to find Stanley standing behind me. He was tearing up the telegram. Into itty-bitty pieces. "You got what you deserved, you know," he said, tossing the pieces of paper in the air like they were confetti or something. "I always thought you needed a good belt in the chops to knock some sense into you, put you in your place!"

That's just what I needed to hear. "Well, why don't you go right on ahead, Stanley!" I really popped a gasket. "Put me in my place! Show us how mucho macho you really are! Go on, Stanley, knock some sense into me! Every woman ought to be beaten up regularly so that she never steps out of her fucking place!" I pushed him aside and stormed into the kitchen. He followed me. The guy obviously had a death wish. "This is my place, right Stanley?" I screamed hysterically as I twirled myself 'round and 'round. "This is where I should be—plucking feathers off capons . . . scraping dirty ovens . . . wiping crummy countertops . . . worrying if my dishes are going to come out of the dishwasher with spots on them—doing my God-given vocation, right Stanley?" I picked up a sopping wet sponge and threw it at him. "Here, Stanley, here's a sponge. Go ahead and flog me with it. Knock some kitchen sense into me. I dare you to. I *want* you to. Knock the crazy ideas out of my head— maybe I'll be happier! Or better still,"—I picked up a potato peeler and threw it at his feet—"why don't you just peel away at my brain until I'm a happily lobotomized little Suzy Homemaker—*everybody* will be happier!"

"Jesus, Shayna Pearl!" he cried. "Calm down, will you? You're hysterical!"

"Hysterical am I?" I started grabbing things off the counters and throwing them around the kitchen. Silverware, glasses, food, dishes—anything I could pry loose. I just couldn't control myself. The rage inside me just kept driving me to smash things. I wanted the whole kitchen —and Stanley—to end up in shambles.

"Cut it out, Shayna Pearl, will you?" he pleaded as he dodged an oncoming bowlful of kasha and bow ties. "Somebody could get hurt!"

"That's the general idea, you fucker!" I picked up a rubber spatula that was dripping with some kind of batter and charged toward him.

"Oh, no you don't!" He grabbed my arms and locked me into a bear hug just as I was about to whack him across the head with the spatula.

"Damn you!" I tried to get away but he had me locked in tight. I bucked; I squirmed; I bit and kicked; I screamed blue murder. It was no use though. He just held on to me until I was too pooped to fight anymore.

"You going to behave yourself now?" He hauled me over to the kitchen table and dumped me into a chair.

All of a sudden I burst out laughing. And then I burst out crying. Then laughing again.

"What are you, crazy or something?" he asked as he brushed off his suit and straightened his tie.

Crazy? Maybe I was crazy. The truth was, I didn't know anymore. I felt so lost. "Oh, God." I put my head down on a place mat and started to really cry. A heaving, nose-dripping, drooling cry. I cried until there was nothing left to heave or drip or drool.

When I finally picked my head up, Stanley was standing over me with a glass of water in one hand and a couple of little green pills in the other. The kitchen was spotless.

"Here, take these Valium," he said, "they'll make you feel better."

I shoved his hand away. "I don't want any. What is it with you people and Valium anyway? You seem to think it's the answer to everything."

"Go on—they'll calm you down."

"G-go away-ay . . ." I sobbed, ". . . leave me alone-ne-ne-ne. . . ."

He shrugged and took the pills himself. "I'm glad everyone's gone," he said as he sat down beside me. "Now we can really talk."

Really talk? What the hell was there left to say? "What do you want from me?"

He reached over and stroked my hair. "You don't stop loving someone just because they're a little mixed up. Just because they're having a few problems."

"Oh, brother!" I bristled. Damn him anyway, did he have to be so bloody noble?

"Look, it's not too late, you know," he went on. "You don't have to go with him. You could patch things up with your family and . . ."

"Forget it!" I rubbed my cheek, which was still smarting from Dad's slap. I'll show him, I thought, I'll show them all. "I'm going upstairs to pack."

"Oh, for crying out loud, you don't want your family to disown you! You're not thinking rationally."

"I'll pack what I can now and send for the rest of my things later."

"You don't have to go to California to write screenplays, you know," he said as he followed me up to my room. "Montreal has a booming film industry. The Hollywood of the North, they call us in the trade papers. In fact, you stand a better chance of making it here than you do out there. In order to qualify for the tax write-off scheme the government offers, producers have to hire a certain number of Canadians to work on films. Screenwriters are in very big demand. Believe me, I know. I *am* a show business lawyer, you know. In fact, I can introduce you to all the right people . . . get you a grant from the Canadian Film Development Corporation . . ."

"I thought all women belong in the kitchen?"

"Well, if you're really serious about this screenwriting business, I could learn to live with it."

"You make it sound like I have a disease!" I cringed. "Anyway, Peter says that you never really make it until you've made it in the States."

"Peter says, Peters says!" He threw his hands up. "You quote him like he's Confucious or something! And what is it with you and this screenplay business all of a sudden? What do you know about it anyway? You've never written one in your entire life."

I reminded him about all the screenwriting courses I'd taken in college.

"Yeah, but you don't have any experience," he persisted. "I mean, you can't go out to Hollywood and expect your idol there—Barbra Streisand—to hire you to write her next picture just like that. It doesn't work that way."

"Yeah, well, Peter believes I can make it. And that's good enough for me." I pulled my tote bag out of the cupboard and tossed it onto the bed.

"Oh, go ahead and pack, you spoiled little J.A.P.!" he cried as I started throwing things into my bag. "Spend your life wandering around, shopping for the perfect existence which doesn't exist. You'll put yourself through hell and end up in the kitchen anyway!"

I gave him an incredulous look. I'd heard of a Wandering Jew. But a Wandering J.A.P.? And what the hell was all that crap about going through hell and ending up in the kitchen anyway? He was making it all sound so pointless. Like a female version of the Myth of Sisyphus. "I see. So I'm just supposed to give up without trying, is that it? Just roll over and die. Forget about discovering what kind of stuff I'm really made of."

"Haven't you heard? You're supposed to be made of sugar and spice and everything nice."

I had to laugh. "I wouldn't repeat that in public if I were you. You're liable to get rounded up and chopped into Bacon Bits. . . ."

"Yes, I'm a chauvinist—and proud of it. A *lot* of guys feel that way these days. We've had it with all that Women's Lib garbage."

"Well, what do I know? I'm just a Wandering J.A.P., shopping around for the perfect existence which doesn't exist, remember?" I threw some more things into my bag. "A Wandering J.A.P. . . ." I repeated it over and over again, my voice sauced in savory sarcasm—egged on by Stanley's Neanderthal comments. "It's kind of romantic, don't you think? A Wandering Jewish Princess: a modern, disillusioned young woman like myself who rebels against life in the kitchen so that she can search for a more fulfilling existence. Just think," I said, warming up faster by the second, "I'll be getting back to my roots, leading the nomadic life of my forebears!"

"Cut it out, Shayna Pearl, you're not making any sense!"

"Sure I am." Suddenly I was feeling extremely giddy. Almost intoxicated. *Freeways. Freedom. Freeman. Mine. All mine!* "Let me explain it to you."

"I don't want you to explain it to me. I want you to stop packing and . . ."

"A Wandering J.A.P.," I went on to explain as I continued packing, "is one who rejects the traditional Jewish woman's role of *baleboosteh*, the role of ideal homemaker in which our mothers, our grandmothers and Jewish mothers for all time have taken so much pride and to which they have devoted so much passion. I guess *baleboosteh*-hood all started with Eve," I cracked. "She kept her house in such perfect order, they called it Eden!"

He buried his face in his hands and let out a strange noise. Kind of like a horse whinnying.

"Now that I think of it, Stanley," I went on, getting giddier by the minute, "my being a Wandering J.A.P. will bring history full circle."

"You've flipped your lid!" he cried.

I ignored him and went on with my story. "It seems to me," I told him, "that Eve was not only the First Baleboosteh of Eden but she was also the first Wandering Jewish Princess in history. She repeated Lilith's mistakes. By plucking one forbidden apple, she fell out of Grace with the Supreme Male Chauvinist Himself, the Man of *the* House who insisted on being referred to as Him with a capital *H*. Because she displayed symptoms of developing a mind of her own and because she broke the sacred Covenant she had made with Him (in which she had promised to be a good *baleboosteh* to Mankind for All Eternity—nothing more, nothing less), she became a threat to His Supreme Male Ego. Hence she committed the Original Sin and was banished from her blissful *au naturelle* existence as Chief Homemaker and Top Kitchen Aid of Eden.

"As punishment for trying to wear the pants in her family, the Almighty He created for her the long-line panty girdle and forced Eve to wiggle her somewhat plentiful ass into it. And as if that wasn't enough torture, He made her put on a brassiere with 'Cross Your Heart' supports and wire reinforcements.

"She must have really summoned all His wrath because before He banished her, He created a second set of underclothes for her to take along: nylon panty hose that tore at the most inopportune of moments and polyester bikini underwear that caused unsightly bulges and didn't breathe at the crotch. He camouflaged all this unsightliness with a smashing flared skirt and a soft, feminine peasant blouse. Before He rested, however, He threw in a pair of six-inch high-heeled pumps with pointed toes and arches that curved like the Golden Gate Bridge.

"Then He tossed her out to wander the earth for all eternity—and on foot yet!

"The Sins of the Mothers, Stanley," I told him as he sat there on the bed, shaking his head over and over, "The Sins of the Mothers.

"Eventually," I continued, "Eve died alone, crippled and neurotic. Some say it was the freedom that did her in. Others say it was the severe case of vaginitis, complicated by ruptured corns of the toes and infected bunions of the feet.

"But somehow, possibly because all roads for women eventually lead back to their roots in the kitchen, Eve's descendants managed to find their way back to the land of *Better Homes and Gardens*. Women once again were allowed to become die-hard *baleboostehs*-in-residence. And just to make sure they didn't go off and do something terribly brilliant, original or creative, charge accounts were invented. Women could then make generous contributions to society while remaining happily and gratefully interned with their heads in a dirty oven.

"I'm picking up where Lilith and Eve left off, Stanley —did you ever think of that?" I cried as I finished packing and zipped up my tote bag. "No one is going to put a girdle on me. And I'm going to be happy, Stanley, happy and creative, original and brilliant, Stanley, because I'm going to keep growing and changing and trying new things. Yeah, I'm going to be happy, Stanley, eternally *happy!*"

"*And you're as loony as a bedbug, Shayna Pearl!*" he cried, his eyes practically popping out of his head. "*Do you know that?!*"

"I've never felt better," I said, stuffing some things into a garment bag, "or saner."

"Tell me something, Ms. Wandering J.A.P.," he sneered, "if you plan on staying out of the kitchen for the rest of your life, just how are you and Peter going to eat? You going to live on Big Macs three times a day?"

"I'm not worried about Peter. He's a very liberated guy. We'll work something out."

"Boy, do you ever have a lot to learn about life."

"I aim to do just that."

"Damn you!" He grabbed my elbow and squeezed so hard that I cried out in pain. "You stupid . . ."

"Ow, leggo of my arm . . . you're hurting me!"

"*I'm* hurting *you?*"

"Let go!"

He shoved me away. "Oh, go on then, go on and ruin your life," he said in that smug, irritating manner of his.

"Just don't come running back to me when things don't work out with that son-of-a-bitch rock singer of yours. Because I won't be here. Do you hear me? *I won't be here!*"

I picked up my things and headed for the airport to wait for Peter's plane, still hours away.

PART IV

Spaghetti Junction

Chapter 12

YOU'D THINK Peter would be a cinch to single out in a crowd.

A guy who is six foot two, lean, bearded and extraordinarily sexy tends to stand out among the mundane folk milling beneath his bearded chin.

So it was only natural that I became slightly hysterical when the passengers of Flight 124 from L.A. began filing into "Arrivals" at Dorval Airport and I couldn't spot him anywhere.

Maybe I've got the wrong flight number, I began to think. Or the wrong day? Or the wrong time? No, no, this has got to be it. I'm sure his telegram said he'd be arriving at Dorval this morning at ten. Or was it Mirabel? Oh, God, maybe I've got the wrong airport! Damn Stanley anyway. Why'd he have to go and tear up the telegram last night? Now I'm not sure of anything anymore.

A second batch of passengers came filing through.

Then a third.

When the bearded likes of Peter Simon Freeman failed

to emerge with the fourth batch, my imagination really began to run wild. Maybe he forgot about me? Maybe he changed his mind? Maybe he met another woman on the plane and they flew off into the sunset together?

I was about to become totally unglued when I heard someone call my name. I looked up to find a tall, jean-clad figure pushing its way through the crowd, heading toward me. It couldn't be, I thought, my hysteria suddenly turning into shock, it just couldn't be! Could it?

"Peter?" I gasped as he stopped in front of me.

"No, Paul McCartney!" He laughed Peter's wonderful, crazy, hoarse laugh. "Who'd ya think?"

My head reeled with confusion. It sounded like Peter all right. "Something's missing . . ."

He glanced around. "Oh, the band took an earlier flight. I had some extra business to take care of . . ."

"No," I blurted, "your hair . . . your beard!"

"Oh, that," he said, grinning. "The guys in my band bet me a year's supply of grass that I wouldn't get a shave and a haircut. It was an offer I just couldn't refuse, if you know what I mean." He stroked his chin, which had a deep cleft in it. Like a miniature rear end. "Whad'ya think?"

I didn't answer. I just stood there blinking my eyes, trying my hardest to absorb the fact that this clean-cut, naked-faced stranger with skin like a baby's tush was the same wild and woolly Peter Simon Freeman I had fallen so madly in love with. No wonder I'd had trouble finding him! I mean, he was still good-looking and everything, no doubt about that. Almost too good-looking. He had all these fine, delicate features . . . sculptured nose, high cheekbones, soft cherry lips . . . sort of like a Ken doll. Impulsively, I reached up to touch his face. It sure *felt* real enough.

"Yeah, it's a shock, I know," he laughed at my stunned reaction. "I'm not used to it myself yet. But what the hell, it's only hair, right?" He dropped his suitcase and pulled me toward him. "C'mere, you. . . ." He scooped me up into his arms and gave me a whopper of a kiss.

A deep sense of shame flooded through me as I kissed him back. He's right, I thought, reveling in the closeness of his body—it's only hair, for crying out loud. I mean, it's not as if he had lost (God*forbid*) an arm or a leg or (double God*forbid*) some other fundamental part of his anatomy. Beard or no beard, long hair or short, Peter is still Peter!

"Hey, I really missed you,"—he stroked my hair—"you know that?"

"Hold me," I said, clinging to him for dear life. God, I just wanted everything to be all right. "Just hold me!"

He gave me a funny look. "What's wrong? You okay?"

Okay? No, I wasn't okay. I had just been through the worst night of my life. First I was screamed at, humiliated, belted in the chops and disowned. Then I spent half the night on an airport bench and the other half with one part or another of me hanging over the toilet with coil cramps. Blood was pouring out of my vagina, my head ached and I was so exhausted I could hardly keep my eyes open. But how could I tell him all that without making him think I was ready for the chronic care services of the Hospital of Hope instead of a meaningful relationship? Damn *Cosmopolitan* magazine anyway, it never prepared me for anything like this!

"Planet Earth calling Shay. Come in, Shay!"

"Huh?" I started. "Oh, yeah, I'm okay. Just tired."

"It's my telegram, isn't it?" he said, his eyes narrowing. "You're not coming with me when I go back to L.A.!"

"Oh, no! I mean, yes!" I cried. "That is, if you still want me to," I added cautiously.

"All *right!*" He scooped me up into his arms and kissed me again. "Fan*tas*tic!"

"Fantastic? Really?" I wasn't feeling too insecure or anything.

"Are you kidding? It's more than fantastic!" he reassured me. "It's perfect! You're perfect! *We're* perfect!"

I was all smiles as we headed for the parking lot. Who could ask for more than perfect? "Hey, I didn't even ask you how your trip was. Did you really record an album out there?"

"Yep," he beamed, "and that's not all. I also managed to line up a couple of other projects too. Backup work and stuff. The big money won't be rolling in for a while, but we'll have plenty to live on."

"Well, of course I plan to contribute my share."

"You just stay home and write screenplays. That's good enough for me."

"Really?"

"Really."

"But what if I don't make money at it for a long time? I mean, I want us to be equal partners. Fifty-fifty."

He shrugged. "You'll do your share. I'm not worried. Do I look worried?"

"No, but . . ."

"Then there's nothing to worry about, right?"

"I—I guess not."

"Then stop looking so worried!"

I let out a nervous laugh. "I can't help it. Ever since I got your telegram, my mind—it's been doing crazy things!"

He laughed. "I knew that telegram would blow you right out of your clogs! I'll bet you never expected it to say what it did in your wildest dreams."

"What, are you kidding? I only had a minor stroke, that's all!"

He laughed again. "Well, if you dug that little surprise, wait'll you see what else I've got up my sleeve."

"What?" I winced. Surprises make me nervous.

"You'll find out later on. God, I love surprises! C'mon!" All of a sudden he picked up speed. Like a turbo-charged race car. I practically had to run to keep up with him. "Let's hurry up and go back to my place. I don't know about you, but I'm horny as all hell."

"Oh-oh," I said aloud without meaning to.

"Oh-oh what?"

"Peter, I . . . we need to . . . there's something . . ." Oh, God, how do you tell a guy who's horny for you that

172

you can't sleep with him for the next few days because sex may be hazardous to your health? Very gradually, I decided. "Nothing, never mind. It can wait . . . I guess." Damn pain-in-the-ass coil! "Say,"—I quickly changed the subject—"are we really going to be leaving for California in ten days, like your telegram said?"

"More or less."

"God!" I stopped dead in my tracks.

"What is it now?" He sounded a little exasperated.

"It just dawned on me. There must be a zillion things we have to take care of before we leave! We have to pack. Make plane reservations. And visas! Don't we have to apply for visas or something? And what are we going to do with my car and your motorcycle? And my job—I have to quit my job. And what about finding a place to live out there . . . ?"

"Whoa, there!" He cut me off. "Take it easy, will you? We have at least two weeks to take care of all that stuff. So calm down, okay?"

"I—I guess I'm just trying to make sure this whole thing's for real, you know what I mean?"

"Yeah, I know." He put his arm around me, and we started out for the parking lot once again. "I find the whole thing kind of hard to believe myself. And speaking of the unbelievable—you never told me how your parents are taking all this. Wait, don't tell me!" he snickered. "They said, 'Over our dead bodies will you go to California with that Svengali!'—right?"

I stiffened. Just thinking about them made my blood boil. "Parents—who needs them anyway? They're nothing but a pain!"

"Especially yours," he agreed wholeheartedly. "To tell you the truth, I'm surprised they haven't locked you up in a tower somewhere—like a modern-day Rapunzel or something. What'd they do anyway? Threaten to take away your credit cards?"

"Do you think it would be okay if I stayed at your place, you know, until we're ready to leave for California?"

"That bad?"

"Worse." A tear trickled down my face. I wiped it away before he could see it. I didn't want to give him the impression that I was some kind of crybaby. "My parents and I are no longer related. I've been pruned from the family tree."

"You're kidding?"

I shook my head. "I spent the whole night in the airport."

"Christ! Hasn't anyone told them that this is the nineteen eighties?"

"I tried to," I shrugged. "But somehow they wouldn't believe it coming from me."

"Ah, they'll come around," he reassured me. "Right now they're just pissed off."

"You—you really think so?" I said, feeling hopeful for the first time since the whole ugly mess started.

"Yeah, they're just playing games with your head, that's all. In the meantime, I suppose I can find room for you at my place." He looked at me and grinned. "Do you do windows?"

"Fun-ny!" I whacked him on the arm.

"Nope," he pinched my ass, "hor-ny!"

Oh-oh.

Who would have dreamed that on my very first day of liberation I'd be faced with the monumental task of cleaning up an entire apartment?

Not me, that was for sure. Simple, naive me. I actually thought Peter was kidding when he made that crack about my doing windows!

But the moment we walked through the door it was hard to ignore the fact that the place was crawling away.

Especially when a brown bug the size of a hamster popped out of one of the dozens of Chinese take-out cartons on the den floor and scurried across my feet.

"What is *that?!*" I screeched, jumping up onto a chair. I'd never seen anything like it before in my life.

"Damn roaches!" Peter said as he stomped on it with his foot. It made a hideous crunch.

I thought I was going to be sick.

"I guess I left here in such a hurry, I forgot to clean up after me and the band. Christ!" He ran his hand over the coffee table. "There must be three inches of dust in here!"

"God!" I was mortified. Cockroaches aside, I couldn't even remember the last time I saw one clump of dust, let alone such a ton of it. In our house, "Germocide Sylvia" always kept that unsightly problem well under control. If ever a clump of dust dared to rear its ugly head, Ma would be quick to whip out the Lemon Pledge and *shpritz* it before it multiplied. As far back as I could remember, our house always reeked of Lemon Pledge. "This place is *Shmutz* City!" I gagged. "And the smell!" It was like a cross between wet clothes and used Kotex pads. "What are we going to do?"

He opened a window. "What do you mean, what are we going to do?" He looked at me like I was nuts or something. "What do you usually do when you find yourself in a dirty apartment?"

"Buy a couple of cans of Lemon Pledge and call a charlady in the morning?"

He laughed. "Cute."

I wasn't trying to be cute. I was dead serious. "Look, I know this terrific char. I bet if I called her right now she'd come right over."

"What's the going rate for charladies these days?"

"Annie charges thirty plus carfare."

He whistled. "Forget the charlady, lady. We need our bread for more important things. Like food."

"I'd rather starve," I wanted to say, but I didn't. I didn't want to sound like a nag. Or a spoiled brat. Or both. "I know you probably think I'm overreacting a little," I told him, "but this is my first cockroach."

"Well, cheer up, kid, it could have been worse. We could have had rats."

"Swell." I didn't know if I should have jumped for joy or out the window. "I can't tell you how relieved I am."

"Just looking on the bright side." He emptied the infested containers into a bag and took them out to the incinerator. "There," he returned, looking pretty pleased with himself, "that takes care of those little buggers."

I shuddered.

"By the way, you can come down off the chair now. The coast is clear."

I stepped down, reluctantly. "You sure?"

"Would I lie to you?"

"Probably!"

He laughed. "If you don't bother them, they won't bother you . . . unless, of course, they get hungry . . ."

"I'm getting out of here!" I bolted for the door.

"Come back here." He grabbed me by the hand and pulled me toward him. "I was only kidding."

"Well, how should I know?"

He took me around and hugged me. "That's what I love about you, you know? You're soooo innocent!"

"I know things!"

"Sure you do." He nuzzled my neck. "When I need the number of a good char, you'll be the first person I ask."

"I'm good for more than that, you know?" I said, getting really flustered.

He kissed me. "Mmmmm . . . I know."

Oh-oh! "Now?"

"*Mmmmmm . . .*"

"*But . . . but we can't! You see, I . . .*"

Cra-aack . . . c-r-a-a-c-k. . . . We both picked our heads up, startled. *Crru-unchchch. . . .* There were some awfully strange noises coming from the den. Burglars maybe? Why not? Everything else was going so smoothly.

"What is that?" I said in a hoarse whisper as I flung myself into Peter's arms. "Let's get out of here!"

"No . . . wait." He took me by the hand and pulled me into the den. "It figures," he laughed, pointing to the couch, where an enormous pair of sneaker-clad feet were dangling over the side, jerking spasmodically as if keeping time to some inaudible beat.

I craned my neck to get a better look. "Oh, for crying

out loud!" I shook my head in disbelief. It was Mac, the drummer with the bright orange fringe of hair that makes him look like Bozo the Clown. He was sprawled out on the couch, a joint in his left hand, two large walnuts he was trying to crack against each other in the right hand. *Cracckkk . . . c r u n c h ch ch. . . .* On his head were two tiny earphones which in turn were plugged into the Walkman slung over his shoulder.

It took him a minute to notice us. "Oh, hey, man,"—he raised his joint in greeting—"welcome home."

I gave Peter an anxious look. What the hell was going on?

"That the new girl singer?" Bozo asked as he removed the earphones and hooked them around his neck.

"No, man," Peter answered, "this is Shay—you remember—we met at our gig at the Cock 'n' Bull a few weeks back. . . ."

"A few weeks back, eh?" He scratched his head. "It's hard to keep track, you know?"

I gave Peter another anxious look. What did he mean by that remark? And what was this about a girl singer? What the hell was going on anyway?

"Well, take it easy, man, see you later," Bozo said as he put the earphones back on his ears and tuned us out. *Cracckkk . . . cr-r-runnch. . . .* Two more walnuts bit the dust and landed in an ever-growing heap on the floor by the couch.

Peter led me out into the hallway and closed the door behind us. "His old lady kicks him out a lot," he explained, "so he just comes here to crash on my couch. No big deal really. Before long you won't even notice he's there. Like the furniture."

"Really, eh?" I said numbly. Somehow this was not turning out the way I'd imagined. Two people in love . . . alone. "And who's the girl singer he was referring to?" I just had to ask, though I wasn't quite sure I wanted to know the answer.

"Oh, yeah, her," he shrugged. "Just some singer we're

trying out for the band. You know, for backup and duets—shit like that. You'll get to meet her one of these days."

"You sure she's *just* a singer?" It slipped out.

He frowned. "Hey, you're not one of those jealous types, are you? The ones who throw a fit every time a chick looks at a guy sideways, are you?"

"Who me?" I stiffened. So much for my next question. Not a good time for me to ask what Bozo meant by his other remark. About finding it hard to keep track. "Naw, I'm not the jealous type. I just thought . . ."

"You think too much." He put his arms around me. "Now, where were we before we were so rudely interrupted?" He pressed his lips to mine. "Mmmmm . . . right . . . mmm, let's go to the bedroom."

I grimaced. "Now?"

"Why not now?"

"Be-be—because . . ."

He stopped nuzzling me and looked around the apartment. "Yeah, I guess you're right,"—he frowned—"this place ain't exactly conducive to the more romantic things in life, is it?"

"Not exactly," I said, though the messy surroundings and Bozo were the least of the problems where lovemaking was concerned. Lousy coil, I thought, it better be worth all the trouble! "Peter, there's . . ."

"Hey, I know what!" he cried. "There's a couple of things I've gotta do anyway. Like stopping by to see my son and picking up some groceries. I'll tell you what. Why don't I go out and do that now? It'll give you a chance to clean up a little."

"What?" I wasn't sure I'd heard right.

"Yeah, that's what we'll do," he said, taking the keys to my car. "That way we'll have a clean place and something to eat for later on."

"What!" I thought he had a lot of nerve to assume that housework was going to be my domain. "I can get groceries too, you know?" Damn, that's not what I meant to say at all. Why can't I ever say what I mean?

"I know you can, Babe. But this way we'll be killing two birds with one stone."

How'd he figure that? I wondered. "But . . ."

"Yeah, this place could really use a woman's touch, you know?"

I shook my head to clear it. Was there something wrong with my hearing? Did that "woman's touch" crapola really come from the very lips of the guy who I thought was going to be the epitome of the Liberated Man?

"The cleaning shit's under the sink. And there's a vacuum in the hall closet. See you later."

Before I could open my mouth to say another word, he kissed me good-bye and took off.

What just happened here? I threw my hands up to God.

Somehow, some way, I had managed to convince myself that living together meant never having to do housework. Of course, the more I thought about it, the more I realized how unrealistic I was being. After all, I'd never been one to live in a pigsty—and I wasn't about to start now. Besides, it wasn't as if housework was going to be my main occupation in life. Once we got to California I'd be writing screenplays and Peter . . . well, maybe then I'd know how to handle him a little better. We're two fairly modern, sensible people, I thought, surely we'll be able to work something out?

Feeling somewhat bolstered, I took a closer look around the apartment to see what had to be done. God, what a mess! Newspapers everywhere. Clothes all over the floor. Enough hair in the sink and bathtub to make a toupee for Kojak. A gross layer of filth on the kitchen floor. Dust on the counters. Dust on the window sills. Enough mold in the fridge to start a penicillin supply house. Sour milk. Had the place been like this when I was here before, I asked myself, or could I really have been just too . . . too blind to notice? Could it be that Ma was right all along? That all men are alike? That they were put on this earth to mess up while women were put here to clean up? No, no, I refuse to believe that of Peter. He's not like other men. He's different. It's just that we're new to each other. We need time to feel each other out. Yeah, that's it. Of course, that *must* be it.

A cramp almost took my breath away. Damn coil. How, I wondered, was I supposed to get anything done with this bloody gizmo tearing at my insides every five minutes? Housework! Where the hell was I supposed to get the strength to do housework? All I felt like doing was lying down and dying.

"Annie? Where are you, Annie?" I cried out to the faithful Polish charlady who's been cleaning our house— or rather, my former house—every Monday, Wednesday and Friday for the past ten years. "Help me, Annie!"

Okay, okay, I admit it. I was finding it difficult to adjust to life without a charlady. In Hampstead, charladies are a fact of life. Just like Italian gardeners, Corvette Stingrays and midwinter Florida suntans.

Each weekday morning between the hours of eight and nine the 161 bus comes down Fleet Road and deposits small armies of these robust creatures at every corner.

As they march down the streets in groups of twos and threes, gabbing away in strange, exotic languages, they sure don't look like anything special. But once they get to cleaning the inside of your house, you have to wonder if you haven't been visited by angels from heaven.

So who could blame me for being upset when I realized I'd have to clean up Peter's filthy apartment with my own two untainted hands? With my ten virgin fingertips that had yet to be touched by common house dirt?

It was only after I recalled a recent conversation I had had with Ma that I stopped being upset and started feeling ridiculous.

The subject was charladies.

"When you get married, I'm going to send Annie to clean your house twice a week as a wedding present," she told me. "A house can never be too clean, you know."

"Is that why you clean the house *before* she gets here?" I replied.

"Don't be such a smart aleck! You'll need a char, believe me."

"Don't tell me what I need. I know what I need."

"You'll sing a different tune once you have to clean your own house."

"I'm never getting married and I'm not having any charlady!"

"We'll see, Princess Grace, we'll see."

After I recalled that conversation, I went straight to the kitchen cupboard and whipped out the Lemon Pledge and a dust cloth. Coil cramps or no coil cramps, there was no way in hell I was going to let Ma have the last word!

I started off by dusting the smaller things—like the turntable. Once I did that, it was a snap to move on to bigger and dustier things—like speakers, end tables and lampshades. Before I knew it, *whammo*, I was overcome by this irrepressible, insatiable urge to clean. Dusting furniture, I discovered, is like eating peanuts. It's impossible to stop at just one.

I don't know what came over me. Maybe I just got a second wind. Or maybe I was just so overtired that I was bordering on insanity. But the next thing I knew, I was putting "Saturday Night Fever" on the stereo and boogying around the apartment (not to mention the prostrate space cadet on the couch), giving a Spray 'n' Wipe here, a Clean 'n' Shine there and a *shpritz* of Lemon Pledge everywhere. The place just didn't smell like home until the aroma of Lemon Pledge permeated the air.

After that, I really got into the swing of things.

I Hoovered to "Stayin' Alive"; Mop 'n' Glowed to "Jive Talking"; Spic 'n' Spanned to "More Than A Woman" and Windexed to "You Should Be Dancin' (Ya!)."

Who would have dreamed it?

Chapter 13

THE AFTERNOON just flew by.

I got so lost in the music and the housework that I never even heard Peter come in.

"If I can't have *you* . . . I don't want nobody, *baby*, ya!" I was singing at the top of my squeaky, off-key voice as I bumped and grinded my way around the bed, laying down fresh sheets. "If I can't have *you-ou-ououou!*"

I wanted to dig a hole and crawl in it when I looked up and saw him standing there. Arms folded across his chest. Watching. Grinning.

"What are you doing here?" I cried.

"I live here, remember?" He laughed. "You really must have been in another world. I've only been standing here for the past five minutes."

"Oh, that, heh, heh," I could feel myself turning purple. "Would you believe I got bitten by a cleaning bug and developed Saturday Night Fever?"

"The place sure is spotless," he marveled. "I see you've got a real domestic streak."

"Yeah, well don't get too used to it!" I cried, afraid he

was getting the wrong idea. "From now on, we share the housework."

"Yes, sir!" He saluted me.

That seemed simple enough. "And one more thing,"—I decided to take advantage of my winning streak—"I don't intend to spend my life in the kitchen either. Planning meals. Cooking meals. Cleaning up from meals!"

"Jeez," he flinched, "what brought all this on?"

"I just want to let you know where I stand, that's all."

"Aye, aye, Mon Capitaine,"—he saluted me again, looking amused—"read you loud and clear."

"I'm serious!"

"I know, I know. Don't worry about it. We'll work it out, okay?"

"Okay."

"Fine."

"Fine."

"Could we change the subject now?"

"Sure." I was feeling pretty cocky.

"Hey, Tiger, come on in here a minute, will ya?" he yelled.

"Tiger?" Were we going to share quarters with Peter's drummer *and* a wild animal?

All of a sudden Peter's son, dressed in full Darth Vader costume and yelling something about dead Wookiees, came tearing into the room and began slashing at me with a plastic sword. "Take that, you Wookiee!" *Smack!* "Take that!" *Whack!*

"Whoa there, Tiger." Peter had to pry him off me. "She's one of us!"

Just the same, "Tiger" gave me another good blow to the stomach before hopping up onto the freshly made bed, shoes and all, and bursting into an imaginary sword fight with Luke Skywalker. "Take that, you Wookiee lover!" he screeched. "Take The Force and shove it!" *Wham!*

"You okay, Babe?" Peter asked me. "I guess he got a little carried away."

A *little* carried away? "I think he wanted to kill me!" I

gasped, rubbing an ugly red welt on my arm where the sword of Darth Vader had left its mark.

"He's really into Space these days. He eats, drinks and breathes it. Wait'll you see the rest of his stuff." He disappeared into the hall and came back with a suitcase in tow. "Just look at what's in here!" He opened the case and we both peered inside. There was a Star Wars glass. A Star Wars lunch pail, Star Wars pajamas, sheets and pillow cases. An "I Love Mork from Ork" button. A "Mork for President" poster. A "Shazbot" T-shirt. "Do you believe what five-year-olds are into these days?"

"What is all this stuff?" I said, bewildered. "Pajamas, sheets, pillowcases . . ."

His whole face lit up. "Remember at the airport I told you I had a couple of surprises for you? Well, this is one of them. Nicky's gonna be staying with us! Isn't that too much, Babe?"

I ducked out of the way just as Nicky's sword was about to slice my head off. "You mean, like for the weekend?" The sword pierced my left tit. Oh, God, I found myself praying, let it only be for the weekend!

"For the weekend? Hell, no!" Peter let out a gleeful laugh. "For keeps!"

"What?" Surely he was kidding? "You're kidding?"

Just then Nicky tugged at his father's sleeve. "Daddy, I have to pee!"

"You know where the bathroom is, Nicky," Peter told him.

"Dad-*dy-yy*, take me to the bathroom; I have to *pe-ee-ee!*" He clutched himself between the legs and did a bizarre little dance around the bed. "I've got to make Number Two too!"

"I'd better go with him," Peter said, and the two of them took off for the can lickity-split.

When Peter got back to the bedroom I was still in the same place, frozen in space and time. Shock does that to me.

"Nicky had a good shit," he reassured me. As if the state of Nicky's vital functions was what was foremost on

my mind! "Now he's in the den watching the tube with
Mac. 'Mork and Mindy' is coming on soon. That'll keep
him quiet for a while." He pulled me down to the bed and
kissed me. "Isn't it exciting? About Nicky coming to live
with us, I mean?"

"I . . . eh . . . uh . . . ga . . ." I was having trouble
getting my mouth in working order. Shock does *that* to
me too. "Gaa . . . uh . . . " First a live-in drummer. Now
this! The "tiger" now seemed desirable by comparison.

"I knew it would blow your mind!" He hugged me. "I
know how crazy you are about that kid. I saw it with my
own eyes that day we all spent together a couple of weeks
back. And you did say, about a dozen times, how you'd
love to have a kid just like him someday."

Oh, Lord, I *did* say that, didn't I? "I—I never dreamed
'someday' would come so soon!" I blurted. Oh, please tell
me this isn't happening, I thought. Please wake me up
and tell me I've been dreaming all this!

No such luck.

"To tell you the truth," he went on, "I didn't think
'someday' was going to be this soon either. Actually, I
had other plans for us this weekend. But when I dropped
by to visit him this afternoon, my ex told me that she has
things to do before she leaves—and would I mind taking
him a couple of days early?"

"Leaves? For where?"

"Japan, of course. I told you about it."

"You did?" That was news to me.

"Sure. You were lying here in this very bed a couple of
weeks ago and I told you how my ex was thinking of going
to some institute over there to study the art of Japanese
flower arranging for a year, maybe more. And I also told
you that if that happened, Nicky would be coming to live
with me."

"Oh?"

"Of course it was all very tentative then," he explained. "We didn't know if she'd be accepted."

"Oh. . . ." I tried to think back but still the conversation eluded me. In fact, most of the details of that night seemed to have eluded me. The state of Peter's apartment. The things we talked about. It was as if I had been in some kind of fog. Sure, he could have told me about his wife and son. He could have told me he was from Mars for all I now knew. The only thing that seemed to have sunk in was his prick, God*help* me!

"Anyway," he continued, "I know we won't be married in the traditional sense—since neither of us believes in that lousy institution—but at least the kid will have a mother-figure around. It'll be healthy."

Suddenly I got a sick feeling in the pit of my stomach. Oh, no, I thought, please don't let me think what I'm thinking! "Peter?" I had to ask him. I had to know. "Would you have asked me to come to live with you even if . . . if Nicky . . ."

"Whoa there!" He cut me off. "Hey, you don't think . . ."

I shrugged. I didn't know what to think anymore.

"Hey,"—he propped himself up on his elbow and looked me straight in the eye—"you gotta know that I'm crazy about you. Kid or no kid, I'd never ask you to come live with me if I didn't love you!"

"You—you really love me?"

"Of course I do! I mean, I know we haven't known each other very long or anything, but hell, I know what I feel. I'm a firm believer in love at first sight. Anyway, I thought you felt the same way about me?"

"I did. I do! It's just that . . ."

The phone rang. He answered it. "Oh, hi. Yeah, no really, it's okay. I said I would and I will." His voice was low and sweet. Almost affectionate. "Nicky? Oh, yeah, right, sure, don't worry about it. Dynamite kid. Yeah, right, I'll catch you later, Babe. . . ."

I raised an eyebrow. Did he say "Babe" or was my mind playing tricks on me?

"Speaking of the devil." He laughed as he put the phone down.

"Your ex?"

"Yeah, checking up on the kid." He shook his head, grinning. "That woman . . ."

I felt a definite twinge. Jealousy maybe. I don't know. Maybe I was crazy, but the way he spoke to her, his tone, the gleam in his eyes—could it be that his ex-wife wasn't all that ex? "Keep in touch often, do you?" I had to ask.

"Well, I was married to the woman for five years. We did have a kid together. I guess there'll always be something between us."

"Oh." I wasn't sure if that was good or bad. Both, maybe. Good for him. Bad for me. Everybody knows ex-wives are bad news.

Just then Nicky came rushing in. "Daddy, Daddy, Mork's coming on soon. You and the lady come watch!"

"The lady's name is Shay," Peter told him, "and Shay and I are kinda busy right now. We'll join you soon, okay?"

"I'm hungry," he pouted, "I want some Ketchup Chips and a Mr. Slurpee."

"It's almost suppertime. You can wait."

"Can we go to McDonald's?" His eyes got as big as Quarter Pounders.

"We'll see."

"Oh, boy!" He ran over and threw his arms around Peter. Then he planted a big, wet kiss on my cheek and skipped out of the room. It was hard to believe that this was the same little monster who had tried to hack me to pieces only moments before.

"He really is adorable," I said, my heart melting. "I wonder if he understands—about his mother going off and leaving him like she is," I added, still trying to make sense of it all myself.

"Look, what can I tell you, Babe?" Peter said. "She's been taking care of Nicky all these years while I've been out chasing my dreams. Now she figures it's her turn. I dunno, maybe she's right. Who's to say? It's a sign of the times I guess." He shrugged. "I suppose some women feel they just can't do justice to a kid and a career."

"And you think I can?" I said in a strangled voice.

"Hey!" He hooked his finger under my chin and tilted my head back. "What's this all about?" He gazed intensely into my eyes. "What happened to the lady with the 'I can conquer the world!' attitude I met a couple of weeks ago?"

Funny, I was wondering the same thing myself. Conquering the world, it seemed, was turning out to be one of those things that are more easily said than done. "I—I just always thought that I'd establish myself first, you know, before having kids. So that I don't end up like your ex-wife."

"You can handle it, Babe, I know you can. I mean, sure you may be innocent about a few things, but you have a helluva lot more on the ball than my ex does. Besides, there are plenty of women in this day and age who manage a career and a family. It's just a matter of pacing yourself."

"You—you really think I could do it?" He was definitely beginning to get to me. Nobody had ever believed in me like that before. "Really?"

"Hey!" he said, his eyes burning into mine. "Do you *really* love me?"

"Of course I do!" I cried. "I left home to be with you, didn't I?"

"Then trust me. You can handle it. You can handle anything if you set your mind to it."

"Yeah?"

"Give yourself a little credit, will ya? You didn't think you could handle the housework either and just look at this place—man, I've never seen it so fucking spotless!"

"Yeah," I found myself agreeing with him, "sometimes I amaze myself, you know?"

"There you have it, Babe. And if you give yourself half a chance, you're gonna find that you're just full of surprises."

"You think?"

"I know!"

Dale Carnegie himself couldn't have been more persuasive. Maybe he's right, I began to think, maybe I can do it all. I mean, every time I pick up a newspaper or a magazine I read about all these women who pursue fascinating, demanding careers yet still manage to have terrific sex lives with their husbands and/or lovers, spend "quality" (as opposed to "quantity") time with their kids *and* keep their homes looking like something out of a *Décormag* cover story to boot. If they could do it, why couldn't I? "Yeah," I blurted, getting carried away with myself for a change, "I can handle it!"

"Now that's the way I like to hear you talk!" he cried, taking me around and hugging me half to death. "You can do it, Babe, no sweat."

"Yeah. . . ." An alarm bell suddenly went off in my head. "No sweat. . . ." My God, what am I saying, I thought, could it really be *that* easy? Hell, my very own sister-in-law once told me that bringing up a kid changes your whole life—drastically. That it demands all your time. Zaps all your energy. God, God, God, what the hell am I getting myself into here? A five-year-old child is such a big responsibility. I've never been responsible for anything more than a turtle—and even then I blew it. Not that I'm worried about flushing little Nicky down the toilet, mind you, but still. Me, a mother? I haven't even learned to take care of myself yet!

"Hey!" He suddenly jumped up from the bed. "I almost forgot. I have another surprise for you."

"Another one?" I stiffened. I didn't think I could live through another one of his surprises. "What is it?" I was almost afraid to ask. "Did you invite the P.M. home for dinner?"

He laughed. "You'll see." He rushed out of the room.

The phone rang.

"Get that will you, Babe?" he shouted.

I picked up the receiver. "Hello?" I said meekly, afraid it might be his ex again—or worse, Ma calling up to make a scene. Another perfect end to another perfect day.

"Shay, thank God!" It was Jo Ann. "I thought I'd find you there."

"What's up?" I asked. There was something in her tone of voice that set me on edge. "Is something wrong?"

"I don't know, you tell me. When I called your house to speak to you just before, your mother—well, she refused to even discuss you. It was almost as if you were dead!"

"Dead?" The hairs on my arms stood up on end. "Oh, God, you don't suppose they're sitting *shiva?*"

Just then Peter came into the room, carrying his guitar. "Dead? Who's dead?"

"I am," I said numbly.

"What?" he cried. "Who the hell is that? Gimme the phone!" He grabbed the receiver out of my hand in that protective, take charge way of his. My knight in shining armor to the rescue once again. "Who the hell is this? Who? Oh, yeah, right, Shay's friend. Yeah, yeah, nice to finally meet you too. Listen, Jo Ann, can Shay call you back later? We're kinda busy right now." He gave me a concerned look. "Yeah, she's upset. Her parents? They had a big fight. Yeah, yeah, she moved in with me. No, no, I'm sure she'll be just fine. California? In about two weeks or so. I have to sublet my place and stuff. Huh? Really? No, I don't think she does. Eight pounds, seven ounces? Yeah, yeah, I'll tell her. Uh-huh, uh-huh, uh-huh —I'll tell her that too. Bye." He rolled his eyes around in his head as he hung up. "If I didn't know better, I'd swear I was just talking to Rona Barrett herself."

"Eight pounds, seven ounces?" Suddenly I snapped out of my semistuporous state. "The baby!" I had forgotten all about the baby. "Is it okay? Is it healthy? Is everything . . ."

"Just take it easy. Your sister-in-law had a very easy labor. The baby's fine. The *bris* is on Wednesday morning."

"It's a boy then," I sighed.

"At least until the *bris.*"

"Huh? Whad'ya mean?"

"Nothing. Never mind. Just a little circumcision humor."

"Oh, yeah, right . . . heh, heh." There was a heavy

feeling in my chest. Like I get every year at Passover from eating Bobbeh Fine's *matzo* balls. "Did you know I was supposed to be his godmother?"

"No, no I didn't."

The phone rang again. It was for him. Business this time. Rehearsals. Amps. Jam sessions. New material. He was a million miles away when he hung up.

"Peter?"

"Hmm?" he started. "What? Oh, yeah, where were we?"

"My nephew's *bris!*" I said, nearing exasperation.

"Oh, yeah, right. . . ."

"I really do want to go. Hey,"—I brightened—"you don't suppose that by Wednesday my parents will have realized how wrong they've been and I could still be . . ."

He made a face.

"Yeah, you're right," I said glumly. I already knew the answer. "Who am I kidding? I'd be about as welcome at that *bris* as a staph infection."

"Hey, this thing is really tearing you apart, isn't it?"

"No!" I cried. Suddenly I got very angry. "I'm not going to let them get to me like this. I was right and they were wrong and I'm through letting them run my life for me. They're not going to get me in their clutches again. No, sir. No way. And I don't even want to talk about it anymore! Okay?"

"You're not going to get any arguments from me," he shrugged. "I don't even know how you stayed with that loony-tune family of yours *this* long. As far as I'm concerned you did good."

Then how come I didn't feel good, dammit! "Peter?"

"Mmm?"

"You—you don't think they're actually sitting *shiva* . . . ?"

"Ah, c'mon," he scoffed, "now you're letting your imagination run away with you! And anyway, I thought you didn't want to talk about your family anymore?"

I was getting on his nerves, I could tell. Which was

kind of understandable really. I was getting on my own nerves. "I'm not handling this very well, am I?"

"Hey,"—he smiled and stroked my hair—"nobody said it was gonna be easy." He sat down beside me on the bed and started tuning his guitar. "That's how come I wrote you this song."

"You wrote a song for me?" I almost floated two feet off the bed. It was like something out of a movie.

He plucked and strummed. "That's the surprise I was telling you about just before. It's still a little rough though. I wrote it on the plane."

"God, nobody ever wrote a song for me before!" It was a fantasy come true. "What's it called?"

The phone rang again.

Another call for him. Business again. Something about guitars and sheet music. A rather lengthy discussion about whose turn it was to bring the grass. The booze? The coke? Chalet Bar-B-Q chicken or Chinese take-out from Yangtze? And how about that new girl singer?

"Sorry, Babe," he said as he hung up, "business before pleasure."

"It's okay," I responded, though not without impatience. Wasn't I ever going to have him all to myself? And how *about* that new girl singer?

"Now,"—he took the phone off the hook and picked up his guitar again—"where were we?"

"The song you wrote for me." I was getting all psyched up again. The mere thought of it—my own song! "You were about to tell me the name of it."

"Right. It's called 'Can't You See?'" He hummed and twanged, twanged and hummed. "Here goes nothin'. . . ."

I'd like to show you things
And take you places
You never dreamed you'd go.
I want to take you up so high
If you'd only let me know,

That you'll spend your life with me
Hey, won't you move on in with me?

For those back home a-worryin'
That I'll taint your virgin mind
They gotta let you go through life and love
And leave them all behind.
It's time they stopped protectin' you
You'll learn from your mistakes,
I'm willin' to let you find yourself
However long it takes.

So won't you . . .

Pack up your things
Say your good-byes
Tell them you're leavin' home for me.
Girl, I need you in my life
Can't you see, oh,
Can't you see?

The times keep changin'
It's near impossible
For woman to know her own mind.
She's gotta take a chance on life and love
And keep growin' all the time.

No, I don't have all the answers,
I can't teach you wrong from right
But, lady, when the whole world comes crashin' down
I'll be 'round to hold you tight.

Commitment is a funny thing to want
In this here day and age
When casual affairs and bein' free
Is more the goin' rage.
Hey, life's just a crazy game we play
There ain't no guarantees

I LOST IT ALL IN MONTREAL

But, Babe, I'm offering you my love,
I'm beggin' you please . . .

Pack up your things
Say your good-byes
Tell them you're comin' home to me.
Girl, you need me in your life
Can't you see?
Hey, can't you see?

"Well?" he said, putting his guitar down on the floor.

"It's beautiful!" I melted into his arms. I was a veritable marshmallow. "The words . . . the melody . . . it's the most beautiful thing in the world!"

"No, you are." He pressed his body against mine, his hands caressing me all over. Suddenly it was as if we were the only two people left on earth and nothing—and nobody—could come between us. Just like the first night we were together. "Mmmm . . ." I found myself writhing under his touch. "Unhhh. . . ."

Before long my shirt was unbuttoned, my pants unzipped. His hands were everywhere—stroking my breasts, rubbing my back, between my legs. More, I thought, spreading my legs wider and wider, more, more, more! A finger plunged up inside me. Then another.

Then it happened. A hideous cramp.

My whole body went rigid. I had to bite my tongue to keep from screaming blue murder. The Coil—I had forgotten all about it!

"Is something wrong?" he asked hoarsely. "Don't tell me you've got your period?" He pulled his hand away as if he had burned it on a hot stove. "I thought I felt a Tampax string!"

"You did. But it's not because I have my period. I had the Coil put in yesterday."

"Well, that's great, Babe!" He nuzzled me. "So what's the problem?" Nuzzle, nuzzle.

"I was waiting for the right time to tell you about it," I sighed. "I guess this is as good as any."

"Tell me what?"

"Well, you see, I'm kind of bleeding from it and the doctor—he said that I shouldn't you know, do it for the next few days or so. And I've got these cramps. . . ." I held my breath as another one passed through me. "They come and go."

"But I can't stop now!" he groaned.

I could feel his hard-on pressing up against my leg. "I'll vouch for that!" it seemed to say. I have to do something, I thought, he just wrote me a song!

I slid down to the floor and knelt between his legs, running my hands over the bulge in his pants.

"Take me inside your mouth," he groaned, "before I come right in my pants!" Without further ado, he arched up, unzipped his jeans and whipped them down in a flash. His position was such that his erection sprang right into my face and landed just about lip level. My tongue snaked out to caress it.

All of a sudden there was a loud thump. Then another. And another.

"Nicky!" I cried, jerking away. "Or Bozo!" I had forgotten all about them.

We both stopped to listen. We could hear nothing except peels of laughter coming from the den. Nicky's and Bozo's.

"They're glued to the TV," Peter reassured me, "don't worry. They won't come in."

"You sure?" I said. "I'll die if either of them walks in and . . ."

He pressed his penis to my lips and cut me off in mid-sentence. "I'm sure," he rasped as he poked and prodded my lips apart. "I know my own kid."

On that reassuring note, I opened wide and took him inside, my mouth and tongue sliding up and down, up and down. Fast and furious. Probing and sucking. Licking and slurping. Bobbing and weaving.

Peter was pretty close to coming when there was another thump. I started to jerk away, but he put his hands on top of my head and held me down.

"You can't leave me hanging like this," he pleaded in a hoarse whisper. "You can't!"

My eyes bulged out of my head as I cast a worried glance toward the bedroom door.

"Don't worry about them," he reassured me once again. "Nothing can tear them away from 'Mork and Mindy'! Nothing!"

Without wasting another precious second, he rammed himself down my throat and started pumping away like there was no tomorrow.

"Nothing . . ." he grunted.

"Nothing . . ." he groaned.

"Noth . . ." he gasped.

". . . ing . . ."

". . . ng . . ."

". . . ggg."

". . . g"

". . ."

Famous last words if I ever heard any.

Just as Peter's semen came spurting into my mouth, "Mork and Mindy" paused for station identification and little Nicky came charging into the bedroom, full speed ahead.

"Make way for Mork from the Planet Ork!" he yelled as he took a flying leap onto the bed and proceeded to jump up and down, up and down. "Nannoo-Nannoo!"

As Peter jackknifed to his feet, he jacked-off all over me. What I didn't swallow got sprayed all over my face and hair.

I wanted to fold up and die.

"Oh, shit, Babe, I'm sorry," he said as we exchanged mortified looks. "Here,"—he reached for a Kleenex—"let me . . ."

I didn't wait around for his help. I zipped up my jeans and, pulling my unbuttoned shirt into some semblance of togetherness, ran into the bathroom and locked myself inside.

"Hey in there, are you all right?" Peter knocked on the door a few seconds later.

I didn't answer. I just stood there with my back against the door, tears streaming down my face, my lower lip trembling uncontrollably. Call me ridiculous for being so upset, but that's the way I felt. I just wasn't used to a five-year-old kid screaming "Nannoo-Nannoo!" into my ear while I'm busy sucking his father's cock! In fact, I'm quite new at sucking cock too.

"Shay?" Peter knocked again.

I reached up and touched the front of my hair. It was all stuck together. And as for the mouthful I had swallowed—I was sick about it! Not that it tasted so bad, mind you. In fact it didn't taste bad at all. Sort of like the sauce on a Big Mac. But the fact that I actually *liked* it made me feel even worse. Swallowing It is considered to be a very un-Jewish thing to do. But Liking It! Liking It is strictly Whore City! Semen is definitely one of those exotic delicacies that our culture deems un*kosher*. Strictly un*kosher*. I mean, it's right up there with pig's knuckles, calf's brains and sheep's kidneys. According to Jo Ann anyway. The fact that I had never had a truly *kosher* day in my life didn't seem to appease my anguish though. It wasn't one of my more rational moments.

"Shay? Why don't you answer me?"

Go away, I thought, go away, go away, go away! Just leave me alone!

"C'mon, open the door!" he pleaded. "You're making a big deal over nothing. C'mon . . . this is childish."

That's all I needed to hear, even if he was right. Furious, I grabbed a magazine from the rack by the john and flung it at the door with all my might. Part of it tore off in my hand. It was a centerfold. A full-blown color picture of a very voluptuous, very nude young woman who was lying on a white bearskin rug and playing with herself. One hand was up her vagina, the other was rubbing her size 44D breasts, and there was a half-peeled banana protruding from her cherry red lips.

"WILLOWMEENA BEATTS," the caption read, "MISS MARCH '79."

Underneath was a detailed biography which said she was a twenty-three-year-old premed student with a "promising" career in neurosurgery who, in her spare time, cooks gourmet meals for her live-in boyfriend and then gives him "Gourmet Blow Jobs" for dessert. Of course Willowmeena, busy as she was, was kind enough to take time out to share one of her "recipes" with her starving readers:

I start off by covering my lover's beautifully thick uncircumcised ten-inch cock with Dream Whip. Then I sprinkle on chopped nuts, syrup—usually chocolate or strawberry—and top the whole thing off with a maraschino cherry. I call it "Willowmeena's Concocktion!"

After I lick off the whipped cream and everything, my lover's hot poker is usually ready to spurt its burning lava into my awaiting mouth. And that's when I give him the biggest treat of all. I wrap my trembling, eager lips around his throbbing tip and I hum a song—usually the theme song from the Ketchup commercial ("Anticipation"). The vibrations drive him wild and when he finally does spurt his luscious come into my mouth—it's slo-o-o-ow good!

After I read that, I didn't know whether to laugh or cry or what. I mean, God, she could do all *that* and brain surgery too?!

"Open the damn door, will ya?" Peter was really pounding by now. "Open it or I'll bust it down!"

I reached over and unlocked the door. I'd already had my fill of high drama for the day without his crashing into the bathroom like something out of "Starsky and Hutch."

"Christ, I was really getting worried about you!" he said, looking truly exasperated. "Why didn't you answer me?"

I plunked myself down on the toilet, still clutching Willowmeena.

"What's that in your hand?"

"The Woman of Your Dreams," I replied, feeling terribly sorry for myself. "Here,"—I handed her over to him—"take her, she's yours."

He gave me a baffled look. "I don't get it. What gives?"

"Nothing . . . never mind. Forget it. It doesn't matter."

"Look," he said, "I know what happened just before was a bad scene, and I'm sorry about that, really I am. If I could go back and prevent it from happening, I would. But I can't. So let's just put it behind us and chalk it up to experience. From now on we'll lock the bedroom door, okay?"

"Yeah, sure." I forced a smile. How the hell could I expect him to understand what was going on inside me if I didn't know myself? There were so many feelings all jumbled up there in the back of my mind, I wondered if I'd ever get them all sorted out. "From now on we'll just lock the bedroom door." Simple enough. One step at a time.

He reached out and touched my crusted-together hair. "Christ, you really are a mess, aren't you?"

"Ah, it's nothing, really." Liar!

Just then Nicky came into the bathroom.

"Daddy,"—he tugged at Peter's pant leg—"I'm hungry!"

"We're on our way, kid." Peter snatched him up and hoisted him onto his shoulders. "Look, why don't you get cleaned up," he told me, "and then we'll go out and grab a Big Mac or something?"

Ugh. I didn't think I could ever look at a Big Mac again! "You two go on without me. I'd really just like to take a nice hot bath and relax a little."

"You sure?"

"Positive. An hour in the bath and I'll be a new person." *Hopefully*.

"Want me to stop by Pine's and bring you back a pizza?"

"Sure, thanks." *Anything, just go!*

"Enjoy your bath, Babe."

"Enjoy your bath, Babe!" Nicky echoed, and the two of them took off, laughing hysterically.

Another first for the kid.

A nightmare in the bathtub.

I don't know. I guess all the heat and steam got to me while I lay there soaking and I just drifted off to sleep. Suddenly I found myself running along a beautiful, sunlit beach with carefree abandon. My jeans were rolled up to my knees; my shoes were in my hands. The feeling of wet sand squishing beneath my feet was glorious. Seaweed wrapped around my ankles like velvet ribbons. The roar of the waves as they came crashing to the shore was like nothing I'd ever heard before.

"I love you, California!" I shouted gleefully. "You're everything I'd ever dreamed you'd be, and more!"

But then, all of a sudden, it grew terribly dark. And cold. God, was it cold! And there was putrid-smelling water swirling all around me. I looked down at the ground and let out a blood-curdling scream. The wet sand squishing under my feet wasn't wet sand anymore. It was shit! And the seaweed around my ankles was actually soggy strands of toilet paper. And the roar of the giant waves crashing against the shore sounded more like the nonstop flushing of toilets.

"No!" I cried. "I don't like it here anymore. I'm going home!" I turned around and started to run. I ran and ran and ran until I got to my former house. "Ma, Daddy, I'm back!" I shouted as I burst through the front door. "Your Shayna Pearl's back for good!" The house was full of people, yet nobody seemed to notice my presence. It was like I was invisible. Then I spotted Ma standing by the main powder room. She was talking to Rabbi Blier, whose services she religiously attends each and every Saturday (when she isn't playing golf) and who usually presides over all our family *bar mitzvahs*, weddings and funerals. "Ma!" I cried, rushing up to her. "What's *he* doing here?" I pointed to the rabbi. "What's going on?" But they didn't seem to see or hear me either. They just went on with their conversation. Like I wasn't even there.

"I'm sorry," said the rabbi. "I'll perform the service, I'll get up and say wonderful things about her, but I won't allow her to be buried in a Jewish cemetery. She died unclean." He shook his head gravely. "You can take your daughter out of the sewer, but you can't take the sewer out of your daughter."

I stood there frozen with horror. They were talking about me!

"Don't worry about it, Rabbi," Ma pooh-poohed him. "when it comes to cleanliness, I'm an expert. I'll have her cleaned up and smelling sweet as Lemon Pledge, and then we can bury her in the Jewish cemetery. Who's to know?"

The rabbi pointed his finger skyward. "He will."

"Oh, don't worry about Him. I can take care of Him!" Ma said. "We're very tight, you know? We have a tremendous rapport, He and I."

"It won't help." The rabbi shook his head gravely again. "Look, I didn't want to have to tell you this, but when I say your daughter died unclean, I mean she really died *unclean*. You see, her insides were contaminated. We found traces of semen in her throat and belly."

"No!" Ma gasped. "You . . . you mean . . ."

"Exactly." The rabbi nodded. "Your daughter Swallowed It like a *shiksa*, so she has to be buried like one—in a *goyishe* cemetery!"

"No!" I cried to deaf ears. "Don't tell her that. I didn't Swallow It on purpose. It was an accident! *An accident!*"

"Why, that . . . that . . ." Ma wailed. "If she weren't already dead I'd *kill* her!"

"It was an accident! An *acci* . . ."

Suddenly I felt myself slipping down. My mouth filled with water. My lungs felt as if they were going to burst. I'm drowning, I thought, oh, God, I'm really drowning!

And then, all of a sudden, a pair of hands grabbed me and pulled me to my feet.

"Shay . . . Shay . . . are you all right?" It was Peter.

"What happened?" I coughed and sputtered.

"You almost drowned in the fucking bathtub, that's what happened!" he cried. "If I hadn't come in when I did . . ."

Suddenly it all came back to me. That hideous nightmare! "Oh, God, Peter, I just had the most awful nightmare. Everybody wanted me dead!"

"Hey, c'mon," he said, wrapping a towel around me and helping me out of the tub, "don't turn into a basket case on me now. I really need you!"

"Need me?"

"I'm afraid Nicky OD'd at McDonalds, and he puked all over the place. I'd clean it up myself, but the smell makes me retch, you know?"

Chapter 14

I PUT MY FOOT DOWN.

"No," I told Peter. "This day has already been too much for me. Fathers have to clean up vomit too these days."

He ran his hand over his face, his fingers tugging at an invisible beard. "Yeah, I guess you're right," he said. "Okay, I'll take care of it."

He cleaned Nicky up and we got him into bed.

Now Peter and I can have some time alone, I thought as we finally turned out the lights and closed the door on the little holy-terror-turned-sleeping angel. Even Bozo had gone out when the batteries in his Walkman died. Not even a cockroach was stirring. . . .

"Well, I'm sure he'll be all right now," Peter said, glancing anxiously at his watch. "I'd better get going."

"Get going?" I stopped dead in my tracks.

"Yeah, the Extinct Species is doing a show tonight at the Cock 'n' Bull."

"You never told me that."

"Didn't I? Sorry. It must have slipped my mind.

Anyway, you don't mind staying here with the kid, do you? I mean,"—he caught me in a yawn—"you look like you could use a little rest anyway."

I responded with a frown. I mean, I knew he had to go and all. Business was business. But still, I couldn't help feeling abandoned—childish as it seemed. "I know you have to go," I said, finally, swallowing my disappointment. "I just wish you didn't have to."

He shook his head. "Sorry, Babe. This is where it's at in the music business. Especially for the leader of a band. And I can't exactly take you with me, the kid being so sick and all." He flashed one of those irresistible smiles of his. "Besides, it'll just be for a couple of hours. . . ."

"Well . . ." I could feel myself melting. Not that he was leaving me much choice. And anyway, I didn't want to sound like a nag, tempting though it was. "If it's just for a couple of hours . . ."

"Thanks, you're terrific, Babe!" He kissed me on the top of my head. "I knew I could count on you." He glanced at his watch again. "Oh, hey, I'm late already. The guys are waiting for me." He turned to go. "We'll see you later."

"We'll?" This was getting better all the time.

"Yeah, me and the guys. We always come back here after a show for some beer and to, you know, hack around with the guitars and shit like that." He gave me another kiss on the head and then he headed out the front door. "Keep the home fires burning and the beer cold, will ya, Babe?"

"But!" I cried helplessly as I watched him disappear. "Damn." I plunked myself down at the kitchen table, shaking my head. Keep the home fires burning? Was that what the crystal ball had in store for me?

By the time he got back home the beer was cold all right. The only thing that was burning though, was me. Slowly but surely.

Only I was determined not to let on. Not yet, anyway. Not until I had a full grasp of the situation. Maybe I was just making rats out of cockroaches again? Maybe I was just tired and cranky? And besides, there was something about Peter. Something that seemed to turn me into mush whenever he walked into a room.

"Hey, Babe!" he said as he came waltzing in alone, bearing a smile, a kiss and a single red rose. "Missed you."

Any woman who can resist that is either on exhibit in a museum or dead.

"For me?" I just couldn't get over it. Nobody had ever bought me a single red rose before. A roomful of flowers, yes, but I always fell for the smaller, more intimate gestures in life. Give me a rose and I'll follow you anywhere. "That's so sweet!"

He laughed that wonderful, crazy, hoarse laugh of his, sending shivers down my spine. "That's cause I'm a pretty sweet guy once you get to know me."

It was a nice moment. I wished it could last forever. "Where's the rest of the guys?" I asked hopefully. "They decide not to come over after all?"

"Naw, they're coming over separately. I couldn't exactly fit them all onto my bike now, could I?"

"No, no, of course not," I sighed.

"Oh, and by the way, there'll be some others too. Besides the band, I mean. Mostly music types. I just love a houseful of people, don't you?"

I swallowed hard. "A house full of people, eh?" Maybe I was going to have to start making appointments for some personal attention. Like a dentist. "Peter, I . . ."

"Oh, hey, is the kid all right? I mean, he didn't puke again . . ."

"No, no, he's fast asleep. Peter, I . . ."

"Great, Babe. You're really terrific with him, you know that?"

"Peter, I . . ."

Just then the troops came marching through the front door. Two by two. Four by four. . . . Before I knew it, the apartment was swamped with people. And not your everyday garden varieties like you see at Nuddick's either. There was a man who looked like a woman, a woman who looked like Barry Manilow, and a couple of hard-to-tells with Iroquois haircuts and blacked-out front teeth—to name just a few. Next to them, the guys in Peter's Extinct Species band looked like delegates to a Moral Majority convention.

I felt strangely out of my element as I sat there, clutching Peter's rose to my face, telling myself not to get into a snit—after all, it was just for a couple of beers and then they'd be moving on.

As usual, I was wrong. The place was full of people all weekend long. In and out, in and out. Coming and going, going and coming. Talking music. Rehearsing. Exchanging everything from ideas to drug paraphernalia to the latest techniques in mascara and eyeliner application.

And Peter. Peter was in his glory. Especially when he was sitting around and jamming with the guys in his band. Then nothing else seemed to exist. Hell, about the only attention I seemed to get from him was when he introduced me to someone new or when little Nicky needed looking after or when the beer ran low. Especially when the beer ran low.

"Get us some Molson Export from the fridge, will ya, Babe?" he'd ask. Or, "Call up the Yangtze and order dinner for seven." Or Pine's for pizza. Or Mike's for subs. Rose or no rose, it didn't take long before this live-in lover began to feel like a live-in *schlepper*.

Okay, okay, I admit that maybe my expectations were a little too high—thinking that Living In Sin was going to be heaven on earth—but hell, being with Peter was beginning to feel about as romantic as living in the Berri Street Metro station. About as busy too.

"Is it always like this around here?" I asked him on one of our rare moments alone, when he came into the kitchen to help me unload a case of Export into the fridge. "We hardly see each other."

He shrugged. "Better get used to it, Babe. This is

what my life is like a lot of the time. Besides,"—he gave me a pat on the behind—"we can't do any messing around until that thing you put in stops giving you problems."

"I'm not talking about sex," I tried to explain, "I'm talking about spending some time together."

"Ah, hell, we'll have plenty of time. You'll see."

"When?"

"Don't worry about it. When we get to L.A. we'll . . ."

"Hey, out there, where's the beer?" someone yelled from the den.

"Yeah, we're all dying of thirst out here!"

"I've got to go." He loaded his arms up with beer and headed out to the den. "We'll talk later. Remind me."

"Oh, yeah, right . . . remind you . . . ha, ha . . ." I stood there talking to myself.

"Have to piss." Steve, the Extinct Species lead guitarist who looked like a wildebeest, passed by on his way to the can, grinning. "Too much brew."

I sat down in a corner, brooding. God, the place was a regular zoo! Ever time you turned around there was someone there. I hated all these people milling about. Occupying Peter's time. His energy. Hell, if I'd wanted a crowd scene I could have stayed home with my family! And if it was going to be like this in California, how was I supposed to write screenplays? Or sleep? Or go to the bathroom in peace? Could I ever get used to group life? Did I want to try?

Enter the wildebeest again, grinning, again.

"Hey, how come Peter leaves a dynamite chick like you alone so much?" he wanted to know.

"Funny, I was wondering the same thing myself," I replied, squirming uncomfortably. I didn't like the way he was ogling me. Just what *do* wildebeests have for lunch anyway? I found myself wondering. "If you're looking for beer, it's in the fridge. Just help yourself."

"Don't mind if I do."

And the next thing I knew, he was all over me. Pawing. Slobbering.

"Peter," I wailed. *"Peee-ter!"*

It took a few tries, but eventually he heard my yelling and came to the rescue.

"Hey, man, you crazy or what?" he asked the wildebeest as he tore him off me. "Have you lost your fucking marbles?"

"But, Peter," he protested, "you never *used* to mind."

My eyes nearly popped right out of my head.

"Yeah, well, not this time, man. Strictly hands off," Peter warned him.

"Oh," he shrugged, "I didn't realize."

"Well, now you do." Peter went to the fridge and pulled out a beer. "Here,"—he tossed it to him—"you're wanted in the den."

He took the beer and disappeared in a hurry.

"Sorry about that, Babe." Peter put his arms around me as I sat there trembling. "He didn't hurt you or anything, did he?"

I shook my head.

"He just gets carried away sometimes, you know? It won't happen again, I promise."

Just when I thought the weekend was mercifully coming to an end, the girl singer made an appearance.

Tall, redheaded and blue-eyed, she had a body that was a highway of curves under a tight knit dress that plunged where it didn't gape. Quite attractive—if you go for that sort of thing.

Peter introduced us, but I guess I was too distracted by the racket the guys in the band were making with their guitars—or was it the way she latched herself onto Peter's arm and didn't let go?—in any case, I never did catch her name.

I did, however, catch her act. In the den. A duet with Peter. She was good. Very good. Peter thought so too. I could tell by the way he got all starry-eyed and touchy-feely.

I could have spit blood. I know, I know, they were only

doing what they do best—making exquisite harmony together—but did Peter *have* to look at her that way?

> So pack up your things
> Say your good-byes
> And come on home to me.

I mean, he was gazing into her eyes with the same intensity he'd displayed to me when he first sang that song only the day before. My song. The one he wrote for me. *"It's your song, Babe."* What was with this guy?

> Girl, I need you in my life
> Can't you see, oh,
> Can't you see.

They were really singing their hearts out and I was really eating mine out, when a striking brunette with furious green eyes came bursting into the room.

"Peeee-turrr!" she laced into him in mid-song. "You and Nicky were supposed to pick me up over a half hour ago!"

What was this now? I wondered. Who the hell was she? This guy had women coming out of the woodwork!

"Hey, lady!" The girl singer was pissed off as all hell. "If you don't mind, we're trying to do a song here."

"Well, excu-use me," cried the brunette, seemingly oblivious of the roomful of people staring at her, "but I do have a flight to Japan to catch in a couple of hours, and Peter is supposed to drive me to the airport. He should have been at my place a half hour ago!"

My ears pricked up like a German shepherd on alert. Japan . . . airport . . . why, of course, Peter's ex-wife!

"Well?" she cried. "Aren't you going to try to explain?"

Peter grimaced. "Sorry, Barb," he said—or was that Babe? "I've been so preoccupied with my music and everything ... I guess it kind of slipped my mind. Nicky's asleep. Why didn't you call to remind me?"

"I did. About a hundred times. Your damn phone was busy!"

He grinned sheepishly. "I took it off the hook so we wouldn't be disturbed during rehearsal."

"How could you forget?" she seethed. "You promised me yesterday. You were supposed to borrow a car and you and Nicky were supposed to pick me up at my place. I waited and waited. Finally I just took a taxi over here. I didn't know what to think anymore!"

God, I thought as she ranted on and on, give the guy a break, will you? He said he forgot ... he was busy with his music. But then again, how could he forget such an important thing? I could see her point.

"I can't believe you forgot!" she cried again.

The girl singer looked at Peter. "Who the fuck is this broad, anyway? And how the hell do you turn her off?"

One of the guys in the band twanged a bass string on his guitar—mimicking the organ music on the soaps. He seemed to find this all highly amusing. I did not.

"Take it easy, you two, will ya?" Peter cried.

"No, I won't take it easy," his ex retorted. "Goddammit, all you ever think of is yourself!"

Peter grabbed her by the hand and pulled her into a corner. "Just cool it, will you?" I heard him tell her. "I said I'd take you ... I'll take you." He reached into the liquor cabinet and pulled out a bottle of something. "Here,"—he poured her a drink—"sip on this while I get Nicky ready and see about borrowing a car."

The minute he left the room the girl singer waltzed up to Mrs. Ex.

"You know, lady, you really ought to cool it before you get your Sergio Valentes out of shape," she told her.

"Why don't you butt out, you little sleaze. This is between me and Peter!"

"Oh, yeah? And what claim do you have over the guy?"

"I have plenty of claim on him. He's *still* my ex-husband, you know! Not to mention the father of my son.

And we happen to be very amicably divorced, if you don't mind."

The girl singer let out a shrill laugh. "Oh, swell, that explains it. That gives you the right to bust in here and break up a song!"

Mrs. Ex let out an even shriller laugh. "So, you're the new live-in, are you? And you think you'll have him all to yourself now, don't you?"

I sat there, stunned. It was obvious that the ex-wife thought the girl singer was me—the girl live-in. I knew I should have gone up there and set the record straight. But something kept me sitting there, listening.

"Have him all to myself?" The girl singer rolled her eyes around in her head. "Even if I were the new live-in—which I'm not, if you must know,"—she said as I shrank further into a corner—"I'm well aware of the fact that I wouldn't have him all to myself. Nobody does."

"Oh, you seem to know him pretty well."

"I do. In fact, I used to know him even better. And I also happen to know that his favorite color is not true blue."

I shook my head in disbelief. Talk about sisters under the skin. Was I going to be one of them too? No, I thought, no, I don't believe that for a minute! Peter loves me. He would never . . . But still, something began to eat away at me. Even after the girl singer left in a huff . . . and mother, father and son left for the airport . . . and the band went home . . . and Bozo was firmly ensconced on the den couch with a week's supply of batteries for his Walkman . . . I still couldn't stop wondering about what I'd gotten myself into with Peter.

"Hey, Sleeping Beauty,"—Peter nudged me—"time to wake up!"

"Huh? What?" I sat bolt upright. "What's wrong now?"

"Nothing's wrong," he laughed. "I just brought you some breakfast in bed, that's all." He set a tray down on my lap. "Orange juice, coffee, bacon and eggs, toast . . . go on, eat, eat, it's getting cold."

I took a sip of the juice. "Oooh." I made a sour face. "What's wrong?" He looked insulted.

"I can't." I pushed the tray away.

"Go on, eat, it's delicious." He pushed the tray back.

"I'm sure it is," I pushed it away again. "It's just that everything smells like vomit, you know?"

"I know, but you've got to eat something or you'll . . . Christ, will you listen to me?" He winced. "I'm beginning to sound like a Jewish Mother!"

"Good." I snuggled up to him. "I could use one right now."

He popped a piece of bacon into his mouth. "I guess I shouldn't have taken Nicky back to McDonald's again. But he was so upset after his mother left for Japan last night that I had to do something to cheer him up, poor kid."

I felt a twinge for him myself. "But did you *have* to let him eat two hot fudge sundaes on top of his Quarter Pounder?"

He laughed. "Not to mention the fries and the Ronald McDonald cookies—I just hate saying no to the kid, you know?"

"So I've noticed." I yawned. God, I was exhausted. I couldn't ever remember feeling so drained. Even my hair felt exhausted. "Is he okay this morning?"

"Oh, yeah, he's back to his old self all right. He's busy turning the place into a disaster area."

"Swell," I said with mixed feelings.

"And it's all thanks to you, Babe. I don't know what I would have done without you." He kissed the top of my head. "You were terrific! Where'd you learn to take care of a sick kid like that anyway?"

"I dunno," I shrugged. "I guess I just did whatever my mother . . . whatever she used to do for me when I was sick!"

"You sound amazed."

"I don't think I ever really gave her credit before, you know. Being a parent is hard work!" Ma, Ma, what are you thinking now, Ma? I wondered, feeling a sudden twinge of sadness. Do you hate what's happened between us as much as I do? Will you and Daddy ever understand that I just need to make my own choices—good and bad? "She's really not such a bad person, my mother," I said, trying to unscramble my feelings. "I mean, sure, she has her *shtik* and everything. She and my father both. But they mean well. You know?"

"Sounds to me like you're beginning to mellow a bit. A couple of days ago the mere thought of them sent you into a complete rage."

"Yeah, I guess I have mellowed, haven't I?" I scratched my head, wondering what it all meant. Was I having a change of heart? Did I make a mistake, turning my back on my family the way I did? Was I doing the right thing? I looked up at Peter, my eyes searching his face. For what, I wasn't sure. All I knew was that I loved him and that I was prepared to follow him anywhere. Or was I? No, of course I was! But what about that scene last night—the one between his ex-wife and the girl singer? Was I supposed to forget it ever happened? Yes, dammit, yes!

"Hey, what are you staring at?" he wanted to know.

"Huh? What?" I started. "Oh, I . . . I . . . ." I couldn't think straight. My mind was all fogged in. God, I thought, letting out a huge yawn, I'm so tired I don't know if I'm coming or going anymore. Bad enough Nicky kept me up half the night with his puking, but what little sleep I had was constantly interrupted by our vegged-out drummer-in-residence. It seems he has this nightlong penchant for tapping out drum solos on the coffee table—that is, when he isn't cracking walnuts into heaps on the floor or singing along with his Walkman at the top of his lungs. Between Bozo and the kid, I was getting old before my time.

"Hello?" Peter waved his hand in front of my face. "Is there anybody home?"

"Huh? Oh, God, I'm sorry!" I shook my head in a vain

attempt to clear it. "I guess I'm just pooped out, you know?"

"I know. That's why I let you sleep in this morning. I would have let you sleep even longer except that we have an appoint—"

"Oh, no!" I cried. "What time is it?"

"Eleven-thirty. Why?"

"Eleven-thirty? I was supposed to be at work two and a half hours ago!"

"Jeez, I forgot all about your work."

"Mrs. Finkelberg's gonna kill me! I promised her I'd be at work at nine sharp. I had an interview to do and, oh, God, she's gonna *kill* me!"

"Take it easy, will ya? You spent the entire weekend taking care of a sick kid, you've hardly slept in two nights, and the night before that you spent on an airport bench. You're in no shape to go to work anyway."

I gave him a piercing look. Is that the way it's going to be from now on, I wondered. Will I ever have time for *my* work? Is that what I want? Is it? Is it? "Shit, I can't believe this is happening!"

"Hey, give yourself a break, will ya? You're not Superwoman, you know?"

My eyes almost popped out of my head. "I can't believe you just said that! You of all people."

"Huh? What are you talking about?"

"I'm talking about . . . I'm talking about . . . oh, hell." I found myself all in a muddle for a change. "I don't know what I'm talking about!" I reached for the phone. "I've got to call Mrs. Finkelberg and explain. Oh, God, she's gonna *kill* me!"

It was just as I suspected.

Mrs. Finkelberg was furious.

"How nice of you to call!" she said. There was so much acid in her voice I thought it was going to eat right through the phone. "I'm almost sorry you didn't decide to show up in person instead. Because then I'd have the satisfaction of *wringing your little neck!*"

Did I call it or did I call it?

"Mrs. Finkelberg, if you'll just let me explain . . ." I was in a complete sweat. Mrs. Finkelberg does that to me. "I can explain."

"Oh, good," she sneered, "I *knew* there was a perfectly *good* reason why you're not sitting at your desk writing up that interview with the mayor as you *promised!*"

"Oh, there is! You see, I . . ."

"And don't tell me you've been ill!" she barked. "Because I know better! When you didn't show up for work this morning, I got concerned. You weren't feeling well on Friday, and I thought maybe you might be dying or something—so I called your house. Not only were you not sick, but you weren't even there! 'Gone bye-bye with boyfriend' is the way your charlady put it, I believe."

"Please," I winced, "you don't understand."

"Oh, I understand all right," she fumed, "I understand that our little chat on Friday didn't even penetrate one little hair of your high-priced La Coupe hairdo, that's what I understand! You sure have a strange way of proving yourself, young lady. A very strange way indeed!"

"But Mrs. Finkelberg . . ."

"I don't know why I bothered wasting my breath on you! You're nothing but a frivolous, ridiculous little J.A.P.! You always were and you always will be!"

"No, you've got it all wrong!" I tried to tell her. "Look, I could be there in half an hour and . . ."

"Don't bother!" she exploded. *"You're fired!"* Click.

"But you don't understand." I sat there numbly, talking to the dial tone. "It's not like you think. You see, I . . ."

"Forget it, Babe." Peter took the phone out of my hand and hung it up. "There's no point."

"You—you heard?" I said, blinking back tears.

"Are you kidding? The way that witch was yelling, I'm sure the entire McGill Ghetto heard!"

"I . . . I can't believe she fired me." The tears began to

flow forth. I felt really and truly awful. Like I had let the whole world down—and myself along with it. "She wouldn't even let me explain . . ."

"Hey, c'mon, don't cry," he said, brushing a tear away with his finger, "you're well rid of her, believe me. Jeez, what a witch! I'll bet she comes to work on a broom!"

"I . . . I know she's a w-i-itch," I sniffled. "But . . . but I . . . she and I . . . we had this talk on Friday, and . . . and . . . and . . ."

"But you were going to have to quit anyway. We're leaving for L.A. in a few days, remember?"

"Yeah, California," I sighed. Ever since that nightmare I'd had in the tub the other night, I was left with this strange, uneasy feeling about California. Sitting there like a lump in my gut. Somebody up there was trying to tell me something. But what? I looked up at Peter, my eyes searching his face for reassurance. But then again, that little nagging doubt. . . . "Everything's going to be okay once we get there, isn't it?"

"Are you kidding?" He took me around. "You just wait and see that little beach house I rented. It's only a stone's throw away from the fucking Pacific ocean, man! I mean, little Nicky's gonna have all that fresh air and sunshine to play in. And we're gonna take long, romantic walks in the surf every night—just like in the fucking movies! And I'm gonna write hit songs and you're gonna write smash screenplays. Now what does *that* sound like to you? Does it sound like heaven or does it sound like heaven?"

"God, you make it sound so wonderful!" I cried.

"That's 'cause it's gonna be!"

"God!" I hugged him with all my might. How, I found myself wondering, could I *not* love this man? He's so exciting! So romantic! So strong! So sure of himself! And yet . . . and yet . . . Suddenly I found myself searching his face again. . . . And yet I couldn't help feeling that something was missing.

"Do I have dirt on my face or something?" he asked me.

"Huh?"

"You keep staring at me."

"Peter?" I just had to get it off my chest. Superficial though it may have seemed, it was bugging the hell out of me. "Are you going to grow your beard back?"

"I dunno. Why? Do you think I should?"

"It's not that you don't look good without it, because you do. Really you do. It's just that, well, it's just that you don't look like you!"

"Well then," he laughed, "I better grow it back fast. We can't have you going to bed with a stranger every night, can we?"

"Hell, no," I giggled, "I'm just not that kind of girl." I was beginning to feel better already. Maybe things were beginning to look up after all? "You know, you haven't kissed me in ages!" I blurted.

"How clumsy of me!" He gave me a whopper of a kiss. "Now," he whacked me on the ass, "hurry up and get dressed, will ya? Like I was about to tell you before, we have an appointment in half an hour."

"An appointment?"

"Yep—we're going to the American consulate to see a Miss Kraut about some immigration visas."

"God, it's really happening, isn't it?"

"You better believe it, Babe!" He grinned.

"You know, I can't believe how fast it's all going. I mean, I always thought it took months to get a visa."

"Not when you've got one of the biggest record companies in the good old U.S. of A. behind you. And anyway, this appointment at the consulate is nothing more than a formality. The whole thing is pretty much all in the bag already."

"Well then, what are we waiting for?" I said with renewed vigor as I slipped into a pair of jeans. "You know," I marveled as a swishing sound caught my ear, "I could swear I hear the ocean already."

He threw his head back and laughed that crazy, hoarse laugh of his. "And I always thought that those were just the pipes gurgling!"

* * *

A funny thing happened during our visit to the American consulate.

I became patriotic.

For Canada, that is!

I don't know. I guess it was the way Miss Kraut, the Processor of Visa Applications, kept referring to us as "you aliens" and "you immigrants" (which she pronounced "ali-*uns*" and "immi-*grunts*"). God, she made it sound like we were about as welcome in the United States as an epidemic of Legionnaire's disease!

"You ali-*uns* will have landed immi-*grunt* sta-*tus*," she drawled on and on, ". . . and you ali-*uns* must register as such each and every January . . . and you ali-*uns* must have green cards to work in these here United States . . . and you ali-*uns* this . . . and you immi-*grunts* that . . ."

Obviously Miss Kraut is extremely good at alienating future immigrants to the United States, because by the time she was through with me, I didn't ever want to set foot in the United States again. Not even to go shopping in Plattsburgh!

But go and tell that to Peter.

He was in seventh heaven.

"Did I tell you it was gonna be a snap or did I tell you it was gonna be a snap?" he babbled excitedly in the car on the way home. "We're almost there, Babe, can you believe it? Isn't it incredible?"

I couldn't bring myself to agree so I didn't answer. Instead I busied myself with the removal of the wad of Double Bubble Nicky had somehow managed to grind into the back seat of my car. "Look at this mess, will you?" I cried, knowing deep inside that it wasn't really the mess that was bothering me. It was something much deeper. A change of heart, maybe? What was I doing, moving to California with this . . . this man?! Who was he anyway? I . . . I hardly even knew him! Could you love someone and not even know him? Everything was happening so fast. So fast! "Just look at this mess . . ."

"Hey, what's eating you?" Peter wanted to know.

"No, Nicky, don't do that!" I wailed as he stuck his fingers into the wad and then wiped them on the carpet, not to mention his hair and clothes. "You're making everything all sticky!"

To which he responded by pulling another wad out of his mouth and imbedding it in the ashtray.

"That does it!" I fumed. "That just does it!"

"Hey, take it easy, will ya?" Peter said. "I'm gonna give the car a good cleaning this afternoon anyway. It'll look as good as new by the time people come around to look it over tomorrow."

"People? What people?"

"Oh, didn't I tell you? I put an ad in the *Gazette* this morning. For your car and my bike."

"Sell my car?" I got a lump in my throat. My mind flashed back to the day Ma and Dad surprised me with it. I could just see it sitting there in the garage, a gleaming white Camaro with a huge blue velvet bow wrapped around it. "To our darling daughter on her 21st birthday," the accompanying oversized card read, "we love you, Mom & Dad." "But this car is like a part of me," I said, my eyes clouding over with misty watercolor memories of the way we were. Sometimes. God, I really did love my family! Despite everything, I still loved them. "It's a part of me."

"Hey, look, I know you're not crazy about giving up your car," he said. "I feel the same way about my bike. But what the hell, right? It's a small sacrifice to make for what we're gonna end up with, isn't it?"

"And anyway, how could you decide to sell *my* car without even bothering to consult me?" I bristled.

"It was just something that had to be done. I'm sorry. I didn't mean to offend you."

"Well, I am offended. You of all people should understand how sick and tired I am of other people making my decisions for me. From now on I want to be included in all the decisions that concern my life, okay?"

"Okay," he nodded. "I get the message."

"Besides, if we sell my car and your bike, how are we gonna get around in L.A.?"

"I thought we'd pool the money we'd make on the sale and buy a secondhand Jeep."

"Oh. *You* thought." I fumed. "Well, wouldn't a flying saucer be more appropriate for the occasion?"

"What?" he cried.

"Isn't that what most ali-*uns* use to get around?"

He gave me a strange look. "Have you flipped your lid?"

"Didn't it even bother you at all?" I asked him.

"Didn't *what* bother me?"

"The way that horrible Kraut-person kept calling us ali-*uns*. I don't know about you, but she made me feel like something out of 'Mork and Mindy'!"

"Nannoo-Nannoo!" Nicky gurgled.

"Yeah, my sentiments exactly!" I sneered.

Peter scratched his head. "Were we just at the same consulate? Anyway, who the hell cares what they call us? The point is—we're going to the United States. The United States! The place where we can achieve the ultimate in fame and fortune in our respective professions. The American Dream is all ours, Babe, all ours!"

It was beginning to sound more like the American nightmare if you asked me. Or maybe even like the nightmare I had in the tub the other night. Or maybe they were one and the same thing! An alien is an alien is an . . . My God, Shay, I thought with sudden horror, will you just listen to yourself? You're beginning to sound nuts! "Damn!" I rubbed my throbbing forehead. "I'm getting a splitting headache from that stupid consulate!"

"Jesus, what's with you anyway? Why are you blowing this whole thing out of proportion?"

Funny, I was wondering the same thing myself. What was really eating me anyway? Was it California? Or Peter? Or his son? Or my family? Or my car? Some of the above? *All* of the above? What? What? *What?!*

"You haven't answered my question, Shay. Why are

you making such a big deal out of this alien business? It's just a term they use for your official status."

To which I responded with an explosion that startled even me: "Yeah? Well, I already feel like a goddamned alien right here and now. I don't have to move three thousand miles away just to make it *official!*"

"Then don't!" he snapped. "Nobody's sticking a fucking gun to your head, you know?"

"Fine!" I cried, wondering what the hell was with me. "Then maybe I won't!"

"Fine!"

"Fine!"

And we drove the rest of the way home in complete and horrible silence.

Whoever coined the phrase "silence is golden" obviously never spent an entire afternoon not speaking to a live-in lover.

By the time evening rolled around I couldn't take it anymore.

I just couldn't bear having Peter so angry with me, what with the rest of my loved ones having cornered that market.

Remembering what that esteemed centerfold and future brain surgeon, Willowmeena Beatts, had said about gourmet meals being the way to a man's heart (not to mention his prick!), I, Shayna Pearl Fine, being of completely unsound mind and damaged body, decided to make the supper to end all suppers.

"Hey, guys!" I cried, bursting into the den where Peter, Nicky and Bozo were watching TV. "How would you like a delicious home-cooked meal tonight?"

They slowly turned their heads away from the tube and stared at me with unblinking eyes.

"I, uh, noticed a box of spaghetti in the kitchen," I babbled on, determined to make peace. "And I found a scrumptious recipe for meat sauce marinara in the latest issue of *Playboy*. Just give me, uh, a few minutes and I'll whip you up an Italian feast you're never gonna forget!" I crowed, despite the fact that I had never whipped up anything more than Lipton's Cup-a-Soup. "So whad'ya say, guys? Sounds out of this world, doesn't it?"

They looked at me as if I was something that had just stepped out of *Invasion of the Body Snatchers*.

"So whad'ya say?" I glanced at Peter. Was that the way he was going to react to every argument? Like a sulky child? And I thought *I* was the immature one. "Well, you can sit here and sulk if you want to. I've got things to do." I did an about-face. *Will the real five-year-old please stand up?*

"Hey," Peter caught up with me in the kitchen, "what's going on?"

"Nothing," I said, hunting through the cupboards for pots and pans. "Can't a woman make a meal for the men in her life without facing an inquisition?"

"I thought you said you were never gonna cook?"

"I say a lot of things I don't mean. I just like to *kvetch* a lot. Ask my moth— Ask anyone who knows me. They'll tell you. I'm Queen of the *Kvetches*."

"Oh, I see," he said, "and this afternoon you were just living up to your reputation?"

"Egg-zactly." I pulled out a huge copper-bottomed pot and placed it on the stove. "This looks spaghetti-ish, doesn't it?"

"Spaghetti-ish?" He burst out laughing. "You know, something tells me you don't know meat sauce marinara from clam chowder."

"Look, I'm just trying to say I'm sorry, okay?" I bristled. "I acted like a shit this afternoon and now I'm trying to make it up to you. Is there anything wrong with that?"

"No, of course not. But are you sure—"

"I think this should be a celebration dinner, don't you?" I rattled on. "I mean, in a few days we'll be getting our visas in the mail and then we'll be off to California to start a whole new life. Now if that doesn't call for a celebration dinner . . ."

"Hey." He grabbed hold of me. "Why don't you just tell me what it is, exactly, that's bugging you?"

I lowered my eyes. "I—I can't."

"Why not?"

"Because . . . because I'm not sure myself . . . exactly," I told him truthfully. *Mixed up* were not the words to describe my state of mind. *Scrambled* might have been more accurate. "Look, it's just something I have to work out for myself. It's not your problem, okay?"

"No, it's not okay! It's . . ."

"Listen!" I cut him off. "I really have to get my cooking started here. I have a zillion things to do."

"Okay, okay," he relented, "I get the message. We'll let it go—for now. You need any help?"

"We could use some wine. Oh, and maybe a loaf of French bread."

"Okay, I'll run down to the corner grocery and pick some up. Anything else you need?"

I rummaged through the pantry for things Italian. "We have Parmesan cheese. And oregano. And . . . do we have any marinaras?"

"Marinaras?" He exploded with laughter. "You're kidding, right?"

"Did I say something funny?" I gave him a puzzled look.

"Did you actually *read* that recipe?"

"I just sort of glanced at it, why?"

"Because there's no such thing as a marinar— Oh, look, why don't you forget about the sauce for tonight? I'll pick up a jar of Ragu at the grocery."

"Well, what am I supposed to do then?" I pouted.

"Make the spaghetti," he said, looking amused. "You *do* know how to make spaghetti, don't you?"

"Well, of course I do! What's so hard about boiling up a bunch of noodles?"

"Sorry I asked!" He turned to go.

"Peter?" I blurted. "Don't hate me, okay?"

"Hate you?" He came back and put his arms around me. "You could never do anything that would make me hate you, don't you know that? I love you!"

"I—I—I—love you too," I said hesitantly. Oh, God, wasn't I even sure of *that* anymore? Suddenly I was filled with panic. Do I? Don't I? Don't I? Do I? And the next thing I knew I was crawling all over him, my hands groping him everywhere, my mouth sweeping back and forth across his face, my lips sucking hungrily at his, sweeping and sucking, sucking and sweeping. Like a Hoover out of control. I do love him, I thought, my mind whirling, I do, I do, I do!

"Mmmm . . . hey, what's this all about?" he said, sounding surprised.

"It's a preview of what's gonna be for dessert," I said in my huskiest voice. Willowmeena would have been proud. "Tonight," I went on, stroking him, "tonight I'm even gonna swallow *all* of it."

"Hey,"—he looked at me rather strangely—"you don't have to do that. I mean, only if you want to."

"I want to!" I said, almost believing it myself. "And then afterwards . . . afterwards we're gonna screw our brains out!"

"What about your coil?" he said. "Doesn't it hurt you anymore?"

"Hurt me? Nawww." Only when I moved! But what the hell, right? If I could cook spaghetti . . . "In fact, I can't wait to try it out."

"Funny, I could swear I saw you popping those pain pills only this morning."

"I *said* it doesn't hurt anymore!" I burst out. "And what's with all the questions anyway? Do you always turn a proposition into an inquisition?"

"Okay, okay, take it easy."

"Look, will you just go the the store already? It's going to close soon and then we'll be out of luck."

He raised an eyebrow. "Are you *sure* you're all right? You sure are acting strange."

"I'm fine! Just go, will you?"

Just then Nicky came into the kitchen. "Is the pizgetti ready yet?" he wanted to know.

"Uh-uh, not yet," Peter told him. "I'm just on my way to the store to pick up some groceries. Wanna come?"

"Uh-uh," he shook his head adamantly, "I wanna stay here and play with my Big Mo," he said, referring to the toy dump truck in his hand.

"You sure?"

"Mrrrrrrrrrrrrrrrr." He got down on the floor and pushed the truck around. "Rrrrrrrrrrrrrr."

"You can leave him here," I said. "I'll keep an eye on him."

"I just thought . . . okay, yeah, why not?" Peter shrugged. "No reason why you can't boil spaghetti and keep an eye on him at the same time." He turned to go. "I won't be long," he said, sounding uneasy.

"Don't worry about a thing!" I yelled after him. "I've got everything under control!"

Famous last words.

Trying to boil spaghetti and keep an eye on Nicky, I soon discovered, was like trying to mix burning charcoal with gasoline.

In both cases you end up with the same explosive results.

Nicky, who had been as quiet as a church mouse all afternoon, suddenly decided to choose the moment of my cooking debut to reenact the Reign of Terror.

"I wanna drink!" he cried as I tried to absorb the instructions on the back of the Valencia Spaghetti box. "I'm thirsty!"

"In a minute, Nicky, just let me get this done and . . ."

"I'm thirsty!"

"Okay, okay, I'll give you a drink." I went to the fridge to pour him some apple juice. "Here now, be a good boy and let me make this spag— Oh, no, Nicky, *not on the floor!*" Somehow, while my back was turned, he had managed to get hold of a box of cherry Jell-O to use as "sand" for his Big Mo dump truck, and then he proceeded to dump the "sand" clear across the floor.

I hardly got that mess all cleaned up when he knocked over the philodendron in the hallway with his Mighty Mite bulldozer.

That I managed to boil the spaghetti at all in the midst of such goings-on was a major miracle.

That I boiled it right out of this world was no small wonder.

But go and tell *that* to Peter.

He really threw a fit when he came back from the grocery store and saw what had become of his supper.

Actually, he wasn't as pissed off about the spaghetti burning to a crisp as he was about the pot melting all over the stove.

Hell hath no fury like a man (even a rock 'n' roll man) whose copper-bottomed spaghetti pot has been destroyed.

"How the fuck did you melt the pot?" he hollered as he inspected its remains, which looked to be about the dimensions of a slightly undersized quarter. *"How the fuck does* anyone *let a pot melt?!"*

"It . . . it was an accident!" I sobbed. "First there was the apple juice . . . and, and, then the Jell-O-o-o . . . and then, oh, God, it was all over the place! And then he, he, he bulldozed the plant and before I knew it—*kaboom!*— the spaghetti caught fire and then the pot caught fire and then . . . and then it just sort of . . . caved in!"

"Oh, my God, Nicky!" His face turned white. "He wasn't in the kitchen . . . ?"

I shook my head. "He's okay. He's in his room."

He breathed a huge sigh of relief and then went back to hollering at me. *"You're just damn lucky the whole place didn't go up in flames!"*

"It's okay. I put it out with the extinguisher before it could spread." I pointed to the little red extinguisher on the counter. "I just pulled it off the wall, pulled the little pin and gave it a couple of squirts and . . . and the fire went out."

"Well, thank God you can do *something* right!" He

wasn't too impressed. "Fuck, I just don't believe this whole thing!" He picked up the remains of the pot with a pair of tongs and flung it into the sink. "Goddammit, Shay!" He turned to me with fire in his eyes. "How the hell could you let something like this happen? I thought you said you had everything under control!"

"I—I thought I did." I stood there quaking in my clogs.

"I—I thought I did!" he mimicked me. "Shit!" he smacked himself on the head. "I musta been crazy to leave my son in the hands of a . . . a goddamned J.A.P.!"

Oooo, that hurt. Coming from him that really hurt. "A goddamned J.A.P., am I?" I exploded. "And what the hell makes you think you're such a goddamned prize?"

"Oh," he seethed, "now I suppose this is all *my* fault?"

"You!" I cried. "You! You promise me beach houses! Fun in the sun! Romance . . . liberation . . . the career of my dreams! And what do I end up with? I'll tell you what! Housework! Motherhood! Male chauvinism! I may as well have gone and married Stanley!"

He grabbed my purse, which was hanging on the back of one of the kitchen chairs, and then he took my car keys out of his pocket and dropped them inside. "Here!" He stuffed the purse into my arms. "I hope you and Louis Vuitton and Stanley will be very happy together. You deserve each other!"

"Happy?" God, I hated him at that moment. I hated him more than I had ever hated anybody in my whole life. "And I was going to be happy with you? You . . . you and your women!" Suddenly the words just burst forth like a dam. "When I saw you looking at that girl singer of yours, I could have sworn it was the same *special* way you looked at me. And that made me wonder, dammit! Do you look at all women that way? And if you look at them all that way, do you think of them all that way? But listen, there's more."

"More? What more?"

"I'll tell you what more, Buster. I learned something from that ex-wife of yours too. I learned that I can trust you as far as I can throw you, that's what. Hell, you've got women coming out of everywhere, don't you? Next thing I know they'll be popping out of the fridge!"

"Are you quite through?" he wanted to know.

"Oh, yeah, I'm through all right . . . better believe I am." I took a deep breath and let it out slowly. "And you know what else? I feel terrific. Like a tremendous weight has been lifted off my shoulders. I feel like a new person now that I've got you off my chest!"

I swung my purse over my shoulder and stormed out of the apartment.

PART V

Home Free

Chapter 15

IT WAS Richard Pecker, husband of Jo Ann and chief psychiatric resident of the Jewish General Hospital, who found me wandering aimlessly through Cavendish Mall (that gargantuan shopping plaza in the heart of Cote St. Luc which some people facetiously refer to as "J.A.P. City"—after those who hang out there).

"Shay, what brings you here so late at night?" he wanted to know.

"I, uh, I dunno," I shrugged. "Nowhere else to go, I guess." I glanced around the nearly deserted mall. "Besides, this place has always been like a second home to me."

"Yeah, you and my wife both!" he laughed.

"Jo Ann, is she with you?"

"Uh-uh. She's at an ORT meeting somewhere out in Dollard Des Ormeaux. I just came here to buy some milk and cigarettes at the bakery. Then I'm going to Nuddick's to pick up a strawberry cheesecake for Jo Ann. She gets these weird cravings . . . well, you know how pregnant woman are?"

"Yeah," I sighed, "so I've heard."

"She's been very worried about you, you know? You haven't returned her calls all weekend."

"Yeah, well, I was busy."

"Mmm . . . I heard about your new boyfriend. Say, where is he anyway?"

"At home, I guess. Crying over burned spaghetti."

"Listen," he gave me a concerned look, "are you all right? You're acting awfully weird."

"Don't start analyzing me, Richard!" I practically bit his head off. "I couldn't stand being analyzed anymore tonight!"

"Well, I am a trained psychiatrist, you know? And if there's something bothering you . . ."

"I'll tell you what," I said glibly, "why don't I just take an overdose of sleeping pills and call you in the morning?"

"Hey! You're not thinking of doing anything crazy, are you?"

"Oh, don't get so excited, Richard," I sighed, "all I have in my purse is a bottle of Pamprin."

"Look, why don't you just tell me what's bugging you? Maybe I can help. Did you and your boyfriend have some kind of fight?"

"I guess you could say we had a parting of the ways," I sighed again.

"Any chance of getting back together?"

"Naw, the princess has been banished from the kingdom forever more." I let out a bitter laugh.

"Has the princess given much thought to going back home to her family?"

"For what?" I had already considered that possibility. "To listen to a lifetime of I-told-you-sos?"

"Well, what about Stanley?"

I shrugged. "What about Stanley?"

"Well, you can't stay here for the rest of your life!"

"Why not?" I was just wallowing in self-pity. "I'll become the 'Phantom of Cavendish Mall.' God knows I've spent enough money in this place to own shares in it. I ought to be able to spend the rest of my life here, don't you think? Who knows? Maybe I'll even become famous and somebody will write a book about me. *The Scarlet J.A.P.*, they can call it."

He raised an eyebrow. "Sounds to me like the princess is feeling terribly guilty about something."

"Not something, Richard. Everything. I mean, I can't seem to do anything right. Twenty-three years old and already I've flunked life!"

"So you're just going to run away from it all, huh?"

"I think it'll be kind of fun living here in the mall, don't you? And besides,"—I wiped a tear away from my eye as I thought back to that nightmare I had had in the tub the other night, which seemed to be haunting me like a bad smell—"my parents have probably already cremated and buried me—in their minds anyway."

"Oh, I don't know about that," he told me. "Jo Ann spoke to your mother only yesterday and your mother, well, all she could talk about was how much she missed you."

"She said that?" My heart leaped right into my throat. "You mean, she doesn't hate me?"

He shook his head. "I'll bet that if you went home right now, everything would be forgiven and forgotten."

"You—you mean, go back to my same old house and my same old room and my same old life?"

"If that's what you want," he shrugged.

"I—I don't know." My head was reeling, for a change. "I need time to think."

"I'll tell you what. Why don't you spend the night over at our house? You look like you could use a good night's sleep, quite frankly."

"Well, I am kind of tired," I said. God, I must have walked the mall a hundred times after I left Peter's. "To be honest, I don't know if I'm coming or going anymore."

"Sure, you get a good night's sleep, and then you can talk things over with Jo Ann in the morning. After all, who knows you better than Jo Ann, eh?"

I looked up at him through tear-filled eyes. "I don't think even *she* can help me out of this one."

"Now I *know* you're tired!" he laughed, putting his arm around me. "C'mon, let's get you to bed, huh?"

A nightmare and a half.

I was sitting on Jo Ann's brand-new couch in her newly decorated living room, waiting for her to make an appearance.

Richard was sitting there in the chair beside me, sipping Remy Martin from a large Boda brandy snifter, talking my ear off about the high cost of Jo Ann.

On and on and on. Suddenly the room got very dark and then it got very bright. The next thing I knew, Jo Ann was standing there in the keyhole-shaped archway, looking her usual exquisite self.

"Shay!" she cried, floating over the plush white shag carpet like an angel would float over a cloud. As she moved toward me, the *House Beautiful* living room seemed to take on new dimensions of beauty. Even a perfect stranger could tell that Jo Ann was in her element amidst the white velours, the soft brown leathers, the dark wood furniture, the fragile Lladro figurines, the breathtaking Heimlich landscapes and the captivating John Little street scenes.

It didn't take much imagination to see that the room, with all its splendor and painstaking detail, was pure Jo Ann. Jo Ann with the shimmering mass of bleach blonde wisps and waves, designed of late by Renaldo of Westmount (formally of Paris and/or Rome). Jo Ann with her eyes as crisp and green as brand new American dollar bills, long mascaraed lashes, heavily blushed cheeks and Delightfully Red fingernails and toenails. Jo Ann with the ever-present gold chain around her neck upon which hung not the usual diamond-studded *J* but three massive initials—J A P—in glittering diamond chunks.

"Shay. . . ." she came up and embraced me, taking the necklace off her neck and putting it around mine. "Welcome back!"

I woke up with a start, soaked in sweat. God, I

thought, touching my bare neck just to make sure, what a nightmare! It seemed so real. I took a look around me. Where the hell was I anyway? Oh, yeah, right, the Pecker's guest room. I was spending the night there—that was all. Or maybe a week or two. Or maybe forever. Shit, where the hell was I supposed to go from here anyway? Back home? The Salvation Army? I lay back in bed, throwing the Bill Blass sheet over my head to block out the encroaching morning light. Maybe I *would* just stay there forever. It sure seemed a lot easier than making a decision about what to do with my life.

But then something happened. Something that changed everything. I guess in her own stupid way, it was Jo Ann who helped to point me in the right direction.

"Oh, no! Shit! Shit! Dammit! Fuck!" Her cries of anguish invaded the guest room like an air raid siren. *"Oh, God, no!"*

Oh, God, I thought, sitting bolt upright in bed, something terrible has happened! Maybe she's having a miscarriage or something! I flew out of bed and ran down to the kitchen, where the cries were coming from. "Jo, are you all right?"

"Oh, Shay!" she wailed, standing there by the kitchen table with the most hideous expression of pain on her face. "I just can't believe it!"

"What is it? Is it the baby?"

"Look!" She held up the middle finger of her right hand. "Look what I did to my nail. I broke it. And it was my nicest one too!" She cast a mournful look down at the table, where her decapitated piece of Delightfully Red fingernail was lying in state on a napkin. "My longest!"

"It's only a nail, for crying out loud!" I looked at her with pure disgust. "From the way you were carrying on I thought you were losing the baby!"

"Well, you know how I am about my nails?" She pulled an emery board out of her bathrobe pocket and waved it frantically in the air. "And Richard and I have a dinner party tomorrow night to top it all off!"

"It's still *only* a nail," I sighed, wearily plunking myself down at the gleaming chrome and glass kitchen table, "and nails do grow back."

"Sure that's easy for you to say!" she pouted. "You bite yours!"

"I don't *bite* mine. I just don't . . . oh, never mind, let's just forget it, okay?"

She didn't answer me. She was too engrossed in wrapping an oversized Band-Aid around the unsightly nakedness of her fingertip.

"Say, is Richard still around? I've got to thank him for being so terrific last night. I don't know what I would have done without him."

"Oh, he left awhile ago." She unwrapped the Band-Aid and then rewrapped it. "Some emergency at the hospital. Some loony jumped out of a fourth-floor window and landed on some doctor's Lamborghini."

"Euwwww," I winced. "That's awful!"

"Yeah, you'd think the jerk could at least have landed on a Honda or a Volkswagen."

I gave her an incredulous look. "I was talking about the guy who jumped out of the window!"

"There,"—she finished bandaging her finger—"that's better."

"It must be awful for Richard to have to look at such a hideous spectacle."

"Yeah, well, I'll go over to Nail 'n' Lash in the mall and get it fixed before he comes home. Jeez, I only hope they can fix it though. It's broken right down to the quick!"

"Jesus!" I cried. "What's gotten into you anyway?"

"Nothing's gotten into me." She looked at me like I was nuts or something. "I'm the same old Jo Ann I always was!" She scribbled a note down on a piece of "Dumb Things I Gotta Do Today" stationery, and then she pinned it to her yellow bulletin board that says PRIORITIES across the top.

Get third nail, rt. hand fixed!!!

it said in bold red letters.

Underneath it was a list of about a half dozen other PRIORITIES which I read with a mixture of horror and, yes, revulsion:

Call char—can she come 3X this wk?

Hair trim—Renaldo of Westmnt. Sat.
    10 a.m. Ask Renaldo to touch up streaks

Pick up plane tickets for Miami!

Pick up new A.K. suit at Lily Simon in
    Westmnt. Sq. Thurs. Also shoes at Holt's!!!

Call Silverman Furs to see if skins are in
    for coat

"Okay,"—she poured us a couple of cups of coffee and sat down beside me at the table—"now that we got all that out of the way, let's get down to brass tacks. What the hell is going on with you? You were already alseep when I came in from my meeting last night, but Richard told me that you've left Peter and that you're thinking of going back home?"

"You know,"—suddenly I felt as if someone had put smelling salts under my nose, awakening me from a dead faint—"ever since I can remember, there's always been a part of me, a very big part of me, that always wanted to be just like you?" But no more, I thought giddily, no more! "No matter how much I wanted to be a writer, no matter now much I wanted to have my own place and my own style, there was always this part of me that used to believe I'd be a complete and utter failure in life if I didn't end up just like you."

"Well, it's not too late, you know," she replied, misinterpreting what I had said—again. "First you'll go back home and kiss and make up. Get yourself back in Mommy's good graces and Daddy's credit rating. Then we'll go

see Renaldo about a new hairstyle—maybe some streaks
... fix up those terrible nails of yours ... get you
hitched up with a decent guy ... marry you off. ...
Don't worry, we'll make a real *mensch* out of you yet!"

I shook my head. "Since when do streaks, nails and a
husband make you a *person?* A *real* person? Who made
up that rule anyway? My mother? Your mother? Who?"

"*Wha?*" She looked at me like I had a screw loose.

"Well, thanks for putting me up." I got up to go. What
was the use anyway? We may as well have been talking
different languages. How could I make her understand?
"See ya."

"Going home?"

"Uh-uh." I shook my head vehemently. "No! Going
back there to live would definitely be a big mistake. Sort
of like jumping from the ... the Mixmaster into the
Cuisinart."

"You mean you're not going home?" she said, amazed.
"After everything you've just been through? Haven't you
learned anything from this whole mess?"

"Don't you understand?" How could I get through to
her? "It's *because* of everything I've just been through
that I can't go back there to live."

"Don't be silly. You've *got* to go home!"

"Oh, no, I don't." I was never more sure of anything in
my whole life.

"You're heading for trouble again, Shay. I can see it
coming."

I went over and kissed her on the cheek. "I love you, Jo
Ann Pecker, really I do. And I know you care about what
happens to me. But you're you and I'm me, and I really
think we can still be friends as long as we don't mix the
two up."

"*Wha?*"

"I have to go upstairs and get dressed now."

"But where are you going?" she yelled after me as I
headed up to the guest room.

"To see a lady about a job!"

* * *

240

I had a hunch that if anyone was going to give me the break I needed, it would be Mrs. Finkelberg.

After all, during out last little "chat," she did claim, in that endearingly snarling way of hers, to be on my side. Now it was time to find out for sure.

"Mrs. Finkelberg!" I burst into her office like I was Peter Pan or something. "I want to talk to you about my job!"

"Oh, really?" She looked up from her midmorning coffee and cheese Danish and glared at me. "I didn't know you had one!"

"Maybe I don't now." I shut the door behind me and then I sat myself down in front of her desk, arms folded across my chest. "But I aim to before I leave here."

"Oh, really?"

"Really!" Even I couldn't believe my own *chutzpa*. But what the hell, right? I had nothing left to lose anyway. You can't fire someone who's already been fired. "Listen, Mrs. Finkelberg, I'm not going to pussyfoot around. I need my job back."

"What's the matter?" she said with mock horror. "Don't tell me Daddy's taken away the MasterCard?"

"As a matter of fact, I don't *live* with Daddy anymore. Or Peter either. And I need my job back so I can pay the rent on the apartment I'm going to be moving into—just as soon as I find one. Not that the salary you've been paying me would be enough to live on, but I'll manage somehow, dammit, even if I have to live in a pay toilet!"

We exchanged startled glances. I guess neither of us could believe what had just come out of my mouth.

"Shayna!" she gasped.

Oh, oh, I thought, bracing myself for the worst, here it comes: Hurricane Yetta.

"Shayna, Shayna, Shayna." She shook her head over and over. "What has gotten into you?"

I took a deep breath and let it out slowly. "Look, I'm sorry if I shock you. But it's sink or swim time for me, and if I'm gonna sink, I'm not gonna go down without a fight!" Okay, okay, so I sounded like something out of an old Knute Rockne film. But it was hard enough trying to be assertive without having to be original too. "I'll fight till my very last breath!"

"*Shocked* is not the word, Shayna!" she cried, her seaweed-colored eyes popping right out of her head. "The word is *de-lighted.*"

"Yeah, well I . . . delighted?" I did a complete double take. I thought for sure she'd been getting ready to throw me out on my behind. "Really?"

"I don't know what's come over you, but whatever it is, it's an improvement."

"Really?"

Her eyes narrowed. "Why do you keep saying that? I told you the other day that I'd be on your side if you proved to be worth siding with."

"I know you said it, but I just wasn't sure . . ."

"If you believed it or not?"

"Well, after everything that's happened to me the past few days, I've learned not to expect too much of anybody —or anything, for that matter."

"The past few days?"

"It's a long story."

"Hmph, aren't they all! I don't suppose this long story has something to do with your failure to show up for work yesterday?"

"Look, I know the charlady told you that I was with my boyfriend—and it's true, I was—but well, that's all over with now. I just want to pick up the pieces and go on, you know?"

She raised a penciled-in eyebrow. "And how do I know that you and this . . . this boyfriend of yours won't get back together and that the same thing won't happen all over again?"

"Because I wouldn't go back to him if he were the last . . ." I sat back in my chair and managed to get a hold of myself. "Because I just want to get my job back, work hard, get ahead in my writing career and earn enough money to support myself . . ."

"Do tell?" Her phone rang and she picked it up. "Yeah?" she snarled. "No! I told you I don't want that color for the front page!" *Slam!* "Incompetence!" She banged a fat fist on the desk. "If there's anything I can't stand it's incompetence!" She took a *nosh* of her Danish. "Now," she growled, spitting food everywhere, "where were we?"

"We were talking about giving me my job back," I said, trying not to look as intimidated as I felt.

"Oh, that." She lapped up the remnants of her Danish from her fingers. "There's just one problem with that. I already hired a new Chief Schlock Processor and Drivel Writer this morning."

"Oh." My face almost fell on the floor.

She gave me a piercing look. "I guess this means we'll just have to give you a different job. From now on, you'll be our Resident Columnist and General Reporter."

"Are you serious?" I cried.

"The starting salary is two hundred and fifty dollars a week. Do you think you could manage to support yourself on that?"

"Are you kidding?" I just couldn't get over it. "That's almost a hundred dollars a week more than I was making before!"

She grinned. "That's because you're going to be working a *hundred* times harder!"

"Oh, yes, ma'am!" I could have just burst.

"I expect your first column by the day after tomorrow. And it better be funny!"

I let out a gleeful laugh. "It'll put Art Buchwald to shame!"

"Hmph, let's not get too cocky, shall we?" she scowled. "And by the way. You have some unfinished business to take care of. I haven't been able to assign anyone else to that 'Poop 'n' Scoop' business with the mayor. Get on it right away, will you?"

"Sure thing," I said without hesitation.

"What, no complaints from the peanut gallery?"

"Don't worry," I reassured her, "when I have something to complain about I'll be sure to let you know."

"And don't think I'm handing you this job on a silver platter! I'm giving you a one-month trial."

"Look, Mrs. Finkelberg, I'm not gonna screw up this time. I really need this job."

"Hmmm, yes," she nodded, "and that, I think, is going to make all the difference in the world. Up until now, you needed a job like you needed another pair of designer jeans!"

"I dunno," I shrugged. "I guess . . . maybe." It did kind of make sense.

"Well, anyway, you get on that interview with the mayor right away and then you can take the next two days to find yourself a place to live and all that. I'll be glad to lend you some money if you need it. But you'll have to pay it back—with interest."

"No, that's okay. I have a little money saved up in the bank. I'll manage . . . somehow."

"Yes . . . yes. I think you will. Tell me something—how are your parents taking this sudden surge of independence of yours?"

"They don't really understand it. I guess you could say that they made their Shayna Pearl a cozy little oyster bed and they kind of expect her to lie in it and cultivate—if you know what I mean?"

"Well, maybe you ought to tell them that cozy oyster beds do not produce very 'shayna'—very nice—pearls. In fact, if you want to get really technical, a pearl doesn't grow at all unless it has the constant irritation of a grain of sand in its oyster bed, if you know what *I* mean?"

"Yes, ma'am. I think I do."

"Hmph, I doubt if you do. But you will!"

I got up to go. "I'm gonna go call the mayor now."

"Oh, and Shayna? I don't know where you picked up that disgusting habit of saying *gonna* all the time, but drop it, will you!"

"Yes, ma'am," I sighed, shaking my head sadly. I knew perfectly well where I picked up that habit. Peter Simon

Freeman. Despite everything, it seemed, he was still very much under my skin. Was I crazy to let him go? Sure, okay, he hadn't lived up to my expectations, but then again, what mere mortal man could?

"It's hardly becoming for the next Art Buchwald to go around saying *gonna*, if you know what I mean."

But then again, I had made my choice, and now, dammit, I was going to stick to it. Come hell or high water!

"Shayna? Will you try to remember that?"

"Huh? Wha? Oh, yes. And thank you. Thank you for everything."

"And remember!" she said as I headed out the door. "You've got one month to prove yourself. One month. *Don't* blow it!"

I had barely put the finishing touches on my "Poop 'n' Scoop" scoop when I heard a deafening roar.

"Damn!" I muttered as I looked out the huge storefront window in front of my desk and saw Peter pulling into the parking lot across the way. "What the hell is he doing here?!" But still, I couldn't seem to take my eyes off him. God, he looked magnificent sitting there atop his gleaming black Norton Commando. My knight on a giant steed.

"Who on earth is that?" cried Dora, the copy editor, whose ever-present squeaky red magic marker suddenly stopped squeaking.

"Looks like Satan's Choice!" snarled Mrs. Finkelberg, who just happened to be standing by the window at the time.

"What a hunk!" drooled Meryl, the receptionist. "I don't care whose choice he is. I'll take him!"

"That must be Shay's ex!" gasped Karen "Assertiveness Training" Biskin, who by now knew the whole story of my "long weekend" and who thought that I was handling the "situation" like a real "trooper." "What do you suppose *he* wants?"

"Oh-oh," murmured Elaine "Brown Belt" Popkin, who also knew the story and who agreed with Karen (and had gone so far as to say that I had scored a touchdown for all Womankind!). "Trouble. . . ."

He came up to the main doors of the tiny shopping plaza that houses the *Register* and he gestured for me to come outside.

I hesitated. It was almost as if I was afraid to get too close to him. Like I didn't trust my own feelings.

He gestured again.

I could feel everybody's eyes on me.

He looked at me and shrugged. Then he made a move toward his motorcycle.

No, I thought, no. I'm not going to run away anymore! I grabbed my purse and ran outside. "Wait, don't go!"

"I didn't think you were gonna come out," he said.

"How—how did you know I was here?" My heart was thumping like a herd of horses' hooves.

"Just a hunch," he smiled awkwardly. "I called your friend Jo Ann to find out if maybe she knew where you were, and she told me that you went to see a lady about a job. So I just kinda figured . . ."

"How come you were looking for me?"

He reached around to the carriage in the back of his bike and pulled out my tote bag. "I thought maybe you'd be needing this," he said, handing it over to me. "You forgot to take it with you last night."

"Oh." I wasn't sure if I was relieved or disappointed. "Thanks."

"So,"—he drew a deep breath and let it out slowly—"how've you been? You all right?"

"Fine," I replied, fidgeting with his handlebar. "You?"

"Fine, just fine."

"And Nicky?"

"Fine too. How are those pains of yours?"

"Pains? Oh, you mean the coil cramps? Better. Gets better every day, you know? I think maybe I'm probably getting used to it being there, you know?"

"Yeah, I mean, no, I couldn't possibly know! I could only imagine. . . ."

There was a long, awkward moment of silence.

"Hey, listen . . ." we both blurted at the same time.

"You first," I conceded.

"Look, all I want to say is I'm sorry I blew up at you last night. I shouldn't have said what I did. I was just angry. I didn't mean to say those things."

"Well, maybe you did, maybe you didn't, but you were right," I admitted, more to myself than to him, "I *was* acting like a J.A.P.! I was obnoxious, self-centered— acting like the whole world owed me a living."

"Hey, no." He waved his hand in the air. "Don't go blaming yourself like that. Like you said, I was no prize either. I mean, I really laid a heavy trip on you. Hell, I led you to believe that we were going to have the most romantic life since Gable and Lombard, and then I saddled you with a kid and housework and all those heavy responsibilities. If anybody was self-centered, it was me."

"Yeah, well I shouldn't have had all those ridiculous expectations. I mean, deep inside I *know* you're not Prince Charming personified, yet I let myself get so carried away sometimes."

"Yeah, well I had some pretty ridiculous expectations myself."

"Not half as ridiculous as mine!"

We looked at each other and burst out laughing.

"Let's just say we both screwed up, okay?" Peter offered me his hand to shake.

"Deal!" I put my hand in his and he squeezed it tightly.

"You're okay, Shayna Pearl Fine." He grinned at me.

"You're not so bad yourself." I smiled back.

"You know what the funny part about all this is? Underneath it all, I think we really care about each other."

"I know I do," I said from the bottom of my heart.

"Well, what do you think we oughtta do about that?"

"I dunno. What do you think?"

"I think," he frowned, "that there are about a dozen pairs of eyes staring out at us from behind that window over there."

"Oh, that!" I laughed. "Those are just my co-workers and my boss, each of whom has a different idea about how I should run my life."

"And you? How do you think you should run your life?"

"Oh, I have a few ideas of my own."

"Do any of those ideas include us getting back together?"

"You mean, to live?"

"To live."

I looked from him to the eyes in the window and from them back to him.

"Well, what are you looking at them for?" he asked me. "Don't you know the *right* answer yourself?"

I stopped to think about it for a moment. I did know the answer. That it was the *right* answer, I couldn't be sure. But deep inside I knew it was the *only* answer. For me. For now. The thought of losing Peter forever hurt like holy hell, but it was just a chance I was going to have to take. "I can't go back to live with you!" I spit the words out real fast, knowing it would be less painful that way. Like when you tear a Band-Aid off a sore at lightning speed.

"Was that a no?" he said. "You said it so fast, I'm not sure I heard you right."

"Yes! I mean, no . . . it was a no!" I forced myself to go on. "Look, I know this is going to sound corny and clichéd, but I really want to live on my own for a while. Find out if I can take care of myself. Don't get me wrong. I don't even know if I can do it. And quite frankly, the whole thing scares me to death. But if I keep running away from everything that scares me, I'll be running my whole life. And then I won't be good for anything—or anybody, including myself. Does that sound terrible?"

"Hell, no," he grinned, "it sounds honest. And that's all I wanted to hear—an honest answer!"

I breathed a huge sigh of relief. "Really?"

"Really. And maybe what you say about yourself applies to me too. Hell, I don't know. But I do know one thing—I think it's a good idea that we give each other some space for a while. Maybe things did happen too fast."

"I—I guess you'll be leaving for California soon, huh?" I said, trying to swallow the gargantuan lump in my throat.

He nodded. "And you? You'll be moving into your own place, I guess."

"As a matter of fact, I'm going apartment-hunting right now. Mrs. Finkelberg—she was very understanding. She gave me a new job *and* a raise. So now I can afford to pay the rent on a studio or maybe even a small one-bedroom."

"You're not giving up on your screenwriting career, I hope?"

"Oh, no! That's still one of my goals in life," I reassured him. "But right now I'm just going to take things as they come. You know, one step at a time. I'm no Superwoman. I admit it. And anyway," I babbled on, trying to postpone the inevitable, "who would want to be? It's impossible to be perfect at everything you do. I mean, you're bound to do some things better than others . . . Oh, hell," I grimaced, suddenly realizing that I was only making things harder, "why don't we just say good-bye and get it over with?"

"Is that the way you want it?" he asked.

"Huh?"

"Well, just because we can't live together right now doesn't mean we have to lose touch. I mean, you know what they say about long distance being the next best thing? And anyway, you could come out to L.A. to visit us on your next vacation. That is, if you'd want to."

"Are you kidding?" I cried. "Just try and keep me away!"

He smoothed his hand over his face. "Maybe I'll even have my beard grown back by then—unless, of course, you don't care anymore?"

"I'm not *that* mature yet," I laughed.

"Hmph," he grinned, "women!"

"Think you'll be back in Montreal at all?"

"I might be. Why? Are you planning to invite me over to your new place for a romantic, candlelight dinner?"

"You're kidding, right?"

"Yeah, right! I'll tell you what. I'll bring the dinner—you light the candles. Fair enough?"

"*Safe* enough, you mean!" I chortled.

"Oh, hey, that reminds me." He reached into his pocket and pulled out an exquisite silver chain—upon which was hanging a rather funny-looking piece of metal about the size of a quarter. "Look familiar?"

"No," I shrugged. "Why? Should it?"

"Wanna take a guess?"

I ran my hand over the smooth, shiny surface. I'd never seen anything quite like it in my whole life. "I give up."

He gave it a twirl. "Believe it or not, this used to be my spaghetti pot . . . once upon a time."

"It's not!" My eyes almost popped out of my head. "I can't believe it." I didn't know whether to laugh or cry or what. "You made a necklace out of it? For me?"

"Yeah, for you. Who'd you think?"

"It's . . . it's . . ."

"You like it?"

"Like it? I love it! And it's so original too. I mean, nobody's ever given me a spaghetti pot necklace before!"

"Well then, we're even." He laughed that wonderful, crazy, hoarse laugh of his. "'Cause nobody's ever *melted* my spaghetti pot before!"

He took the necklace and hung it around my neck. "Go get 'em, Babe!"

He gave me a whopper of a kiss, and then he started up his motorcycle and took off.

"Hello, Ma? It's me!"

There was no reply.

"You know, your daughter?"

An audible gasp! "Shayna Pearl?"

She remembered my name. Good sign. "Yeah, it's Shayna Pearl, Ma."

"Where . . . where are you?" Audible weeping.

"In a phone booth on St. Paul Street."

"What are you doing there?"

"Calling you!"

Audible nose blowing.

Ditto at my end.

"Jo Ann . . . Jo Ann tells me you and *him* are no longer . . ."

"No, Ma, Peter and I aren't living together anymore, if that's what you mean."

A huge sigh of relief could be heard all the way down St. Paul Street.

"But we're still going to keep in touch. We just won't be living together . . . for now anyway." Presenting: the New/Assertive/Honest/Nonwhining Me.

"I'm sure you did whatever you thought was right, dear." Presenting: the New/Calmer/Nonnagging/More Tolerant Mother.

"In fact, I may be going out to L.A. to visit him next Christmas."

"Over my dead bod—"

"Maaaaa!"

Okay, okay, so nobody's perfect.

Count to ten and start again. "Ma, listen, there's something you should know."

"When are you coming home?"

"Ma, this may come as a shock to you but a lot has happened to me these past few days. I guess you could say I've grown up overnight."

"What do you mean, you've grown up overnight?" she wanted to know. "When are you coming home?"

"Ma, I think I'm grown up enough to be on my own now."

"What do you mean? What are you talking about?"

"Ma, listen, I'm not coming back there to live."

"What? But where else do you have to go?"

"Well, like I said before, I think I'm old enough to be on my own now . . . so I went out this afternoon and found myself an apartment. Signed the lease and everything!"

No answer. But the silence was deafening.

"Ma, c'mon, deep inside you've got to know it's the best thing for all of us."

A heavy sigh. "Where . . . where is it?"

"Here on St. Paul Street. As a matter of fact, I'm standing in front of it right now. My phone hasn't been connected yet, so that's why I have to use the phone booth out front."

"What? You rented an apartment in Old Montreal? With all the separatists and whatnots?"

"Oh, Mother, really! All kinds of people live around here, not just separatists. It'll be a real experience, don't you think?"

"But Old Montreal, of all places! Couldn't you at least have found something a little closer to home? How about those lovely apartments around the Cavendish Mall? Now there's . . ."

"Ma, I'm only twenty minutes away by car. Ten if I take the expressway. It's not like I'm out in James Bay or something! Don't worry, I won't be a stranger."

"I worry . . . I worry . . ."

"Oh, Mother, just wait until you see it! It's a fabulous little studio in this renovated warehouse and . . . and it's got wall-to-wall carpets and an exposed brick wall, and even a fireplace! Oh, Mother, it's so beautiful—and the rent isn't as bad as you'd think. Of course, it's a small place but, oh, Mother, I just fell in love with it at first sight. I mean, it was only the second apartment I looked at, but the moment I saw it I just knew . . ."

"But how are you going to support yourself?"

"I knew you were going to ask that! And you don't have to worry. Mrs. Finkelberg gave me a big raise. Of course it'll be a while before I can afford to fix up my apartment the way I'd like to, you know, brass bed . . . rolltop desk . . . stuff like that. But I can wait. I'll do it a little bit at a time."

"And just how, might I ask, do you plan to live in the meanwhile? You can't live in an unfurnished apartment. At least a bed!"

"Don't worry. I'll manage."

"At least . . . at least let me ship over the furniture from your room. I know how much you hate it, but . . ."

"Hey, great, Ma!" Beggars cannot afford to be choosers. "That's a terrific idea. I can strip it down and stain it dark brown—if that's okay with you?"

"That's . . . that's a very sensible idea. I'll have it shipped over as soon as possible. Maybe even tomorrow."

"Well, thanks Ma!" I didn't know if it was my imagination or what, but there seemed to be a new note of respect in her voice. Suddenly she was talking to a person instead of her Betsy Wetsy doll. She was trying. She really was. And while I didn't dare delude myself into thinking that everything was going to be hunky-dory from now on, I did feel as if I had overcome a hurdle of some kind. It was a beginning anyway. "Say, you wouldn't happen to know of a place where I could buy a cheap set of dishes and some cutlery, would you?"

"Sure, Kaplow's always gives a good deal on di—only *one* set?"

"Oh, Ma, you don't expect me to keep *kosher*, do you?"

"Well, why not? You were brought up in a *kosher* home!"

"Ma, I don't know how to break this to you, but there are many honest-to-God observant Jews out there who would hardly consider your home *kosher* just because you keep separate sets of dishes for milk, meat and Chinese take-out."

"It wouldn't kill you to . . ."

"Look, Ma, you have your ideas and I have mine. I won't tell you how to run your house, and you won't tell me how to run mine, okay?"

Heavy sigh. "And when do I get to see this wonderful apartment of yours?"

Delighted laugh. "How about tomorrow? I thought maybe I'd come to the *bris* and then you could all come down afterward and take the grand tour. Say, what time is the *bris*, anyway? Jo Ann only told me the date but . . ."

"It's at ten. Ten in the morning. At the Jewish General."

"It is okay if I come, isn't it?"

"Well, what do you think? You're a part of this family, aren't you? Though, of course, they've already picked a new godmother."

"That's okay. I just want to be there, you know? I really do care about my family."

"And we care about you too."

"What about Daddy?" I was almost afraid to ask. "Is he still, you know, furious with me?"

"Well, you did give him a terrible shock, Shayna Pearl. You gave us all a terrible shock."

"Well, you seem to be recovering."

"I'm trying," she sighed.

"And Daddy?"

"He says he's given up trying to understand you at all, but what he says and what he does are two different things. Do you know that I actually caught him reading *Cosmopolitan* the other night?"

"Daddy?" I laughed.

"He's trying, Shayna Pearl. In his own way he's really trying to understand."

"Well, I guess I'll find out how he really feels when I see him at the *bris* tomorrow."

"What do you mean tomorrow? You'll see him tonight—when you come home to sleep."

"Ma, I thought you understood. I've got my own place now. And tonight especially—it's my first night in my very first apartment and, well, I just want to spend it here."

"But where will you sleep? You don't have a bed! And where will you eat?"

"Not to worry, Mother dear." I had it all figured out. "Believe it or not, someone left this old overstuffed couch behind. I can sleep on that. And after I get off the phone with you I'm going to run over to Eaton's to buy myself a quilt—I need a new one anyway. And as for eating . . . well, there's this little restaurant—a greasy spoon, sort of—almost right next door to my apartment."

An audible cluck of disapproval. "I can just see it already. You're going to waste away to nothing!"

"I'm not going to waste away to nothing! Say,"—I glanced down at my watch—"my watch has stopped. What time is it anyway? I have to get over to Eaton's before it closes."

"It's four o'clock." Long pause. "I see you left your new Cartier watch in your drawer."

"Well, I didn't think . . ."

"I'll bring it to the *bris*."

"You mean, you still want me to have it?"

"Well, what good is it going to do sitting in your drawer?"

"Oh, Ma, I . . . you're . . ."

"I really wish you'd come home to sleep tonight, Shayna Pearl. At least come for supper. We're having barbecued chicken. It's your favorite."

God, I thought, my mouth watering, Ma's barbecued chicken! "It sounds great, Ma, really," I said, trying to get a hold of myself, "but I . . ."

"And then you can take a nice, long hot bath in our sunken blue marble tub."

God, a hot bath in the sunken blue marble tub! No, no, I had my own tub now. Sure, it wasn't blue marble. Or sunken. Grimy gray was more like it. But it was mine! "Look, Ma, it's all very tempting and everything, but I really want to tough it out on my own. It's like Mrs. Finkelberg says—I need some sand in my oyster."

"You what?"

"I need some . . . oh, never mind. I'll explain it to you when I see you. I really have to go now."

"Are you sure . . . ?"

"Ma, I'll be okay. Really."

Another deafening silence.

"I . . . I love you, Ma. See you tomorrow." I hung up.

I was lying there in my apartment thinking how great it was to finally be on my own for the very first time. My very first evening of freedom. No one to answer to. I could come and go as I pleased. Take a bath in peace. Have uninterrupted sexual fantasies.

I thought for sure I had died and gone to heaven.

And then, all of a sudden, I heard a creak. And then another. I don't mind saying that I got a little scared. Okay, okay, *a lot* scared. Scenes from every horror movie I'd ever seen began flashing through my mind. From *He Knows You're Alone* to *The Texas Chainsaw Massacre*. I ran to the door to make sure the lock was secure. It was. I took a deep breath and let it out slowly. It was probably just the floors creaking. Or the walls. Yeah, of course, it was just the walls. Silly me.

I returned to the overstuffed couch I had inherited from the previous tenant, and I plunked myself down. I scanned my apartment, thinking of the different ways I could decorate it. And then, 1,001 decorating ideas later, I got bored. And yeah, a little lonely. Okay, okay, *a lot* lonely. I mean, all my life I had lived in a house full of people and all kinds of goings-on. And now there was just me and the four walls. Creaky ones at that. Maybe I had made a terrible mistake? Maybe I wasn't cut out for all this freedom and independence? Maybe I was the baby everybody thought I was? Suddenly I felt this urge to grab my purse and run home to Mama and Daddy. Talk to them. Have an argument. Raid the fridge. Take a steaming bath in my beloved blue marble tub. Yeah, sure, sure, I had my own tub now. But there was something about that blue marble tub. Something secure.

Another creak.

I bolted for the door. I was half way out before I managed to get a hold of myself. What was I doing? Was I really going to let a couple of creaks and a little loneliness spoil everything I had fought so hard to gain? No, I couldn't. I was going to tough this thing out, dammit! I wanted to. God, I really wanted to. Maybe if I just had some company. . . . Jo Ann! I could call Jo Ann and ask her to come down and . . . no, no, I was through being so dependent on her for every little thing. And besides, Jo Ann had her own life. I couldn't expect her to come and baby-sit with me every time I heard a noise. I had to get used to being alone if I was going to live in my own apartment. Living alone was probably an acquired taste, I decided. Like caviar or beer. Or Swallowing It. After all, this was only my first night in my apartment. I had to give it time. Maybe I'd get used to it once it was all fixed up. Maybe I'd never get used to it. But I had to try.

I went back to the couch and sat down. My stomach growled. God, I was starving. My mouth was watering for some of Ma's barbecued chicken. It was tempting. Very tempting. But of course I couldn't run home every time my stomach grumbled either. And so, feeling somewhat apprehensive, okay, okay, *a lot* apprehensive, I went down to the corner greasy spoon for a sandwich. As hard as it is to believe, I had never eaten alone in a restaurant before. This was definitely a first for the kid.

"A grilled cheese sandwich and coffee please," I said, smiling timidly at the proprietor as I sat down at the counter.

"Quoi?" he said.

"Oh, je m'excuse!" Having grown up in the predominantly English-speaking West End of Montreal, you sometimes tend to forget that the rest of the city is predominantly *français*. *"Un,* uh, um, *sandwich de,* uh, *fromage grillé,"* I sputtered in my rusty French. It sure was hard to believe that I had studied the language for years in school. It seemed they had taught us "Everything You Ever Wanted to Know About the French Language"—except how to carry on a decent conversation. "Oh, and, uh, *un café, s'il vous plaît."*

Three workmen turned around and grinned at me. *"Grillé,"* one of them said, and they all smiled more broadly.

I sat there stiffly, hoping that if I just ignored them they'd go away.

But they just sat there guzzling their Labatts from the bottle and continued to send occasional glances my way.

Unable to shake my feeling of uneasiness, I gave the proprietor a pleading look, hoping he would come to my rescue.

He just smiled and went to make my sandwich.

I glanced nervously over at the workmen. They were all huddled together, whispering, and then one of them got up and headed toward me.

"Mademoiselle, est-ce que je peux te demander un question?"

"Huh?" A question. He wanted to ask me a question. That was all. No reason to call out the Mounties. Nothing I couldn't handle. Besides, he was kind of cute. *"Oui? Qu'est qu'il y a?"* I replied, feeling more relaxed. Both with him and his language.

He looked over at his friends and then he turned back to me. *"Je pense que tu veux un bec, oui?"*

"Huh?" *Bec . . . bec.* What the hell was a *bec?* Some kind of Québecois dessert he wanted me to try? Maybe he thought I was a tourist and was just trying to be hospitable?

"Oui?" he coaxed me.

"I, uh, okay, *oui,*" I found myself saying, not wanting to seem like an idiot.

All of a sudden he grabbed me and gave me a big kiss. Right smack on the lips.

"Ah! Hey! What, are you crazy?!" I cried, feeling a mixture of rage, fright and humiliation. "What did you do that for?"

He shrugged. "I h'ask you if you want h'a kiss, h'and you say yes!" he replied in broken English, and he and his friends burst out laughing.

I didn't know whether to laugh or cry or have a nervous breakdown or what.

"C'était un grand plaisir de faire ta connaissance,

mademoiselle!" He gave a deep bow and then returned to his table, looking mighty pleased with himself.

A hand touched my arm. I almost jumped right out of my skin.

"*Mademoiselle?*" It was the proprietor. "*Est-ce que tu manges ta sandwich ici ou bien que tu l'emportes avec toi?*"

"Huh?" I glanced over at the workmen, who were looking at me, still grinning. I started to shake.

"*Ça fait rien,*" the proprietor reassured me, "*ils font juste du fun avec toi.*"

I tried to smile, only it came out more like a nervous twitch. I knew he was right. They were just having a little fun at my expense. But somehow I didn't find that very consoling. If anything, the whole incident made me realize how vulnerable I was. A woman on her own. No parents or Peter or Stanley or any other knight in shining armor to come to the rescue. Fair game to anyone and everyone. Suddenly I felt as if I had regressed ten years. Oh, God, I thought, wanting to run home to my family as fast as my legs could carry me, am I kidding myself or what? Do I really have the stuff it takes to survive out here in the Real World? Is somebody always going to be packing me a sandwich?

"*Mademoiselle?*" The proprietor nudged my arm. "You h'eat da sandwich 'ere or you want h'I should wrap h'it to go?"

For a second I looked at him, wondering. "Here," I said. "*Ici.*"

ANTON MYRER

A GREEN DESIRE

Available wherever paperbacks are sold. or directly from the publisher Include 50¢ per copy for postage and handling: allow 6-8 weeks for delivery Avon Books. Mail Order Dept., 224 West 57th St. N.Y. N Y 10019   Green Desire 1-83

"FUNNY, SEXY AND FULL OF DEVASTATING INSIGHTS."
—New York Daily News

BABY LOVE
Joyce Maynard

In a picture-postcard New Hampshire town, young mothers and would-be mothers are trying to live out America's TV and Top 40 fantasies. Trying to act more grown up than they feel. Dreaming of true devotion. Wondering where love's gone.

Sandy had to give up teen romance when backseat love brought Baby. Now she has a little-boy husband to baby, too.

Tara has nobody to love but her precious infant daughter, and she is not going to let her mother give "it" away.

Wanda has plenty of boyfriends, her own place, too much fattening food-stamp ice cream, and a baby that's getting her down.

Carla left the New York scene for "quaint" New England and desperately wants a baby, now that her lover doesn't.

Before the week is out, the lives of these frustrated young women, their unready men, and disquieting outsiders will erupt in a climax of emotional devastation far too real for prime-time America.

"SMASHING"   —People

"Joyce Maynard has an unswerving eye, a sharply perked ear, and the ability to keep her readers hanging."   —The New York Times Book Review

A Main Selection of Book-of-the-Month Club

AVON Paperback   59550-8/$2.95

Available wherever paperbacks are sold, or directly from the publisher. Include 50¢ per copy for postage and handling; allow 6-8 weeks for delivery. Avon Books, Mail Order Dept., 224 West 57th St., N.Y., N.Y. 10019.

Baby Love 8-82